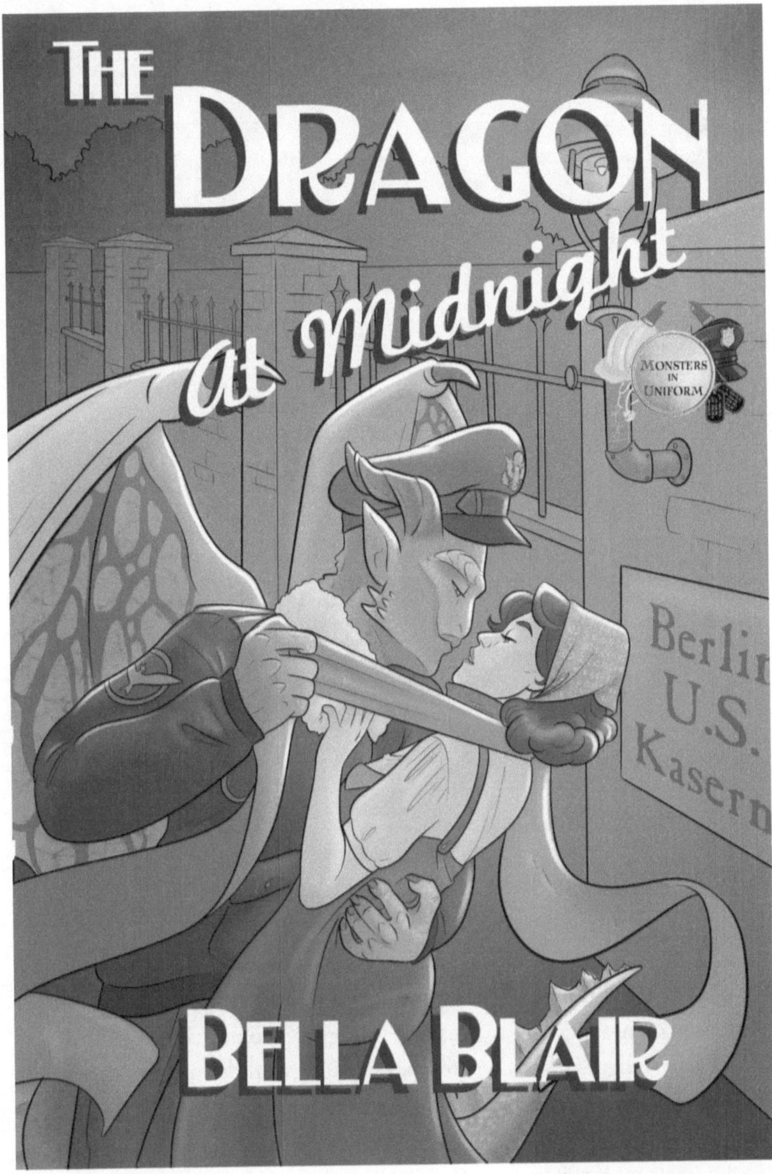
THE DRAGON
At Midnight
MONSTERS IN UNIFORM
Berlin
U.S.
Kasern
BELLA BLAIR

Book Cover by Kit Fox

Editing and Proofreading by: Evil Comma

ASIN: B0FQ3GH2WC

ISBN:

AUTHORS NOTE

I grew up in Berlin, two houses down from the Wall in a sleepy suburban street that felt anything but ordinary. Where other children had swings or tree forts, we had something far more thrilling: a tall, creaking wooden American watchtower, manned two or three times a day by U.S. soldiers.

They arrived in jeeps with mounted machine guns, climbed the tower, and peered over the Wall toward the East. On *their* side, there was nothing but fields, woods, and a lone metal guard tower glaring back.

To us children, that wooden watchtower became everything: a pirate fort, a spaceship, a detective's hideout, the Death Star. And when the soldiers arrived and found us playing, they'd slip us candy and chewing gum, the earliest and most effective propaganda campaign ever deployed.

It clearly worked. I married a GI.

My family's history is woven into this book in deeper ways, too. My uncle, much like Klaus in the story, was six years old when the war ended. He remembered the *Rosinenbomber*—the raisin bombers—and told me how Berlin's children would race to catch the tiny parachutes of candy drifting from American planes. His stories stuck with me my entire life, and this book exists because of him.

My grandmother also lived through unimaginable horror. When the Russians stormed the bunker where she hid during the final days of the war, she was pregnant with my mother. She would have been killed if not for my uncle's terrified cry. Some spark of mercy surfaced, and the soldier spared them both.

My grandfather's story is another thread woven into this novel. Captured by the Russians, he survived harsh POW conditions by playing a role: he pretended to be a communist, earning slightly better rations and treatment. When he was eventually released, he returned to Berlin as a driver for Soviet officers, risking his life every day as he secretly siphoned gas from their vehicles, just enough to keep his family warm and fed, never enough to be noticed.

Dangerous, clever, stubborn.

Very German.

So when I first met my husband on his first night in Berlin, newly stationed at McNair, I probably never stood a chance. It was destiny wrapped in camo.

Writing *The Dragon at Midnight* allowed me to honor the history I grew up with—the fear, the resilience, the hope—while telling a story about love rising from ashes. The *Berlin Blockade* was one of the most terrifying periods for families like mine, and I hope that, through Inga and Gideon's journey, you felt even a fraction of what Berliners lived through and how profoundly grateful they were for the help they received.

Even today, the Berlin Airlift is remembered.

There is no official public holiday called *Tag der Luftbrücke* (Airlift Day), but its significance is commemorated every year in Berlin, with memorial events, museum exhibitions, and sometimes even flyovers of historical aircraft. In 2023, the 75th anniversary was honored with major celebrations at Tempelhof Airport and across the city. Berlin never forgets what was done for it.

Neither do I.

Thank you for reading this story of survival, courage, and love.

And thank you to the Rosinenbomber pilots—real heroes—whose kindness changed a city and inspired a little girl growing up near the Wall.

SUMMARY

I swore I'd never fall for a man in uniform.

Then a dragon shifter pilot claimed me under the lantern light.

Berlin, 1948.

The war is over, but the city is still starving.

I'm Inga Weber—eighteen, German, and raising my little brother in the ruins. By night, I work in a bar for American pilots. By day, I stand in ration lines and pray the Soviets don't come back for what they already took.

Love isn't an option. Survival is.

Then Gideon Griffin walks in.

He's dangerous in a way that has nothing to do with his uniform—scarred, controlled, watching me like he's holding something back. When Russian soldiers corner me in the dark, Gideon steps in with a fury that feels ancient.

Inhuman.

Because Gideon isn't just a pilot.

He's a dragon shifter—one bound by fire, secrecy, and a mating instinct he can't deny.

And somehow… I'm his.

As Berlin becomes a battleground again, Gideon's enemies close in, and the bond between us tightens— hotter, deeper, impossible to escape. He wants to fly me out of the ashes, claim me as his mate, and build a future far from war.

But loving a dragon comes with a price.

If I stay, I risk my life.

If I leave, I lose everything I've ever known.

And if Gideon fails to protect me… the city will burn.

- Dragon shifter pilot
- Fated mates
- Possessive protector
- Found family & war-torn romance
- Steamy paranormal romance set during the Berlin Airlift

*Would **you** fall for a monster in uniform?*

Gideon

Berlin — June 28, 1948, Monday

THE CITY LOOKED like a broken jaw. From a thousand feet up, Berlin was nothing but gray teeth and dark gaps, whole blocks punched out, streets stitched together by rubble and the glitter of shattered glass.

The dragon in me remembered when it all glowed. When the firestorms I helped unleash rolled over rooftops and turned the sky molten. Now there was only dust. Ash. A cold wind, dragging itself across the ruins.

I banked the C-47, making the old girl groan under the weight of flour, milk powder, and salt. Two years ago, I'd dropped bombs over this city. Tonight, I was dropping calories. The world had flipped itself inside out. Or maybe I had.

"Easy Two-Four, cleared to land. Keep it tight." The tower's voice snapped through my headset. Tempelhof's runway glowed below like a wet match in the dark. At the fence, the usual crowd waited—mostly women and kids—faces tilted up, hoping for something to fall from the sky that wasn't fire this time.

They wouldn't touch our cargo. It went to depots, bakeries, and ration centers. Counted by the ounce. But they still came. They stood in the streets to watch the landings, to hear the engines, to remind themselves someone still remembered them.

Halvorsen—Uncle Wiggly Wings—had started dropping candy on tiny parachutes. Wiggle the wings, drop the sweets, make a child smile, was his mantra. Hope with a tail number.

I didn't wiggle my wings. Never had. The kids watching didn't expect anything from me. They just stood, quiet and steady by the fences. The dragon didn't like fences. He liked open skies and clean targets. He rumbled when we passed over the Tiergarten, the hacked-down trees, the broken spine of the Kaiser Wilhelm Church.

We did this, he whispered. *You did.*

My jaw tightened. The war was supposed to be over, but it didn't feel over when the city still smelled faintly of ash. I'd buried brothers in that fire. Good men who'd sworn we'd never come back to Berlin unless it was to finish it. Now I was flying mercy missions over the same damn rooftops I'd once turned into flames, satisfying the beast inside me.

After Germany surrendered, the victors carved her up. Four zones: American, British, French, Soviet. And because no one wanted to hand over the capital, they carved Berlin into quarters, too. A neat little island dropped in the middle of Soviet territory.

It had looked clever on paper, and politicians love paper. But paper doesn't feed people.

Then, on June 24, the Soviets shut everything off—roads, rails, canals—cutting two million civilians off the supply chain and waiting for Berlin to starve into submission. Waiting to claim the prize they'd wanted from the start.

But they'd underestimated one thing. Us. We answered with engines.

Operation Vittles, it was called, because apparently, saving a city needed a cute name. Day and night, every two minutes, another plane came in like mine, loaded with: flour, coal, medicine, hope. Measured not in lives, but in tons.

In retaliation, the Russians threatened to shoot us down.

We kept flying.

Apparently, the threat of the Reds was greater than that of a country who had started WWII not too long ago.

I adjusted the trim and felt the plane settle beneath my hands. "Easy Two-Four, final approach," I said into the mic.

The C-47 sank toward the runway, obedient as a tired dog. The load shifted with a heavy thud. Later, we'd haul coal, black dust getting into everything, but right now, the city needed bread more than heat. They said each Berliner needed about 1,700 calories a day to survive. I'd seen men fight on half of that.

The wheels hit hard. Smoke curled off the tires, the dragon purred deep in my gut at the smell of scorched rubber. Ground crewmen waved me in, efficient and fast as always, no wasted motion. The airlift was a machine that couldn't afford to break its rhythm.

I cut the engines, and the sudden silence felt wrong, like a heartbeat skipping. The cargo doors opened. Thin men with ropey arms started unloading sacks into waiting trucks. The rations would be sorted, counted, and passed out across the Western sectors. The people at the fence got nothing but the sight of it. But sometimes, that was enough.

A little boy on his mother's hip caught my eye. Knit cap. Hollow cheeks. He waved, two fingers sticking out like wings. Without thinking, I waggled the C-47's rudder once, a small salute. The boy grinned like I'd handed him gold.

You should hate them, the dragon murmured. *They are the enemy.*

I knew that without needing a reminder.

Hell, I remembered every tracer round, every night we limped home missing another man. But the kid at the fence wasn't the enemy. He was just hungry.

Politicians, though, they were fair game. They were the bastards who'd sliced Germany into pieces, then acted shocked when the edges bled. They'd stuck Berlin—the damn *capital*—in the middle of Soviet land and called it balance.

Now Berlin was the golden goose everybody wanted to claim, and the ticking time bomb that could start World War III. All it would take was one mistake. One collision in the air corridor. One trigger-happy Russian fighter.

The dragon liked that idea.

I didn't.

"Gideon!" the loadmaster yelled, smacking my shoulder. "Turn time's eight minutes."

"Make it six," I muttered, scribbling my signature on the manifest.

I glanced through the windshield one last time. The boy was still there, waving. I felt something loosen in my chest, something I thought the war had burned out of me.

I pushed the throttles forward. The C-47 roared, eager to climb back into the sky. Berlin fell away beneath me, gray and broken but still breathing.

The dragon coiled around my ribs, warm and heavy, whispering about fire and glory.

But I kept my eyes on the horizon.

We could haul food, coal, medicine—whatever the brass wanted.

But what we were really hauling was *time*.

And I prayed to God that, for now, that would be enough.

Inga

Berlin — June 29, 1948, Tuesday

I WOKE before the light and lay still, listening for the creak that meant the ceiling was ready to fall. Thankfully, it didn't come; there were only the small, thin breaths of my brother and the restless scrape of wind against cardboard. I eased off the old mattress and tucked the blanket around Klaus's shoulders. He slept with one hand under his cheek the way he had as a baby, lashes black against hollowed skin. Six years old and already he knew the rule: if he woke and I wasn't there, he stayed put. No wandering. No talking. No opening the door for anyone.

The apartment had been grand once. I remembered it scrubbed and shining because my mother used to clean here, and sometimes, she'd taken me along. *Inga, hold the bucket; Inga, wring the cloth; Inga, look how marble becomes a mirror when you polish it.* Now half the walls were gone, and what was left leaned at odd angles, like a drunk who'd fallen asleep standing up. The marble was gray and would make my mother roll over in her grave if she had one. I'd patched the gaps with planks, flattened crates, and sheets of cardboard scavenged from the bar. The wind still found a way in. Dust had worked itself into everything: our skin, our hair, the mattress springs.

But at least here, no one looked for us. The ruin was too ruined to bother with. It might collapse at any hour, and people preferred buildings that pretended they wouldn't.

I pulled on my Kittelschürze—a sort of apron with pockets made to be worn over dresses to keep them from getting too dirty. It was June; normally, there would be a hint of spring in the air, but there was only ash. The air coming off the canals was a bit chilly, and shards of open rooms could be damp and sharp at dawn, a chill that would settle in your bones if you let it. I pushed my feet into shoes that had belonged to someone richer and dead, kissed Klaus's hair, and slipped out.

Outside, the courtyard was filled with rubble. Brick heaps crouched like sleeping animals. The streets were already thick with people heading in the same direction I was, moving quietly, shoulders forward, the way you do when you've spent years flinching at sirens. No bombs fell now, but the city still walked like it expected them.

You had to line up early if you wanted your ration, earlier still since the Russians closed the roads and rails. They said the Americans and British were flying in food, sacks and sacks of it, and coal would come too. I believed it because I'd seen the planes grumble across the sky and slide down into Tempelhof like silver fish returning to a dark pond. I believed it because I had to. Belief and bread were both thin, but one made the other easier to swallow.

The queue outside the grocer's looped around the corner, thin bodies wrapped in thin coats. A little cough here, a sniffle there, just enough to prove we were alive. I found my place behind Old Manne, who nodded without turning. He'd come back six years ago with one arm and a face that looked carved from a softer kind of stone. He kept the stump of his sleeve pinned neatly, the way my mother had kept ribbons straight.

"Morning, Mädchen—girl," he said. "You look tired."

"I worked late," I replied. "Some English pilots came in and stayed late."

"Good tippers," he nodded with a sideways smile. "Bad singers."

"Very bad," I agreed. Some were worse at other things, but Manne and I knew not to say this out loud. These men were our *liberators*. But he was right, they did tip well.

Money didn't buy much now, but tips still meant cigarettes to trade or a bit of meat if you knew the right person or the right back door.

Mother Olga stood three people ahead, a sturdy woman with a baby tied to her chest and four more children orbiting like hungry moons. Her husband, like my father, was missing in Russia. Missing meant you kept a plate on the shelf and a story at the ready. It meant the ache never scabbed over.

The line shifted, a quiet, stubborn inch. Further up, I saw Elke on tiptoe, craning to see how much stock the shop-keeper had. She spotted me and sent a quick wink. Of everyone I knew, Elke had the fewest ties left. Her grand-mother and mother had both been killed when the Russians came through, and her father and several uncles were either dead or gone. She was pretty in a way the city still recognized: clean collar, sharp cheekbones, a laugh like a dare. *Berliner Mädchen are the prettiest*, my mom used to say. Elke worked with me at Die Ecke—The Corner—bar, and she had a plan for her life that involved leaving Berlin on the arm of anyone with a uniform—French, English, American—she didn't care as long as they took her away. I didn't judge her for it. She wanted a ticket out. I wanted a roof that didn't fall and a stomach that didn't ache. We all wanted something.

"Did you sleep?" Elke asked when I edged close enough.

"Some, I finished at midnight."

"Midnight," she huffed. "I was finished at ten, and then I wasn't." She rolled her eyes. "Americans. One of them promised me Chicago. Have you heard of Chicago?"

"It sounds far."

"That's the point," she said, grinning. Then her mouth softened. "How's Klaus?"

"Sleeping. He knows to stay put." Saying it out loud didn't make the fear smaller. The building could crack itself open while I was gone. A stranger could step through the cardboard and find a boy too obedient for his own good. I kept talking anyway. "He was three when the war ended. He learned quick."

Elke murmured. "As if the war ever ended, as if it ever will."

Old Manne nodded his agreement and sighed loudly. We were quiet after that. The city made you superstitious. If you said you were safe, the ceiling fell. If you said you were hungry, you learned quickly that hunger could get worse.

Rumors cracked like ice beneath our feet. The Russians had closed everything—roads, rails, barges—because the Western sectors had changed the money, because the Soviets wanted Berlin to kneel, because men who never had to line up for bread liked to show how big their dicks were. Some said the Americans would fly food in forever; some said they'd stop as soon as it got hard. Some said the Russians would take the whole city any day now and that the Red Army would come house to house like before, taking what they wanted and killing what they couldn't carry. My mother died in the spring, three years ago. For me, the rumor wasn't rumor. It was a memory that liked to wake with the dawn.

The line breathed forward again. The shopkeeper stood behind a counter that had once held pyramids of oranges. Now there was a chalkboard with numbers on it, and a pair of scales he polished as if they were a church relic. Rations were written in little squares in a booklet, boxes ready for stamps, grams and grams that added up to hunger: flour if you were lucky, a smear of fat, ersatz coffee that tasted like burnt rubber. The new money from last week looked crisp and untrustworthy. People still traded with cigarettes and favors and the careful nods that meant you owed someone a little piece of your future.

"Your Kittelschürze is thin," Old Manne observed.

"So am I," I retorted, and we both pretended to laugh.

I thought of Klaus under our scratchy blanket, the mattress springs that squeaked if you breathed too hard, the way I'd propped one leg of the bed up on a brick to make it level. I thought of my mother's hands, slick with polish, rubbing at a marble sill until our faces appeared in it like ghosts. I thought of the roar of planes overhead and the men in their cockpits who had flown to kill us and now flew to keep us alive.

Someone at the front of the line lifted her chin. "Listen," she said.

We all did. It was a sound we'd learned to tell apart in the war: friendly or enemy, bomber or fighter, low or high. This one came like a steady hum, growing to a throatier growl, then slid lower as if the sky were exhaling. A plane taking off at Tempelhof. Another after it. Another after that. Every two minutes, people whispered. Every two minutes, another belly of sacks of flour, salt, milk powder, dried eggs, sugar—the most essential necessities.

"When the pilots wiggle their wings, they'll drop sweets for the children," Mother Olga's oldest boy said, wide-eyed. "I saw it last night. He did it just for me."

"Not for you, Hans," she scolded gently. "For all of us."

I imagined Klaus's face when I'd tell him about the candy parachutes. I imagined him believing it, which was sweeter than the chocolate itself. He liked to stand on the broken balcony and wave at the planes, as if his small hand could tug them closer. I hated leaving him, but it would be worse to drag him here and let him yawn for hours and watch my cheeks burn when we reached the front, and there was less than we'd hoped for.

"We'll manage," I whispered, to no one and everyone, to my mother and to the city, to the ghost of myself who used to carry buckets up clean stairwells and think the world was heavy but fair. "We always do."

Elke bumped my shoulder. "You hear about Die Ecke? The owner says Americans from the airfield will be coming more often. More tips."

"More hands," I said.

"Take the money. Keep your hands to yourself," she snickered, which was as close as anyone came to a prayer anymore.

I nodded. I wasn't going to marry a uniform. I wasn't going to trade myself for nylons or chocolate or a ticket to anywhere. Survival was not the same as surrender. I would stand in line and count grams, keep our patched walls from falling, and teach my brother how to stay quiet and small until it was safe to be loud.

In the distance, the familiar sound of jackhammers started up as another day of putting Berlin back together began.

The line moved. The scales dipped. When it was my turn, I set my ration card down, smoothing the wrinkled edge with my thumb, and watched as my booklet thinned by a few squares. When I stepped away, I held a sack that felt too light for the hope I wanted to put in it.

Outside, the engines rolled over us again, and I lifted my head. The plane slid like a silver knife across the gray. For a moment—just a moment—I let myself imagine the man inside looking down at our street, at our ruin, at me.

Then I tucked the sack under my arm and went home to wake my brother.

Berlin — June 30, 1948, Wednesday

WEDNESDAY NIGHT, and for the first time all week, my name did not appear on the flight board. I'd racked up nearly fifty hours since Sunday—flying the corridors into Berlin, skimming low on approach to Tempelhof or Gatow, then turning straight back toward the western zones, Frankfurt, Wiesbaden, Celle, or Fassberg. Filling up on flour, coal, sugar. Rations measured by the ton. The same shattered city beneath me every time, until Berlin still glowed red and white behind my eyelids when I tried to sleep.

The brass called it efficiency.

I called it penance.

'. The thing inside me—call it instinct, or dragon, or just some fucked-up part of my brain that needed to be in motion—didn't know what to do with a slack leash. My senses were still tuned to engine whine and ice in the slipstream, to the pulse of the Berlin skyline stitched by searchlights and burning in the haze. I caught myself pacing the tarmac in front of my barracks, boots crunching over gravel, and tried to ignore the tug in my chest that wanted to climb straight up and disappear into the night. The dragon itched to be let out and take flight. I told myself I was just cold. I told myself a lot of things.

The other pilots were trickling back from the night flights, still high on adrenaline and cheap American cigarettes. Even from ten yards away, I could hear their laughter, bright and tinny. Someone had a wind-up phonograph out near the steps, and a German singer's voice, *Lale Andersen*, I thought, floated over the drizzle like a broken lullaby. The song, called *Lily Marleen*, was popular with the troops. It was a scene I'd seen a hundred times, but tonight it felt staged, like we were actors in a play where everyone said their lines a little too loud, a little too fast. The only thing real was the hunger, and I wasn't talking about food.

Most of these guys were kids, good kids, some of them, but still kids. They'd signed up at eighteen or nineteen, saw a year or two of Hell from the air, and now we were feeding Berlin instead of flattening it. The turnaround would have given anyone whiplash. One month, they're dropping bombs on anonymous cities in the lines of fire; the next, they're ferrying sacks of sugar to the same streets, and all the rules about the enemy are suddenly gone.

Me? I'd learned there were no rules. Not for people like me.

"Griffin!" I heard my last name, and when I turned, I saw Carter hustling toward me, already halfway through a Lucky Strike and grinning as if he'd just won the lottery.

Carter was a redhead from Valdosta, Georgia, with a constellation of freckles so dense it looked like he'd been dusted with cocoa powder. He called everyone sir, even when he was half-drunk, and had a way of making trouble without ever seeming to get *into* trouble. I liked him in the way you like a stray cat that won't stop following you around. You know it's not good for you, but there's a kind of comfort in the persistence.

"We're heading to a bar," Carter said. "You in?"

I glanced back at the barracks, at the dim glow behind the blackout curtains, and pictured the darkness waiting inside, sweat and metal, the hiss of nightmares sliding through the cracks in my skull. I imagined lying on the cot, trying to remember what sleep was supposed to feel like. I knew exactly what waited for me. It was always the same: burning houses, screaming engines, wings sheared off in midair. The ghosts were punctual as hell.

"I don't drink much," I said, even though the thought of a cold beer was already making my mouth water.

Carter just laughed. "That's what you always say, and then you're the last one out the door." He flicked his cigarette butt into the rain. "Come on, man. You can't just sit around here all night. Besides, these *Krauts* might be starving, but they know how to make a damn good pilsner."

He said *Krauts* the way you'd say *Huskers* or *Tarheels*, like it was a sports team and not a city full of people picking through rubble for a place to sleep. I didn't hold it against him. Everything in this place was a joke if you wanted to survive, especially for the ones who'd never had to see the inside of a German city before the bombs stopped falling.

He jerked his thumb toward a knot of pilots forming by the gate. "Come on, Griffin. Die Ecke. You know, the corner bar? Heard the waitresses are easy on the eyes."

I did know. Word spread fast in the American sector. Most of those so-called waitresses were girls who'd learned a little English before the war and were now learning a lot more after. If you had a ration bar and a pack of Camels, you could forget about the rest of the world for a few hours. The other guys loved to talk about it, about how easy everything was here, how different it was from home. In the States, girls still needed chaperones. Here, all you needed was a smile and the right uniform.

I'd never joined in, but not for the reasons people assumed. I hated the idea of trading favors for flesh, of taking something from someone who had nothing left to give. The Germans didn't mean much to me, not after what I'd seen, but that didn't mean I should treat them like souvenirs. Maybe it was guilt, or maybe it was something worse, but I tried to stay out of the games. Still, a bar was a bar, and I wasn't about to spend another night alone with my nightmares.

"Fine," I said, and pulled my jacket over my shoulders. "But I'm not carrying anyone home this time."

Carter's smile widened. "That's the spirit!" He clapped me on the back, and for a second, I wondered if he felt the twitch under my skin, the way the dragon in me was starting to stretch out, restless and hot.

We met up with the others at the gate, five pilots, all with the same look in their eyes: the search for something to fill the emptiness. Some had been here since the start of the war, others were fresh from the States and still trying to figure out why the girls in Berlin didn't look like the girls in New Jersey. I nodded at a couple of men I recognized, and we started the walk into town.

The city was different at night. In the daytime, the ruins looked like mountains, a horizon of broken teeth shrouded in dust and exhaust. At night, the shadows covered the worst of it, and you could almost pretend it was a real city again. People came out after sunset, kids in torn sweaters, women in patched-up Kittelschürzen, old men with faces like paper, all moving quietly, lips zipped up tight against the cold and the memories. Sometimes I thought about what it would be like to live here, and the thought made me sick.

We walked in a loose formation, boots making puddles splash, the only sound Carter's relentless commentary about local women, imported booze, and the insanity of American brass. The others joined in, laughing too loudly, shoving each other with the nervous energy of men who knew tomorrow could be their last flight. I hung back, letting the conversation wash over me like a second language.

About halfway down the Hauptstrasse—Main Street— Carter fell back to match my stride. He looked at me sideways, like he was trying to figure out a magic trick.

"You ever think about going home?" he asked quietly, keeping his voice low enough that it wouldn't carry.

I shrugged. "I try not to. My contract isn't up for a while."

Carter grinned. I said it as a joke, but there was an edge to it, and he heard it. He always did. "You're not as weird as you think you are," he said. "We all got something following us around these days."

I let it go. The truth was, Carter had no idea. No one did. If he knew what I really was, he'd have been the first to run, or worse, the first to try to use it. That was the risk you ran, every day, with every face you met: sooner or later, someone was going to find out. In the close quarters of the barracks, secrets never stayed buried, especially one as dangerous as mine. There were always eyes, always questions, always someone listening a little too closely.

It was one of the reasons I missed Montana so fiercely. Back home, in our small mountain town, I didn't have to pretend. I could be what I was born to be without fear, without judgment, without wondering if tomorrow would bring a noose or a firing squad.

Before we reached the bar, I watched a tired-looking woman pushing a stroller down the street. One wooden wheel squeaked with every step, making me wonder how she managed to get the kid to sleep with that sound.

The bar was tucked into the side of a half-collapsed building, a neon sign in the window barely holding on. The inside smelled like beer and boiled cabbage, and the tables were crowded with airlift crews and a few French soldiers in civilian clothes. Behind the bar, a girl poured drinks with one hand and took cigarettes with the other. She couldn't have been more than twenty, with hair cut short and a face that looked like it had forgotten how to smile.

We pushed through the crowd, staking out a table near the back. Carter ordered a round of beers, and I sat with my back to the wall, scanning the room out of habit. The dragon didn't like closed spaces; it wanted to be out, above, always moving. He curled tighter inside me, his scales whispering across my bones.

He missed home, the mountains, the quiet community where being what we were wasn't a secret to hide, where I could shift under the moon and not have to come back covered in blood.

Once, I'd thought joining the military would make me a hero. I was seventeen and full of fire, my mother's shaky signature was still wet on the enlistment papers. *Go make them proud, Gideon,* she'd said. *Go protect the world.*

By nineteen, I was flying escort over France, shooting down men who looked just like me except for the flag on their wing. By twenty, my best friend Mark—another dragon—was gone, shot down somewhere over Saxony.

By twenty-one, the war was over.

And I was still here, fighting something that wouldn't die.

The noise level climbed as more crews staggered in. English mixed with a smattering of Russian, and both blended with the sharp, clipped German of the locals. People smoked, drank, fought, and made up in the span of a few sentences. It was chaos, but it was a familiar kind. You could pretend the world was normal here, if only for a little while.

Carter returned with a pitcher and six pints, distributing them like a priest giving out communion. "To the Berlin Express," he announced, raising his glass. The others echoed him, and for a minute, I almost felt like a person and not a machine. I raised my own glass, said nothing, and let the beer do the talking.

A few minutes later, Carter nudged my shin under the table. "Check six, Griff. Two o'clock. That one's new."

I followed his nod past a haze of cigarette smoke and the hunched backs of half a dozen flight engineers. Not much to see at first. A girl in a worn gray dress—nothing fancy —but her long chestnut hair caught the dim light and held it, like it refused to let go once it was noticed. She wore it curled at the ends, old-fashioned, almost like something you'd see in a *Life* magazine ad back home. Her face was carved thinner than it should've been, hollows under her cheekbones that weren't there for beauty, but for survival.

She was pretty enough.

Pretty in the brittle way of someone barely keeping ahead of gravity. Pretty in the way that made your chest ache if you looked too long, like something already half-lost.

Then the dragon stirred. Not a roar. Not fire. Just a low, unmistakable pull beneath my ribs, heat curling, scales shifting in warning or recognition, I couldn't tell which. My attention sharpened without my permission, my focus narrowing until the rest of the bar dulled around the edges.

She moved between tables, balancing a tray with practiced ease, ducking a grabby hand without breaking stride. She didn't look up often. When she did, her eyes were large and dark, shellacked with something harder than mascara.

Resignation, maybe.

Or the kind of cold that sank into your bones and never quite left, no matter how warm the room was. My dragon watched her the way it watched the sky before a storm. Alert. Intent.

Certain that something important had just crossed our path.

And for the first time since the war ended, since I'd learned how to lock every dangerous part of myself down tight, I had the uneasy, undeniable sense that whatever this was, I wasn't going to be able to walk away from it.

"'You see what I'm seeing?" Carter said, turning his glass so the pale beer made a warped lens between us. "That one's trouble."

"She doesn't look old enough to be here," I said, though she was probably my age, maybe a year or two younger.

"Old enough to break hearts," someone else said—Schmidt, I think, the only German-American in our squadron, blond and baby-faced and doomed to be a translation joke forever. "Or your teeth, if you get fresh."

More laughter, but it was a thin layer over something else. The German girls made everyone just a little uncomfortable, even the ones who acted like kings in the ruins. Some of the guys had wives waiting stateside, pictures folded into four and carried like talismans, and I'd seen more than a few promises unravel on the night tram to Steglitz or in the back rooms of bars like this. The girls were never the problem. It was always us.

The second time the waitress passed by, I caught her eye, just for a moment. She didn't smile or give me a line. She just looked at me like I was another piece of broken furniture to step around and kept moving.

Carter noticed. He always did. He leaned over, pitched

his voice low. "Bet you five packs of Lucky Strikes you can't get her name before midnight."

I grunted. "What makes you think I'm interested?"

"What makes you think you're not?" Carter's grin was all teeth. "I hear the new ones are looking for real connections. Nylons, chocolate, a way out. You got nylons, right? In your room? You always have everything, man."

He said it like a joke, but I could feel the eyes of the table swing my way, checking if maybe I did have something they didn't. In their heads, it was still a race, still a contest, even here at the edge of the world. The dragon didn't understand contests. He understood only claims.

So I lied. "I'm fresh out."

The lie tasted wrong the moment it left my mouth, like smoke swallowed the wrong way.

Carter clapped my shoulder, unconvinced. "Don't sweat it, Griff. She's out of your league anyway."

The others joined in, laughing, ribbing me the way men did when they were bored and restless and trying to forget where they were. The warmth of it should've been good. Should've grounded me. Instead, the dragon under my skin rolled and flexed, a low warning ripple that had nothing to do with Carter's words and everything to do with the girl across the room. My shoulders tightened. All I wanted was air. Space. Sky.

The night moved fast after that. Glasses refilled. Voices climbed. Smoke thickened. The tiny bar warped until it felt like all of Berlin had been pressed into one room, breathing the same sour steam, clinging to the same fragile hope that the Americans would leave enough behind to drink again tomorrow.

When the girl came by our table, Schmidt tried his German on her. She cut him off in perfect English. "We close in half an hour," her eyes flicked over him—then to me—and away again. "Last call."

The dragon stilled. Not relaxed. Focused.

Carter leaned in. "What's your name, anyway? For our friend here, not for us. He's shy."

She gave him nothing but the faintest shake of her head. "Inga," she replied, not looking at any of us.

Her name landed low and solid in my chest, like it had always belonged there.

"Inga," Carter repeated, rolling it around like a new flavor of gum. "Pretty name for a cold night, huh, Griff?"

I felt her glance at me, quick, sharp, assessing. A look that made something hot and instinctive coil tight under my ribs.

"We'll take one more round, Inga," I said, because I had to say something, keeping my voice level by force of habit alone.

She turned without a word.

Schmidt watched her move away and murmured, "That one... she is not like the others."

The dragon agreed.

"None of them are," I mumbled, but no one heard me.

By midnight, most of the crowd had thinned out. Carter and Schmidt were drunk enough to start singing, arms locked around each other's shoulders, God only knew what language it was supposed to be. I heeled my chair back against the wall and watched Inga wipe down the bar.

Her movements were spare. Mechanical. Efficient. She never smiled. Never flirted. She poured another drink only when someone asked and counted the cigarettes before she took them, every single time.

The dragon watched her, too.

It recognized something in the way she held herself, not weakness, but discipline. A refusal to break. Like if you looked close enough, you'd see the cracks, but she kept fitting the pieces together and daring the world to try her again.

When the bar finally emptied, I stood to leave. Carter was passed out cold, his cheek mashed into a puddle of spilled beer. Schmidt was arguing with the jukebox in slurred German. I left more money on the table than I needed to and thought about saying goodnight to Inga.

But she was gone, vanished through a door behind the bar. I'd noticed the Russians all night. Noticed them noticing her too. And now I didn't like the way they followed her out the back. I told myself it wasn't my concern. That this would only bring trouble. That I didn't care about Germans. Or Russians.

The dragon huffed at the lie. Because I knew exactly what those men were about to do.

And I knew—just as surely—that I couldn't let it happen. Not to her. Not to any woman. Not on my watch.

Inga

Berlin — July 1, 1948, Thursday morning

I DIDN'T SO MUCH NOTICE the American staring as I felt it, a slow burn on the side of my face as I wiped down the sticky bar and kept my eyes on the always-filthy glassware. He was one of those men who never seemed to tire; even this late at night, he still had a clean-shaven jaw, a cap set like a challenge, and a bomber jacket creased in all the right places. In some other life, maybe, I would have found that interesting. But after a day like mine, standing in line all morning for minimal rations, a cold pot of barley soup re-boiled for the third day and portioned between my brother and me, followed by a slog through algebra by candle-end, I had no energy left for noticing and even less for caring.

Americans stared, but so did the British, the French, the Polish, and every other uniform in this city's kaleidoscope of armies. Every pair of eyes landed with the same hunger, the same calculation. Sometimes they'd try to soften it with a compliment or a joke, but it always boiled down to who would offer what, and at what price. I'd learned to tune it out, to act as if my body was already a ghost, transparent and untouchable. I'd learned to keep my face flat and my steps quick, to fill the orders, collect the coins and cigarettes, and slide out the back before anyone could get clever. On a night like this, with rain sluicing down the windows and the stink of wet wool and mold thick enough to choke you, I just wanted the shift to end.

By midnight, the tips of my toes were numb, and my heels ached as if ground into the floorboards by a giant thumb. Every muscle in my legs was trembling with exhaustion. I was running out of patience and warmth, and the only thing keeping me upright was the thought of home: kicking off my worn shoes, peeling down my last clean pair of stockings, and wrapping Klaus in the threadbare blanket until the shivering stopped, if only for a few hours. There was nothing to look forward to but sleep, and the hope that maybe, maybe, tomorrow's ration line would be just a little shorter.

I shucked off my apron—still wet where beer had sloshed over my wrist—and counted the cigarettes I'd managed to squirrel away. Two Lucky Strikes, one half-smoked Chesterfield, and a local brand that tasted like burnt rope. Not bad, really. I tied them into a corner of my kerchief and ducked out the back, the bar's low yellow glow dying behind me as the heavy door swung shut.

The alley was a tunnel of cold, with walls that sweated rain and reeked of a thousand spilled secrets. The air slapped me awake, all raw, wet brick and the chemical sting of cabbage, rain drawing smoke from the ancient cracks. Even the rubble here was alive, piled shapes that looked like sleeping dogs, or maybe piles of discarded coats hugging themselves against the cold. I hunched my head, tugged my coat collar up, and quick-marched toward the mouth of the alley, my heels skidding on the slick cobbles.

I was barely out when a voice like velvet and vodka sang out behind me. "Fräulein," it called. The *r* was buried in the tongue. Russian. I didn't slow. I didn't turn. Russians were never alone. I'd learned to tell the difference between the regulars and the *specials*, the ones who wore their uniforms with a kind of practiced menace, whose eyes never stopped looking for an opening, a soft place, a weak spot. These were the kind that came in pairs, or worse.

A second voice joined the first, laughing, throwing out half-understood German with the rhythm of a joke gone sour. "Jemand hat es eilig," it said. *Someone's in a hurry.* The footsteps behind me quickened, one, then two, then three, a shuffling syncopation as the men closed in, boots scraping grit and puddles.

My heart went sideways. The city's ruins were full of warnings, and I'd grown up hearing all of them: how to vanish when you need to, how to make yourself invisible, how to recognize the footfall of a friend or a predator. But sometimes, even the best warnings can't save you. I tried to widen my stride, but the alley narrowed up ahead, funneling me toward the street. The only light was a spill from a window above, barely enough to see the shapes that moved ahead of me. Two figures slipped out of a doorway, blocking the exit as neatly as a lock snapping shut. The one in front wore a cap low on his brow, the red star almost invisible in the wet. The other toyed with a packet of cigarettes, flipping it in his palm like he was practicing a trick.

"Trade," offered the one in the cap. His German was better than his friend's, but not by much. "Cigarettes. Good ones. Lucky Strikes." He shook the pack at me, and for a second, I thought maybe it was just a shakedown. But then his chin flicked toward a dented metal trash bin tucked into a recess. "You lie there. Two minutes. Fair, fair."

The taste of old soup came back up my throat. For a moment, I thought about screaming, but I'd tried once before, years ago, and learned that the world could swallow a scream whole and never spit it out. I tried to push past him, but a hand darted out—fast, practiced— and hooked my elbow. The grip was iron. I yanked back, and my purse slipped and hit the stones, scattering the cigarettes and what little money I'd earned. The other men went for my coat hem, not rough but deliberate, tugging it just enough to remind me of who held the cards.

The alley closed in, and the walls loomed higher, the wet bricks sucking away every sound but their laughter. I tried to swing with my free arm, but he caught that wrist, too, and twisted it until the bones creaked. "No fight," he said, grinning. "Pretty girl. Just quick, okay?"

My body froze, but my mind sprinted backward, years and years, to the bomb shelter behind a ruined building where we'd hidden during the last horror. I could hear it all again: the stampede of boots, the pounding on the door, my mother's hand clamped over my mouth to stifle the noise. The memory was a dark river, and it dragged me under, back to the day when the Russians came to our shelter and pulled women out by the hair, laughing the whole time. My mother's eyes had locked on mine, empty of fear, just cold and clear, like she'd always known that would happen. Then the door had ripped open, and hands had swept her away, and I'd never seen her again.

I flailed, but the men laughed louder. "Nice," said the one with the cigarettes. "She has spirit." He pinched my cheek, hard, and I spat in his face. He howled, and the man in the cap slapped me, hard enough that my ear rang and the world spun sideways. I landed on my knees, scraping them and my last nylons raw on the grit.

"Stop," I said. It was the smallest sound, a whisper, but as soon as it left my lips, it ballooned into something much bigger. I tried again, louder, and this time it came out edged with panic. "Stop!" The word ricocheted up the brick walls, desperate and ugly and useless.

He clapped a hand over my mouth, squeezing my jaw until my teeth dug into my own lips. I bit down, tasting blood, and he cursed and shoved me against the wall. I crumpled to the ground, the dragon-shape of terror unfolding in my chest, claws raking, wings beating. I couldn't breathe. I couldn't think. I could only remember, and I remembered everything, me and the woman with the braid, the night we crawled upstairs and found the bodies spread like broken dolls outside the bunker, left like trash.

For a moment, I thought the world might just end right there, in that wet alley, curled into a ball while the men decided what to do with what was left of me. But then, from somewhere behind us, a new shadow cut through the lantern light, and the whole night shifted.

"Let her go." The voice was American. Flat, unhurried, deadly calm. The kind of voice that didn't need to shout, because it had already won the argument.

The men paused, just for a heartbeat, and I saw them trying to judge whether this was a bluff or a real problem. The cap guy turned, eyeing the American up and down. "No trouble," he said in English, the accent thick as soup. "We are friends, Amerikanets. We offer trade."

The American didn't move. He didn't even blink. "You're going to drop the cigarettes," he said. "And you're going to walk away. Now."

The men looked at each other. The one with the cigarettes tried to laugh, made a show of lighting up right in the American's face. "You want trade?" he said, blowing smoke. "We can trade."

The American's hand moved—a flick, almost lazy—and the cigarette snapped out of the man's mouth and into the gutter. Before he could even yelp, the American punched him, just once, but with the kind of force that made the wet air vibrate. Cap guy lunged. The American twisted sharply, slamming his shoulder into the man and driving him sideways with his full weight, sending the Russian crashing into the trash bin. Metal rang. The Russian swore and came up swinging, and the American put him back down with a short, mean punch that made my teeth ache just watching. He looked in my direction for a moment, and in that fraction of time, I could have sworn his eyes flashed golden. But I put it away as a trick of the light and my stressed mind.

It took less than a handful of seconds. Then there was only breathing, mine, ragged and wet; the American's, steady, loud in the narrow space.

"Go," he said without looking away from them.

The men picked themselves up, spat words I couldn't hear, and shoved off into the street, shoulders hunched against any more consequence.

I hadn't realized I'd crawled into the corner until my spine felt the cold of the wall and my palms felt grit. My whole body shook—knees knocking, teeth clicking like a little machine—and I hated it, hated that they would have seen it if they'd stayed one second longer.

The American crouched, slow, like you do for a dog that might bite. "Hey," he said, voice roughened down to something almost gentle. "You're okay."

But I wasn't. When his hands hovered and then settled, warm and careful, on my arms, I grabbed his sleeves like I was falling off a roof. I didn't want to. I did it anyway. I pressed my face into a jacket that smelled like rain and oil and the high metallic tang of airplanes, and my breath stuttered against his chest in useless, ugly sobs.

"There," he said, because what else was there to say? "There. There. You're safe."

I didn't know his name. I didn't care. I clung harder, shaking so badly I thought my bones would come apart, and he held on like he had nothing better to do than hold me together. He was so warm. So incredibly warm, and the way his heart beat under my ear had a calming effect.

"Breathe," he said, low against my hair. "That's it. In. Out."

I did what he asked because the alternative was drowning.

Against everything inside me, I heard my own voice say, very small, "Don't let go."

"I won't," he promised.

And—for the space of a few heartbeats in a city built of ruins—he didn't.

Berlin — July 1, 1948, Thursday morning

I KEPT hold of her until her shoulders stopped trembling like a leaf in the wind. Her fingers dug into the fabric of my jacket, clinging to it like a promise the coat itself had made to keep her safe.

"Did they—" I started. The question was blunt. Stupid. Useless. I wanted to find the men who'd cornered her and turn them into ash where they stood. I closed my eyes before I could finish the thought, because the dragon inside me was already roaring, already imagining bone and fire and screams cut short. "Did they hurt you?"

She shook her head so slowly it felt like watching someone move through water. "No," she said, her voice small but steady. "You came just in time. Thank you."

It wasn't the word *no* that soothed the dragon. It was her voice. The sound of it slid through me, through the heat and the rage, and something ancient in my chest stilled. Never in my life had a voice affected me like that, not a command, not an order, not even fear. The dragon quieted, not gone, not forgiving, but listening.

Her hands loosened their grip. The shivering slowed, fading to an afterthought. I eased her back until she could stand on her own. She was so slight. Her coat was little more than a suggestion of warmth. I shrugged out of my leather jacket and had to crouch to settle it around her shoulders. The fabric smelled of fuel and rain and the faint iron tang that clung to everything I owned. When I wrapped it around her, she swallowed hard, like warmth was returning to places that had forgotten what it felt like.

"Let me take you home," I said, because the words felt safer than thinking.

She looked up at me then, eyes huge and raw in the alley light, and the fear flared again, sharp and animal, like someone had yanked a string tight inside her chest.

"It's okay," I said quickly. "I won't hurt you." I hesitated, then added, softer, "I'm Gideon."

"Inga," she answered automatically, as if the name had slipped out before she could stop it. She blinked, surprised by the sound of herself saying it.

She nodded—not to me, but to herself—then looked away. For a heartbeat, her body said *no* even if her mouth didn't. Then her chin tipped, just slightly, pointing down the lane to the right.

She started walking. I fell in beside her.

At first, we passed streets where people had tried to pretend life might return. Boarded shopfronts. A café with two lonely tables beneath a patched canopy. A stretch of cobblestone swept clean enough to be ashamed of the dirt pushed into the gutters. Someone had nailed glass back into window frames, hung tarps that tried very hard to look like curtains. A tram clanked past in the distance, carrying people who looked more like ghosts than passengers.

But the farther we went, the more the city stopped pretending. The lights thinned. The streets narrowed. Small fires smoldered in the ruins, casting crooked shadows against walls that might collapse tomorrow or stand another year out of sheer spite.

The dragon stayed close to the surface as we walked, muscles coiled, fury banked and waiting. Because even if she'd been spared, they hadn't been. Not yet.

By some ruins, she stopped, "This is it."

"This is...where?" I asked because saying it out loud made it sound less like an accusation and more like a question.

She glanced at me and shrugged. "It's fine," she said. "Thank you." She tugged at the jacket, as if to return it. "I can go alone from here."

'She held out my coat like an offering, eyes locked on my face to see what I would do. I didn't take it. She didn't want me to see where she lived. I knew that. I also knew I couldn't leave her here.

"If you want me to——" I began, and she hesitated, then pointed toward a darkened block where a building hung together by timber and tape and prayers. It looked like a paper house someone had tried to mend with glue and stubbornness.

"I'll be safe," she said, thrusting my jacket into my hands, and it read like a lie she didn't seem to believe either. "Thank you again."

She moved faster then, ducking over piles of masonry, climbing the broken steps of what had been an apartment block. Once she stumbled on a loose slab, and I wanted to leap across that gap in one stride. I wanted to catch her, to be the man whose hands never missed. But I held myself back because the truth was ugly and simple: if I went with her inside, I'd be forcing my way into a life I hadn't been invited to, and that would be worse than walking away.

She looked back over her shoulder once, frowning, and in that instant, I realized I was still too close. I had been holding her back without meaning to. Her face told me not to follow. So I stepped back into the dark and watched.

She disappeared through a doorway patched with planks. The light inside was thinner than the streetlight; it looked like hope kept to a single candle. When the door closed, it sounded like the last hinge on a house trying to survive the night.

For a second, I stood rooted, jacket in my hands, rain on my shoulders. Then I walked to the curb and flagged a battered taxi. The driver squinted at me through a cloud of smoke, then nodded and opened the door. The cab smelled of old leather and sweet, cheap perfume. I gave the driver the address of the McNair barracks, which he seemed to know well. The vehicle jolted, and we pulled away, the cab's taillight a candle floating through Berlin's broken spine.

On the way back to the barracks, I thought of a lot of things I didn't like. I didn't like the Russians, men who could make an alley into a courtroom and sentence a woman without a trial. I didn't like myself for how easily I wanted to answer force with force. I didn't like how all the old certainties had been unstitched the day the war ended.

Most of all, I didn't like the way my hands had trembled with the urge to burn the men where they stood. Not in a cold, tactical way. In a raw, animal way I'd never felt before, even on the day Mark had gone down. Fire had felt methodical then; this was blood in my mouth and claws under my skin. I wanted to shift, big and terrible and hot, to unmake them as easily as the world had been unmade in 1944. The thought was almost beautiful in its completeness.

And then there was Inga. She was a small, stubborn flare in a city that had learned to snub out flares. When she'd clung to me, I'd felt something I hadn't allowed myself to feel in years, not pity, not even exactly protectiveness, but a fierce, sharp heat that made my head spin. It scared me because I had no room for complications. I had duties and ghosts and a contract and a rhythm that kept the darkness at bay. I didn't need a girl who smelled of rain and scared breath to complicate my life.

I ran my hand through my hair until my fingers came away damp. I told myself a hundred times in that taxi the reasons why I should forget her: rules, distance, the stupidity of getting attached in a city that could fall apart again tomorrow. I said I didn't want anything to do with anyone who lived in these ruins.

The truth was different—softer and more dangerous. I liked the look she'd given me when she'd said *Thank you*, like it was a word she'd never expected to say again. I hated how much that small thing mattered.

"How long have you been in Berlin?" the driver asked, going for small talk.

"Too long," I answered, not in the mood for conversation.

He nodded, maybe out of politeness, maybe because he knew better than to pry. In the faint glow of the dash, I saw the missing stump where his left hand used to be. A war souvenir. Maybe he'd lost it to one of my bombs. Maybe he was the one who shot Mark down. We'd never know, and it didn't matter. Three years ago, we would have shot at each other and not thought twice. Now we were supposed to trade small talk like it was just another night.

The city thinned out as we drove south, past darkened shopfronts and piles of brick that used to be houses. The rain had turned the streets slick and quiet. Ahead, the road narrowed where the checkpoint squatted across the boundary between the American and Soviet sectors: a wooden barrier, a shed with a lamp burning low, and a pair of Russian guards in gray coats watching every car that passed.

The driver slowed, fished out his papers, and leaned out the window. One of the guards stepped up, his flashlight cut across my face, then down to the insignia on my jacket. His eyes were like glass, no curiosity, no warmth, just the kind of emptiness you learn from too many winters.

"U.S. Airlift," I said, holding his stare.

He studied me a second longer than he needed to, and I could tell he wanted to detain me. My dragon almost dared him to give it a try, but something in my eyes must have unsettled him, and he waved us through with a flick of his fingers. The barrier lifted, creaking, and the car rolled on.

I let out a breath I hadn't realized I'd been holding. The driver didn't look at me, just muttered, "Always the same. They like to remind us whose road it is."

He wasn't wrong. Every inch of this city belonged to someone else. Every mile was borrowed from the ruins.

The drive wasn't long after that, and the driver must've picked up on my tone, because he didn't say another word until the barracks loomed up out of the dark. McNair Barracks, solid and gray and pretending to be American now.

By the time he stopped, my coat felt heavier than it had when I'd taken it off the hanger. I paid the fare, nodded once, and walked the rest of the way alone. The sound of my boots on wet stone was the only thing I trusted to tell me I was still me.

In the cot that night, sleep didn't come easy. I lay with the hum of the barracks around me and the memory of a woman shaking in an alley, and I knew the dragon inside me was as awake as the man. I didn't want the trouble she promised. I didn't want the ache.

But somewhere, under the noise and the restlessness and the stale cigarette smoke, a small part of me had already started to shift its plans.

Berlin —July 1, 1948, Thursday

I WOKE to the sound of plaster dust settling, soft, like someone sifting flour through their fingers. And for a blissful moment, I was transported in time. Back to when the world hadn't ended, when nobody thought of a war yet. When I was in the kitchen with my mother and she was singing Christmas songs while decorating cookies.

For a long moment, I lay still and counted Klaus's breaths and thought of how sad it was for him that he never got to experience that. He didn't even know what Christmas cookies were, and I told myself that I had to do better. For him. He deserved so much more. He made the little whistle sound he made at the end of each exhale, and my eyes filled with tears before I let myself move.

Morning was always the same list, even when the weather or the rumors changed: sweep, heat water, check the walls, see if the world had remembered us.

I swept first. Dust was a second skin here; it found your lungs and your hair and the cracks in your knuckles. I pushed it toward the hole where a wall used to be, then covered the gap again with our patchwork of boards and cardboard. One of the planks had slipped in the night; I hammered it back with the heel of my shoe until the draft grew smaller.

Klaus rolled over; his hair was sticking up, making him look like a hedgehog. "Food?" he mumbled.

"Food," I promised, and put the kettle on the iron plate we used for a stove. We were down to the last knob of fat and a scoop of barley. I fried a sliver of onion in the pan for the smell, then stirred in water, barley, and a pinch of salt. Steam made the room feel almost kind. I set a cracked mug of ersatz coffee near the hot plate to warm my hands.

While the porridge thickened, I checked our stash: two slices of dark bread, hard as a lesson; a spoon of jam for Klaus's birthday, assuming I could keep it from him another week; three cigarettes wrapped like treasure for trading. On the windowsill, I kept the ration booklet under a stone. I touched it the way some people touch a cross.

We ate sitting on the mattress, sharing the bowl and pretending not to notice the grit between our teeth. "Chew slowly," I said. "Tell your belly it's a feast."

"That's lying," Klaus said, and I laughed because he needed me to.

After, I made him do schoolwork. He dragged his heels like a mule. The book we used had a blackened corner and pages that smelled faintly of smoke. I had found it in a stairwell with the spine scorched, and it felt like a miracle to save any words at all.

"Copy the sums," I said, setting the stump of a pencil in his hand.

He groaned. "Can't we go out? Just for a little? I'll be fast."

"You'll be careful," I corrected. "Fast boys break bones."

He bent to his numbers with a sigh so deep it rattled the window. Outside, a cart clattered over broken cobbles; somewhere, a woman shouted a name as if she could call a person back from whatever swallowed them. In the courtyard, the water pump squealed, then came the cough of someone trying to start a fire with damp coal. Life here was made of small noises and keeping your balance.

When the last sum was done—crooked, but done—I let him go. "Ten minutes," I warned. "And I'm coming. I need some fresh air too," I lied, because the truth was that I couldn't bear not having my eyes on him.

We stepped into the courtyard where the building's stumps bit at the sky. Children drifted in like sparrows from the neighboring ruins. A knot of orphans—*Trümmerkinder*—rubble kids—were already there, throwing rocks at a bottle and swearing like old men. I didn't like Klaus near them. The world had made them hard too early; hardness rubs off like charcoal. I tugged him toward the steps instead.

That's when I saw Axel at the far wall. Ten years old and small as a five-year-old, his left shoe was worn down at the heel where he dragged his bad leg. He watched the others the way a hungry dog watches a butcher's window, trying hard to keep emotions from his face. The boys didn't let him play. They mimed his limp when he looked away or, sometimes, even when he didn't.

I felt the old ache open in my chest. Some days, when we had more food—if we ever had more—I let him sleep on our floor with Klaus, two small bodies curled like commas in the same sentence. Not tonight, though. I had no idea what we would eat tonight yet.

"Can I run to the fence?" Klaus asked, bouncing on his toes. "Please?"

"Stay where I can see you," I relented. "If you lose sight of me, you freeze. You remember?"

"I'm not a baby," he said, already grinning.

We went out to the street where a strip of sky showed between the broken roofs, pale and low. The first plane announced itself with a long, throaty hum that set a ripple through the children like wind through grass. They pointed, shouted, forgot to pretend they weren't excited. A C-47 slid into view, belly fat with sacks, coming in low for Tempelhof. Klaus ran to the edge of the rubble pile and waved both arms like a semaphore. I waved, too, because: why not? Some habits are older than war.

I told myself not to think about last night, about the Russians in the damp dark and a hand on my elbow like a trap. I told myself not to think about the American with the clean blond hair and the serious blue eyes who'd said *you're safe* like he believed he could make it true.

But my mind pried at the memory anyway, in much the same way one can't stop picking at a loose scab. He had looked like a poster—what the Reich used to promise us a man should look like—and I'd spent years hating that face. It should have made me cold. Instead, his jacket had been warm on my shoulders, and something in me I thought ruined had…loosened. Kindness was dangerous. Kindness got you to open a door better kept locked tight. I had learned that under the ground, while the boots hammered the stairs. Still, when he wrapped his coat around me, some brittle piece gave way. Not love. Not even hope. A simpler hunger I hadn't let myself feel: the need to be held without being taken.

Another plane came in low, the sound deep enough to press against my ribs. Klaus jumped and shouted up at the sky. Across the yard, Axel stared like he wanted to swallow the whole airplane. The other boys shoved past him, whooping; one cuffed the back of his head as if to test whether he'd fall. He didn't. He just tilted, then straightened, mouth set.

I thought of the Americans who wagged their wings and dropped sweets on little parachutes. I thought of the Russians who traded Lucky Strikes for dignity. I thought of the way the American—Gideon, he'd said his 'was—

had held me while I shook like a child and remembered the way his heartbeat felt under my cheek, steady as the new timetables the Allies pinned up wherever people gathered.

"Can I go closer?" Klaus asked, already inching toward the fence that used to be a garden gate.

"Fine," I said, because he'd been penned up all week, and boys are not plants; they don't grow without sky. "But you stop at the street, and you look both ways. Twice."

He nodded solemnly and sprinted.

I turned to Axel.

"If you get cold tonight, come on by." A little bit of warmth was all I could offer the kid.

His face flickered, went from longing to suspicion, then back to the blank he wore like a coat. I didn't ask to touch him; some children here were all nerve ends and no skin. Instead, I stepped close enough that he could lean if he wanted. After a moment, he did, the smallest lean, a bird testing whether a branch would hold. I put an arm around his sharp shoulders. For one heartbeat, he softened into me like wax, then remembered himself and sprang away. He half-ran, half-limped after the others, chin high, pretending he'd planned the retreat.

"Yes," I said to the space he left. "Like me."

I hadn't run from Gideon last night, but it had been close. None of us were trained for gentle. Kindness here could be a trap door. You learned not to step where the floor seemed strong.

Klaus whooped. The plane sank lower; its wing lights blinked. Somewhere, a woman crossed herself. Someone else spat and said the Americans wouldn't keep it up; someone swore the Russians would starve us yet. I stood with my hands in my Kittelschürze pockets and watched my brother holler at the sky like he could call it closer by force of will. I loved him so fiercely it made my chest hurt. I would carry the whole city on my back if it meant he slept warm. But love was heavy, and some days my shoulders ached from its weight.

The plane's engines changed pitch, a warm-down growl I now knew meant wheels to concrete, Tempelhof's big mouth swallowing another bird. Klaus turned back to me, his face lit with the kind of joy that made everything else look like a trick of bad light.

"Did you see?" he shouted, as if I could have missed it.

"I saw," I called. "Of course I saw."

He ran back and grabbed my hand, his fingers small but sure. Behind him, Axel paused at the top of a broken step and looked at us, hollow, lonely, the city's echo made into a boy. I lifted my free arm, a question that could be refused. He shook his head once and then limped away, shoulders hunched against the wind.

I watched him go and thought of a stranger's jacket around my ribs and the way my body had remembered how to lean. Then I pushed the thought down where I kept other dangerous things and steered Klaus home, counting our steps by twos to make the road seem shorter.

Berlin — July 3, 1948, Saturday

FOR TWO DAYS, I tried to scrub her out of my head. I flew double shifts. I ate standing. I slept in pieces. I walked the flight line until my boots hurt. I stayed away from Die Ecke, though every night my eyes flicked toward that direction, like some part of me expected her to step out of the rubble and look at me with those tired, fierce eyes.

None of it helped.

Every time I blinked, I saw her pinned in that alley, breath shaking, eyes wide with terror. Every time I inhaled, I smelled her hair under my jacket. Every time I steadied my pulse, I heard her whisper: *You came just in time.*

And every time I thought about those Russians, the dragon inside me bared its teeth. Let me out, it murmured. Let me burn them.

I slammed the door on that thought. Couldn't afford it.

Not in this city. Not in this uniform. But I couldn't shake her.

I told myself it was because she was vulnerable. Because she was living in a ruin held together by despair and rust. Because this city would swallow her whole if someone didn't look out for her.

But that wasn't the truth.

The truth was that Inga had gotten under my skin, deeper than shrapnel, deeper than guilt. And now I was carrying her with me into the sky.

Which made me dangerous.

The weather wasn't helping. The northern corridor was choked with clouds thick as wool, and the sun had already sunk behind the gray horizon by the time Reynolds and I taxied out for our last run of the day.

"Feels like a cursed night," he grumbled beside me.

Berlin felt like that every night.

We climbed into the soup, instruments glowing faintly in the gloom. The engines were steady; the old girl was humming with the regular heartbeat of a machine that refused to die.

The city unfolded beneath us in smudges of shadow and broken geometry, a wounded thing curled on itself. The Tiergarten was black and skeletal. The Reichstag was a toothless skull. And the Soviet sector was a darkness even deeper than night. I breathed in through my nose. The dragon stirred, restless.

I tried to distract myself, but that didn't work. Inga rose up again, soft as a bruise.

"Easy Two-Four, maintain heading," the tower crackled.

"Roger," I said.

We leveled out at 4,500 feet, the air, cold and thin, humming against the fuselage.

Reynolds flicked a switch, frowned at the radio hiss. "Interference again."

"Soviets?" I muttered.

He shrugged. "Either that or ghosts."

Knowing this city, I wasn't ruling out either.

Five minutes later, I felt it, a shift in the air pressure, a flutter in the yoke.

And then: a shadow sliced across the clouds like a shark fin.

A Soviet Yak.

Flying too low. Too close.

Too damn fast.

Reynolds cursed. "Jesus—he's right on top of us!"

The Yak dove across our bow, a deliberate buzz so close I could count the rivets on its belly. Turbulence slashed across us like a whip. The Dakota bucked hard. Cargo straps groaned in the back. My pulse detonated.

"He's not supposed to be in the corridor," Reynolds hissed.

"No," I growled, gripping the wheel tighter. "He's not."

The Yak circled us once, twice, like a wolf sniffing prey. Then it peeled off toward the Soviet sector, and that was when I saw the flash. A tiny spark on a rooftop ruin. A muzzle flare.

CRACK.

Something slammed into the starboard fuselage, metal screaming as the bullet tore through skin and frame. The plane jerked violently.

"Christ!" Reynolds shouted. "We're hit!"

My dragon roared awake so violently, I nearly blacked out. Heat surged under my skin. My vision sharpened unnaturally, edges turning gold.

Every instinct screamed at me to turn, dive, obliterate the threat.

Burn them, the dragon snarled. *Let me burn them.*

I pulled back hard on the yoke, forcing breath through my teeth. "Hold steady!"

Another flash.

Another shot.

Another metallic shriek as a bullet punched the underside near the cargo bay.

Reynolds gaped at me. "They're firing on us, Griff! They're SHOOTING at us!"

"Don't say it on the radio," I barked. "Do not—say— anything."

"They're trying to kill us!"

"If we broadcast this," I ground out, "the Soviets get exactly what they want."

Reynolds paled. "You think they're trying to start something?"

I thought of Inga. Of the night she almost died. Of the Russian smirk as he grabbed her wrist. Of how this city was a fuse waiting for a spark.

"Yes," I said.

We limped toward Tempelhof, the Dakota shuddering with every mile. The right wing hummed with damage. One of the gauges trembled in the red.

"We're losing altitude," Reynolds informed me.

"Not if I can help it."

I coaxed her, begged her, prayed to gods I didn't believe in. The engines rattled but held. The runway lights finally appeared through the haze, thin, flickering, desperate. With a shudder, we hit the tarmac hard, bouncing once, twice, then grinding to a stop with a squeal that ripped through my spine.

Silence.

Then Reynolds exhaled shakily. "We're alive."

"Barely."

The ground crew swarmed the plane, eyes going wide as dinner plates when they saw the bullet holes. Two MPs hauled us toward Operations before anyone could even ask a question.

Colonel Jamison's face was the color of an imminent heart attack.

"You two," he said in a low, deadly voice, "will not mention this."

Reynolds blinked at him. "Sir—they SHOT at—"

"No," Jamison snapped. "They did not."

"Sir—"

"They. Did. Not."

He slammed a folder shut so hard, dust jumped. He pointed between us, jabbing the air as if stabbing invisible ghosts. "Do you have any idea how many incidents I've buried in the last month? The French nearly exchanged fire with Soviet MPs last week. A British truck was rammed near the Tiergarten. A French corporal ended up in the hospital after a *misunderstanding* at a checkpoint. And now this."

Reynolds swallowed. "Sir, with respect—"

Jamison sliced the air with his hand. "Respect? Respect went out the window the moment Stalin shut down the roads. We're dancing on a razor's edge. One spark—one goddamn bullet acknowledged—and this whole city goes up like kindling."

His voice dropped lower, darker. "And trust me, gentlemen... Washington will gladly sacrifice two American pilots rather than answer that bullet with another."

A chill ran down my spine that had nothing to do with the dragon. Jamison leaned closer, eyes sharp as broken glass. "You saw nothing. You heard nothing. Your plane hit debris. Do. You. Understand?"

The dragon clawed under my ribs. The injustice burned. But I understood. The last thing anybody needed was the beginning of WWIII. Two dead American pilots would be a low price to pay to stop it from happening. We were flying in food and other essentials this city needed to keep it alive. The Russians wanted it. The Russians were itching to start WWIII.

I stood straighter, "Yes, sir."

Jamison exhaled. "Good. Now get out of my sight."

Outside, the night was damp and metallic. Another plane roared overhead, unbothered, unaware. A baby cried near the fence, a thin sound lost in the engines.

And all I could think was: If the Soviets were willing to

shoot at me in the sky over a city still bleeding from the last war, what would they do to someone like her?

The dragon whispered: *Find her. Make sure she's safe.*

I didn't listen.

Not yet.

But oh, God, I wanted to.

Berlin — July 4, 1948, Sunday

I'D CONTINUED to keep my distance. Avoided Die Ecke, the alley, the very idea of her. Not that it helped any. She kept turning up anyway, in the quiet between engines, in the part of my chest that wouldn't go still. I flew my runs, signed the manifests, drank bad coffee, and pretended not to look at every Russian uniform I passed. I told myself I didn't have time for complications, and that was almost true.

On the Fourth of July, the field felt different, flags taped to office doors, a sheet cake frosted with a crooked map of the States, a guy from Supply trying to grill bratwurst on a dented oil drum while Glenn Miller bled from a tinny phonograph. No fireworks, not with half the city held together by a string. But some idiot had scrounged up some sparklers, and the bright light scratched against a low sky.

I finished my last flight just before dusk, logged it, and told myself I'd sleep. I had rotation again at dawn. Then

Carter hooked an elbow through mine and grinned like mischief. "Come on, Griff. Independence Day. One beer won't kill you. Die Ecke?"

I should have said no.

I said yes.

The bar was the same. Loud, the way only people trying not to think can be loud, English and mostly French and German braided together, laughter with a hard edge. The neon hum at the window made the room look underwater. She was there behind the bar, hair pinned up, face thinner than I remembered, which could've been my imagination or just the light. For a second, I thought she smiled when she saw me, small and gone in an instant, and that one flicker unspooled something I hadn't meant to bring with me.

I took a table near the wall and tipped heavy—cigarettes slid under the glass like a message. For her, they were a fortune; for me, they were ration paper with different ink. When she brought my beer, I heard myself ask, too gently, "Have you eaten?"

She went still, the way a bird goes still. "Yes," she said, and the word had corners. She turned away before I could make it worse.

I didn't chase. I sat and watched the room fill and empty around me. Someone put on *Lili Marleen,* and half the bar groaned and sang anyway. Outside, a tram rattled past with its windows open, the bell dinging like an apology. Men in party hats cut from Stars and Stripes newsprint toasted each other and talked about home as if it were a place you could buy a ticket to: Fort Worth and Spokane, Scranton and Mobile, the Mississippi like a road of light.

I waited until closing. Carter had peeled off with a girl who laughed like she was trying it on; the other pilots were arguing about baseball they hadn't seen in two years. I paid for the table and stepped into the alley air that tasted like wet brick and coal smoke.

She came out a minute later, shoulders drawn, the night pressing close.

"What do you want?" she asked, not afraid this time, just exhausted. "Payment? For being nice the other day?"

I shook my head. "I only wanted to make sure you're okay."

"Well," she said, and the word bent like a beam under weight. "I am." She slipped past me, quick, as if speed could make truth of it.

I'd promised myself I wouldn't follow. I followed anyway. "I'd like to get to know you," I said, hating how clumsy it sounded in the dark. "Better."

She stopped, turned, brows up. "Why?"

I shrugged because I didn't have language for the thing that had set its teeth in me. "Be damned if I know," I said, honest for once. "I don't even like Germans."

She laughed, a real, sudden laugh that felt like a match struck in the dark. "That makes two of us."

We stood there with the city listening. In the distance, someone tried to play "*Yankee Doodle*" on an accordion and lost their nerve halfway through. A woman called a child's name, and the echo brought it back smaller. I thought about home without meaning to: my mother on a porch swing with a dish towel over her lap, fireflies stitching light in the tall grass, the county fireworks shaking windows, my kid sister sneaking a second piece of pie and pretending it wasn't in her hand.

"It's our Independence Day," I said, because I needed to say something that wasn't her name. "Fourth of July. Back home, there'd be a parade. Grills in every yard. Kids running with sparklers until somebody gets burned and laughs anyway. You ask a hundred people what it means, and they'll all give you a different answer, but everyone shows up."

She tilted her head, thinking it over like a riddle. "I wouldn't have known it was July if you hadn't told me; the calendar burned."

"Yeah," I said. "I guess it did."

We started walking without deciding to, side by side, along a block where two streetlamps had survived and made a little island of light. A boy on a bicycle with no chain pushed past, shoes scuffing, a loaf of bread strapped to the rear rack with twine. In a doorway, someone had chalked a date and a crude drawing of an airplane with a smiling face. The wind came up and smelled like rain over stone.

"I keep thinking I should leave," I said, half to her, half to myself. "That it'd be smarter to go home to a town that remembers my name. Then I fly another load and see a kid wave at my wing like it's the answer to a question I don't know how to ask."

"And you stay," she said.

"And I stay," I confirmed.

She looked at me then, really looked, as if searching for the trick in the sentence. "We get used to staying," she said. "Even when leaving is the thing that would save us."

I didn't know how to touch that without breaking it. "If anyone bothers you again—" I started, and she lifted a hand.

"I know," she said. "You'll come burn them down." The corner of her mouth twitched. "That's not how this city keeps breathing."

"I won't burn anything," I said, and the lie tasted like metal. "I'll…show up."

She nodded once, sharp, as if we'd agreed to something that didn't have a name. For a heartbeat, we stood close enough that I could feel the heat coming off her like a coal banked under ash. Then she stepped back.

"I have to go," she said. "Klaus will be waiting."

"Klaus?" I felt a stab of jealousy run through me like a knife. Of course she had a man in her life. A woman like her had to. The urge to find that man and burn him to a crisp, though, surprised me. Not bothered, just surprised.

"My little brother." She clarified, and the amount of relief that rushed through me was ridiculous.

I dug into my pocket without thinking and came up with a pack of chewing gum. I held it out and then felt stupid. She looked at my hand, then at my face. Not under-standing.

"For your brother... Klaus." I tried.

She blinked, as if not comprehending the idea of someone giving her something for free. I pushed the pack toward her, took her hand—it felt so light and cold, and so right—and pressed the gum into her palm. "For Klaus." I reiterated.

She moved away, not fast, not afraid, just turned and let the dark take her in gentle pieces. I stood in the mouth of the alley and watched until she was a shadow in a city of shadows.

Behind me, a drunken Navy officer whooped "Happy Fourth!" at nobody, and somewhere a bottle popped like a small firework that had lost its way. I thought about my father's hand steady on my shoulder the first time I lit a sparkler, about my mother's voice telling me to be careful, about my sister sleeping under a flag we'd hung. I missed them in a sudden, bone-deep way that made me want to walk back to the field and keep flying until distance did what sleep couldn't.

Instead, I shoved my hands into my pockets and turned toward McNair. My boots made that hollow midnight sound on the cobbles, the sound that proves the ground is still there. I didn't like Germans, and I liked Russians less, and I liked least of all the part of me that had reached for her without permission.

Damned if I knew why. But it was July 4th, and for the first time in a long time, I let myself want something that wasn't survival.

Inga

Berlin—July 6, 1948, Tuesday

IT HAD BEEN two days since the American—*Gideon*—gave
me the gum. Two days of replaying his voice in my head
when I didn't mean to, two days of pretending the whole
thing had meant nothing.

I gave the strips to Klaus as soon as he woke the next
morning. For a moment, I thought I'd keep it, save it for
his birthday. But the truth was sharper: It wasn't mine to
keep and give. Gideon had given it to me for Klaus.
Klaus's eyes had gone so wide I thought they might spill
right out of his face.

"Gum?" he'd whispered like it was a magic word.
"For me?"

"Yes," I said. "Try it."

He'd held the little stick like it was treasure from another
world. When he finally put it in his mouth, he chewed
once, twice, then grinned like the sun had broken right
through our collapsed ceiling.

"It's sweet!"

"Only a little," I warned.

"I love it!" He broke the stick in half the way I'd shown him and held the other piece out. "You can have the rest."

I shook my head. "No. I want you to enjoy all of it." I watched as he carefully wrapped the broken stick back up and secured it in his pocket.

We came outside today after lessons, and he popped a piece in his mouth, chewing happily, then noticed me staring across the courtyard. Axel was there, half-shadow and half-boy, pressed against a wall like he wanted to disappear into it. Klaus followed my stare. "You want me to give the other half to *him*?" he asked, incredulous.

I nodded.

Klaus sighed like an old man, but he walked over. Axel recoiled before Klaus even spoke.

"Here," Klaus said, holding out the gum.

Axel's eyes narrowed, darting between my brother's hand and the other kids in the courtyard. The Trümmerkinder were watching, snickering, elbowing each other, whispering cruel things they'd learned too young.

Axel backed up, shaking his head. "What do you want me to do for it?" he muttered, suspicious.

"Nothing!" Klaus said, offended.

But Axel didn't believe it. None of them ever did.

I stepped closer. "Axel, it's a gift. From my brother."

He hesitated. Just for a breath. Then he turned and limped away, shoulders hunched tight. Something stung behind my eyes. Not anger, just that deep, endless sadness this city had carved into us all.

"Stay away from them," I told Klaus softly as the other boys laughed. "They're desperate. Desperation can be dangerous."

But watching them, boys and girls with dirt-smudged faces, torn coats, and no parents to hold them steady, I felt sorry for them too. There were so many. Too many. I had no idea how any of them kept breathing.

Klaus tugged on my sleeve. "Do you think the pilot will wiggle his wings today?"

I swallowed hard. *Gideon.* His smile flickered in my mind, just a flash from the doorway of Die Ecke, the heat in his eyes when he looked at me.

I told myself I didn't care.

A low hum rolled across the sky. The kids jerked their heads up all at once, like a flock hearing a signal. Then came another hum—deeper, louder—the familiar thrum of engines hauling hope. The plane dipped low over the rooftops, and then—wiggle, wiggle.

The courtyard erupted.

The children exploded forward like someone had cut a string. Even the wary ones. Even Axel, hobbling at the edge. And Klaus turned toward me, eyes bright as coins.

"Go ahead," I told him. "But stay where I can see you."

I watched him sprint with the others, heart hammering. The world beyond the courtyard was treacherous, more treacherous than he understood. Several Trümmerfrauen —rubble women—shoveling bricks stopped what they were doing and watched the kids. Their faces were streaked gray from the dust, but a smile lit all their tired faces as they watched the children fly over broken glass that glittered between loose stones.

Whole slabs of concrete shifted underfoot like they were tired of carrying the weight. And farther out, beyond the intact blocks, were the places that scared me most, collapsed cellars, their floors hollowed like animal traps, bomb craters that collected debris and hid deadly drops, the occasional unexploded bomb, half-buried and forgotten, and stairwells that led nowhere, their iron rails rusted through.

Every week, you heard one of the duds go off. A single muffled boom somewhere in the ruins, followed by silence. Someone stepped wrong. Someone ventured too far.

"Klaus," I whispered under my breath, "look where you're going."

But he was already gone with the tide of children, chasing the possibility of chocolate falling from the sky.

I started after him, picking my way over the rubble. The air stank of old smoke and wet stone. Somewhere beyond the next block, a woman was calling a name over and over. Somewhere else, a hammer struck metal, repairing something that would probably break again tomorrow.

The kids streamed toward the open lot near the collapsed tram depot. It had once been a street, but now it was a maze of broken walls and mangled tracks, danger disguised as a playground.

Klaus slowed at the edge of a jagged break in the pavement.

"Careful!" I called. "That's one of the old cellars, don't go near it."

He waved as if he'd heard me, but his eyes were on the sky, not the ground. A gust of wind pushed warm dust through the ruins. The plane circled, lining up for another pass, and all the children surged forward at once toward the safer part of the courtyard where the ground was mostly solid and the rubble had been cleared by hand over the last months.

Still, my heart lodged in my throat.

You didn't relax in Berlin.

Not even for a second.

A ripple of sound rolled through the kids. "Look!" one of them shouted. "Look, look!"

Tiny parachutes—made from scraps of tissue, handker-chiefs, maybe even old ration wrappers—floated down from the sky like little ghosts dancing on the wind. The courtyard erupted.

Whoops, squeals, shrill laughter, the real kind, the kind that hit me straight in the chest. For a moment, I forgot how to breathe. How long had it been since I heard kids laughing without fear?

My heart soared with them.

Klaus came running toward me, holding a parachute above his head like a trophy. A Hershey bar swung from the string in triumph.

Before he could reach me, one of the Trümmerkinder lunged at him, a boy I had seen before who was older and so much stronger than Klaus. His face was sharp with a hunger that should never be seen in a kid's eye, and it wasn't for food. Klaus stumbled back, nearly falling.

"Hey!" I snapped.

I caught the older boy by the ear, not even trying to be gentle. "No," I hissed. "Leave him."

He scowled but backed off, rubbing his ear. The other Trümmerkinder watched, some laughing, some whisper-ing, all with eyes too hollow for their age. Too broken. Klaus barely noticed. He was too busy staring at the miracle in his hands.

"Can I keep it?" he asked breathlessly.

That one question nearly cracked me open. He was only six, but he already knew the truth: chocolate like that could fetch bread on the black market. Oats. Maybe even a proper blanket or a shirt that didn't choke his wrists. It could keep us fed for a week.

A week.

My stomach twisted painfully. I thought of our empty pantry. I thought of the nights I pretended I wasn't hungry so he wouldn't worry. But then I looked at him, really looked. At the light in his eyes. At how he trembled with excitement. At how long he had waited to be a child again.

And I knew.

"Yes," I said, my voice soft. "It's yours. You go ahead and eat it. Just…not all at once, okay?"

His mouth fell open. "Inga?"

Everything emotion reflected in that single word—everything he feared, everything he wanted, everything he hoped—hit me like a tidal wave. I fell to my knees and hugged him so tight he squeaked.

"You decide," I whispered into his hair. "It's yours. But understand this: sometimes it's more important to live—really live—even for one minute…than to save everything for a future we can't promise."

It nearly killed me to say it. To tell him to be wasteful. But I wanted to see his face when he tasted something good. He pulled back, solemn as a priest, and broke off a small square. He looked at me again for permission. I nodded. I watched him place it on his tongue, and his whole body reacted. His eyes rolled back. His shoulders rose. He sighed—this deep, ridiculous sound of pure joy —then laughed like he couldn't hold it in.

He laughed.

"Ingaaa," he groaned dramatically, "it's soooo good."

I laughed too, tears stinging my eyes. Then he held out another piece he'd broken off. "For you."

I shook my head. "No. It's yours."

But he kept his arm out, stubborn as a mule, his little jaw set. "Sometimes you have to live in the moment," he said very seriously.

I barked out a laugh, the sound surprising both of us. "You're right," I said, taking the chocolate. "You're absolutely right."

I put the piece on my tongue and closed my eyes. It was like falling backward through time. I remembered a Christmas, lights, a tin of sweets, my mother humming as she stirred something warm on the stove. I must have been five. Six. Before my father lost his job... before everything. He had been an architect, fired for refusing to join the Party. Because he wouldn't design the grand new buildings the Reich demanded. Courage cost people their lives back then. I suppose we were lucky that it only cost us our home.

The chocolate brought all of it back, bright and warm and unbearably precious, and for the first time in a long time, it didn't hurt when I allowed myself to do so. It was a warm memory, one I would cherish for the rest of my life.

When I opened my eyes, Klaus was watching me.

"Happy?" he asked.

I nodded, swallowing past the lump in my throat. "Yes. That made me really, really happy."

He beamed. "I'll get you more tomorrow," he promised somberly, like a knight making a vow.

A tiny laugh escaped me. "I know."

And as I looked at him—his teeth still stained with chocolate, his eyes shining—my mind flickered back to the words I'd told him about living in the moment. A pair of blue eyes rose in my thoughts. A quiet smile. A jacket, warm on my shoulders. Gideon.

My stomach fluttered, traitorous and warm.

I shook myself back to reality. "Come on, Klaus," I said. "Let's go home. I need to get ready for work."

He grabbed my hand, the rich scent of chocolate still lingering on his fingers, and we headed back through the ruins, one miracle lighter, but somehow, impossibly, heavier with hope.

Berlin — July 10, 1948, Saturday

Four days. Four miserable, restless, engine-screaming days. Four days of flying, eating whatever passed for food in the mess, pretending to sleep, and doing everything in my power *not* to think about her.

Didn't matter. She was under my skin like shrapnel.

I didn't know why. Hell, I didn't even know what to *call* the thing clawing at me. I'd landed in burning cities, I'd lost half the people I cared about, I'd watched my own hands do things I still woke up sweating from, but this?

This was unbearable.

Maybe it was her absence. Maybe my mind had polished her until she gleamed 'because I hadn't seen her again. Maybe my dragon had decided she belonged to him, and my human half was just along for the ride. Or maybe I was simply losing my goddamn mind.

I hadn't even made it off the tarmac when I saw him—the man in the gray suit. No one wore suits in Berlin unless they wanted to bake, freeze, or get shot. This one looked like he didn't care which.

He stepped out from behind the hangar like he'd been waiting for me.

A shadow that decided to walk. "Captain Griffin?"

I didn't slow. "You need something?"

"Just a moment of your time." His voice was rich American with a Southern accent. He fell into step beside me, hands in his pockets, like we were out for a casual stroll instead of walking through the most heavily contested airfield on earth.

"I'm with Special Activities," he said softly. "You can think of us as… observers."

I snorted, pretending not to know that he was a spook. That he worked for a new organization called Central Intelligence Agency. Not many people knew about it yet but I had my sources. "That supposed to mean something to me?"

"It will." He cut me a sideways glance. "Tell me about the incident."

My stomach went cold.

"What incident?" I asked, keeping my voice bored, lazy, even though my pulse had started a low, furious throb.

The man smiled. Not kindly. "Good. Colonel Jamison said you were smart."

Jamison.

So this wasn't a trap. It was worse: it was sanctioned.

I crossed my arms. "If Jamison told you anything, then you already know there's nothing to report."

"Nothing," the agent repeated. "A damaged plane. Bullet-like punctures. Two pilots who swear they saw nothing unusual."

I gave him my best cold stare. "That's right."

A standoff stretched between us, hot air shimmering on the tarmac, men shouting in the distance, propellers whining. The agent didn't blink.

Finally, he exhaled. "Okay. Fine. I'll be the one to talk."

He glanced around—habit, not fear—then continued in a low voice. "The Russians want Berlin. Badly. They're probing every weakness we have. Air corridors. Supply lines. Morale. If they can push us into firing the first shot, they win. If they can make us blink, they win. If they can *accidentally* down a plane and make it look like our fault…"

His eyes settled on me. "That's how world wars start."

Heat prickled at the back of my neck. "Jamison said the same thing."

"Jamison says what he's allowed to." The agent leaned in. "I'm telling you what he isn't."

The dragon surged under my ribs. Not in anger, just an instinctive reaction to danger and threats. My vision sharpened until I could see every bead of sweat on the man's temple.

"How dangerous are we talking?" I asked quietly.

His expression changed, something like sympathy, something like a warning. "We're one mistake away from losing the city," he said. "And maybe the whole damn world."

For a moment, the only sound was the growl of engines overhead. I thought of Inga. Of Klaus. The ruined building they slept in. The Russians, stalking the streets like wolves in a broken forest. The bullets that had torn through my plane.

I clenched my jaw. "So what do you want from me?"

"Nothing," the agent said. Then added, "Yet."

He stepped back, smoothing his suit jacket.

"Just keep your eyes open, Captain. Report nothing. Notice everything. And for God's sake..."

His voice dropped. "...watch yourself."

He turned and walked away, swallowed by the hangar shadows. I watched him go, and the knot in my chest tightened. Berlin wasn't just wounded. It was rigged with explosives. And the fuse was burning fast.

I'd like to say that it was the conversation with the stranger that drove me back to Die Ecke, not the urge to see that she was okay. But I'd be lying. It was a need. Deep and primal. I didn't go inside. I wasn't in the mood to watch people pretend the world wasn't on the brink of another war, that this city wasn't seconds from being run over by the Reds, who wanted nothing more than to rape and plunder it. If only to say, *We won. Berlin is ours.*

I didn't go into the bar; instead, I stood across the street and waited until the door finally creaked open and she stepped out. She looked tired. Not worn down exactly, just weighed down. Like gravity wanted more from her than from anyone else.

I stepped forward.

She gasped and pressed a hand to her heart. "You startled me."

"Sorry," I said, even though I wasn't. I'd been waiting for that moment.

She narrowed her eyes. "Is this how you get your kicks? Waiting out here for me?"

A smile tugged at my mouth, completely uninvited. "Maybe."

Flirting?

Was that what this was?

I'd never done it. I'd joined up at seventeen, enlisting in what was still technically the *Army Air Forces* back then, because the Air Force wasn't officially born until '47. Before that, the extent of my romantic experience had been awkward hand-holding behind a barn and a kiss so quick it barely counted. Then I was in England. France. Italy. And war does things to people. Makes them reckless. Makes them hungry. Makes certain kinds of arrangements feel simple, transactional, necessary. Girls had liked me, some because I had rations, some because I had wings, some because I was gone the next day. But that wasn't flirting. That was survival dressed up like intimacy.

I'd never, *ever*, used a woman. Never taken something that wasn't freely, soberly given. There were lines I didn't cross, even when the world was on fire and everyone else seemed to be stepping over their own shadows.

But this?

This felt like something entirely different.

She crossed her arms, uncertain but... not leaving. "So what is this?" she asked quietly. "Is this... our thing now?"

Something inside me tightened, pleasure, fear, longing, I didn't know. "If you like."

Her lips parted. A shift happened, small but real. Like she gave herself a nudge from the inside.

"I think..." She exhaled. "I think I'd like that."

We started walking. Side by side. Awkward as hell. Every

time our sleeves brushed, my heart thumped like a rookie's first jump.

"So," she said after a few strides, "where are you from?"

"Montana." Saying out loud the name of my home state felt good. "A little nowhere town with more cows than people."

"Montana," she repeated softly, like she was tasting the word. "That sounds… far."

"It is." I glanced at her. "Where are *you* from?"

She gave me a wry look. "Here. Unfortunately."

We kept walking, the silence settling into something less sharp.

She pointed at the dark sky. "Do you miss it? Home?"

More than I ever let myself think about. The mountains. My mother's cooking. My sister racing me across the fields. The way the wind smelled like pine instead of diesel and dust.

"Yeah," I said. "I do."

"And yet you're here," she murmured.

"Someone has to fly the food," I said. "And the city… it grows on you."

She snorted. "Like mold."

A laugh barked out of me before I could stop it. God, it felt good to laugh.

We turned a corner, and it hit me where we were headed. I recognized the pattern of bombed-out walls, the sag of the broken rooflines, the street lamp that leaned just a little to the left. I'd walked her most of the way home the night I rescued her.

My steps slowed.

"You live near here," I said quietly.

She nodded, eyes flicking toward the ruins. "Yes. Don't worry. You don't have to come all the way."

"I want to," I said before I could stop myself.

She looked up at me, shocked, but not displeased.

"We're close," she murmured.

Closer than she knew. Closer than *I* should be.

But the street didn't feel dangerous tonight. Her presence didn't feel dangerous. Only the way my chest ached when I looked at her.

This time, for once, I didn't push it away.

"So, Inga," I said softly, "can I walk you the rest of the way?"

She hesitated. Then, so quiet I almost didn't hear it. "Yes."

The walk passed too quickly. Every step with her felt... easy. Even the silences. Especially the silences. I kept trying to memorize the sound of her breath, the way her fingers brushed her coat, the way she glanced up at me like she wasn't sure if she should trust me, but wanted to try anyway.

She stopped suddenly and pointed into a cluster of half-collapsed walls and twisted beams.

"This is me," she said softly.

I stared. "That?"

She nodded. My brows drew together. "Inga... that isn't a building. That's—"

"Ruins," she finished. "I know."

"It's dangerous."

She shrugged one shoulder, weary but resigned. "It's... private."

Private.

Right.

No neighbors. No drunks. No watchful eyes.

Just darkness and dust and the possibility of the whole thing collapsing on her in her sleep. Then something colder dawned on me. A young woman. Alone. In a city crawling with men who had nothing left to lose.

"How old are you?" I asked before I could stop myself.

"Eighteen."

Eighteen.

Jesus Christ.

A girl her age should've been worrying about dances or school or whatever German girls did before the world caught fire. Not this. Not sleeping in a ruin like a trapped animal.

"Unprotected," I muttered before I could catch the word. "In a place like this…"

She stiffened, but she didn't argue. Maybe she didn't have the energy.

And maybe—dammit—maybe she wasn't wrong. Maybe the ruins hid her better than any crowded street would. It was a shitty kind of safety, but it was the only kind she had. Before I could say anything else, a voice called from somewhere inside the rubble.

"Inga?"

Her spine went rigid. "Klaus?"

A small figure appeared between broken bricks. Then another behind him, also small, keeping back like he didn't want to be seen. Klaus clambered forward, clutching the edge of a wall for balance, his clothes dusty, his face drawn.

"Inga," he said shakily, "I'm sorry…"

She rushed toward him. "Klaus? Are you hurt?"

He shook his head too fast. "Bastian and his friends came. They… they trashed our home."

My blood turned to fire. "They what?"

Klaus looked at me shyly and ducked his head. "They took my chocolate."

"He caught a Hershey bar a couple of days ago," Inga looked up for just a moment before she turned back to her brother. "Are *you* okay?" Urgently checking him over with quick, trembling hands.

"I'm okay," he whispered. "I just—wanted to save some. For later. They grabbed it. I couldn't stop them."

The shame on his face... It hit me straight in the gut.

"Who is Bastian?" I asked, my voice low, dangerous. I already felt the dragon shifting under my ribs. The bastard would rue the moment he dared mess with what was mine. *Mine?*

Before I could go any further with that particular train of a headache, Inga explained, "He's the leader of the Trümmerkinder."

"The Trumm—what?"

"Trümmer... rubble. Rubble children." She sighed. "Orphans. Kids who live in ruins. They survive in packs, like stray dogs."

I stared at her. "Wait—he's a *child?*"

She nodded. I felt fury coil so tight in my chest I had to take a breath to keep from growling. "A kid did this to *him?* To *you?*"

"They're desperate," she whispered. "Hungry. Angry. Lost. It's just how things are. I'll take it from here—"

"The hell you will," I cut in.

Her eyes widened.

"Show me," I demanded.

Because I didn't care if they were six or sixteen, no one hurt this little boy.

No one terrified Inga. Not while I was anywhere in this godforsaken city.

And the dragon inside me?

He lifted his head, hungry for justice.

"Take me to them," my voice surprised me with its roughness. "I'm not letting this happen again."

She didn't answer right away; her mouth opened, then closed again, like she couldn't decide whether to tell me to go to hell or to thank me. But before she could find the words, Klaus looked up at me with wide, shining eyes. There was no fear in them; it was like he was staring at Superman.

The same look my little sister gave me when I walked through the door in uniform the first time. Molly. God, I hadn't let myself think her name in weeks.

"Hier lang," Klaus said suddenly, gesturing into the maze of rubble—this way.

"Klaus," Inga warned sharply. "Nein."

But the kid shook his head. "Komm."

He didn't speak English, but I didn't need a translator. The meaning was clear enough. He meant *follow me*.

Inga sighed, defeated. "He wants to show you," she murmured. "Our—what's left of our home. And... what the boys did."

We began to climb through the rubble, Klaus scrambling like it was familiar terrain. Inga kept close behind him, explaining under her breath, "He was so proud of that chocolate. He's eaten a small bit each day and said he'd save the rest for tomorrow." Her voice cracked. "He... he was trying to save it for me."

The dragon inside me stirred, furious, pacing behind my ribs like he wanted out. Before I could speak, a movement flickered in the corner of my vision, small, quick, darting between the rubble. The same shadow I had noticed earlier. I tensed, ready for trouble. Until the shape stepped into the moonlight.

It was just another child. Maybe ten. Maybe younger; Berlin shrunk its kids terribly. Thin as wire, limp in one leg, eyes too old for his face.

Inga exhaled. "Axel," she said softly.

He approached hesitantly, then held out something in his dirt-smudged hand. A melted, smashed, but unmistakable bar of chocolate.

Klaus gasped.

Axel thrust it toward him awkwardly. "Hier... für dich." His voice cracked.

Inga translated quietly. "He... he says he got it back for him."

Klaus stared at the bar, then at Axel, unsure. Hope and disbelief battled across his little face. My teeth clenched. I wanted to demand how, wanted to know what those other boys had done to him. But I already sensed the answer.

Inga knelt, and the shaking of her voice hit me in my core. Even more so when she looked up to me to translate what she had said to him. "Axel... they'll hurt you when they find out you took it back."

He lifted one shoulder, half a shrug, half resignation. "Sie tun mir immer weh."

"They always hurt me," she translated, her throat tight.

His next words were choked, just like Inga's when she explained what he said, "He says, at least this time..." she swallowed hard, "At least this time, it'll be worth it."

Every part of me went still. The dragon rose—slow, dangerous—like smoke curling through my bones. I'd seen beaten-down men in war zones. Prisoners. Refugees. Soldiers with nothing left.

But a child?

A child saying they always hurt me, like it was a weather report?

Something inside me tore.

Inga reached for Axel, her face raw with compassion and anguish. "Axel…"

Klaus pressed the chocolate back into Axel's palm. "Halb?" he offered shyly.

Inga blinked back tears. "Half?"

Axel looked stunned. Then he nodded, so gratefully, as if Klaus hadn't handed him candy but a crown. My throat burned.

This wasn't what I had pictured years ago from the cockpit of my bomber. Back then, the world was clean lines and orders, targets on a map, red circles marking where the enemy lived. I'd told myself it was soldiers down there, factories, rail lines. Men fighting men.

But here it was—what war really hit.

Small hands. Thin shoulders. Kids who fought over chocolate because childhood had been ripped out from under them. A cold weight pressed against my ribs. The dragon inside me shifted uneasily, as if even he didn't know what to do with the guilt swelling in my chest. I shoved it down. Focused my anger somewhere safer.

Toward the boys who had done this, who'd hurt these kids, stolen from them, terrorized them. But it didn't stay anger.

Not for long.

Because looking at Axel and Klaus standing side by side —two half-starved boys offering each other the only sweetness they'd seen in years—I felt something tear open. Something protective and dangerous. I realized, with a force that knocked the wind out of me, that I'd never wanted to shield anything the way I wanted to shield these two kids. And *her*. Inga.

I looked up.

She was staring at me with an expression she'd never shown me before; it was unguarded and raw. A glimpse of the soul she'd been fighting to protect with every breath she took. In that one look, I saw everything. The pain she carried like a second spine. The exhaustion carved into her bones. The hopelessness she hid from her brother. The fierce, stubborn determination that kept her standing in a world designed to crush her.

And the truth hit me like a cannonball: She wasn't just *a German.*

She wasn't the enemy. She was a *person*. A survivor. A sister.

Someone worth protecting, worth saving, worth… more.

I'd never been this torn in my life.

Part of me wanted to scoop Axel and Klaus up right then, carry them away, feed them, build walls around them until the bruises faded and the fear went quiet. But the other part—the soldier, the dragon, the man who understood what hungry packs of boys could turn into— knew this wasn't finished.

And wouldn't be.

"Show me," I said again, my voice rougher, deeper, something less human bleeding through.

This time, Inga didn't argue. She just nodded, a tiny broken motion, and turned to lead me deeper into the ruins.

Berlin — July 11, 1948, Sunday, early morning

I DIDN'T KNOW what to say to him. Gideon stood there like some impossible pillar of strength in a world made of dust and broken edges. His jaw was tight, his eyes dark and burning with something that wasn't anger alone. Something heavier. Something that made my stomach twist in a way I didn't understand.

"Show me," he'd declared.

Not asked.

Declared.

For the first time in a long while, something shifted inside me, something that whispered *I don't have to do everything alone.* I wasn't sure if that scared me or relieved me.

I swallowed hard, nodded, and motioned for Klaus and Axel to follow. "Kommt."—Come—I said in German.

The boys obeyed instantly. Axel's limp was more pronounced than usual, and I suspected he hadn't told us quite the truth about how he had liberated Klaus's chocolate. Klaus stuck close to Gideon, glancing up at him with those wide, hero-worshipping eyes. He'd never looked at anyone that way before.

Our Papa had been gone before he could have formed any memories. The party hadn't wanted to give him a job, but he was good enough to be cannon fodder. There weren't many men around, at least not under seventy. It hurt me to think that not only had Klaus been lacking male influence, but that he would never know his father. With everything I had been worrying about, this had never crossed my mind until now. At least I had some memories of our parents; Klaus had none. Not even a picture. The day they took my mom, our apartment had been bombed too. There had been nothing left but ash and smoke.

The ruins swallowed us as we walked, once-apartments now reduced to jagged silhouettes, rooms with no walls, walls with no roofs, doors that opened into nothing. The air smelled of damp stone and old smoke, and every few steps my boots crunched over broken glass.

"This way," I murmured, stepping carefully over a collapsed beam.

Gideon was behind me, his strides sure, his presence too large for the narrow path we walked. I felt him even when I didn't look back; his heat was a strange comfort I didn't want but couldn't shake.

We slipped into what had once been our building's court-yard. Nothing was recognizable anymore. Just heaps of rubble where flowerbeds had been, a staircase still standing on one side, its steps choked with bricks and ash, leading nowhere. An old bathtub lay overturned in the dirt, its white enamel cracked and blistered from the heat of explosions, like the skeleton of a domestic life no one remembered how to use anymore.

My throat tightened. "This… is where we live."

Gideon stopped short. His breath left him in a sharp, wounded sound. "You sleep here?"

I nodded. "Inside that."

I pointed toward what had once been the laundry room. Three walls remained, stubborn as teeth. The roof was a patchwork of scavenged boards, cardboard, and a torn tarp someone had discarded. It leaked when it rained, but not as badly as you'd think. I hadn't been ashamed of it before. It was shelter. It kept Klaus dry. It kept us alive. But now I saw it through Gideon's eyes, and for the first time, the shame crept in, quiet and poisonous.

"This place," I said quickly, before he could speak, before he could ask why, "it's hidden. People don't come here."

That was the truth of it. The intact buildings were dangerous. Everyone wanted them. Squatters fought over rooms with locks on the doors. Men noticed girls. Russian patrols noticed movement. Anything that looked *livable* drew attention, and attention got people hurt, or worse.

The ruins were different. The well-meaning stayed away. The predators didn't bother. No one wanted a place that might collapse in the night.

"I tried other places," I added, softer now. "Basements. Shared rooms. But they were crowded. Loud. And Klaus…" My voice caught. "He was so little. He cried at night. People don't like crying children." I swallowed. "Here, no one listens. No one looks." I turned to Gideon then, forcing myself to meet his gaze. "I can leave him alone here when I work nights. No one ever comes, only the Trümmerkinder. Not once. That's why we stayed."

Because in a city of broken walls, sometimes the most ruined place was the safest.

For a moment, he didn't say anything. He just stood there, staring at the remains of my careful, fragile world, at the place where I'd taught my brother to sleep without fear.

He didn't speak. But he went very, very still.

Suddenly, I knew. He wasn't judging me. He was grieving.

And that somehow hurt more.

Klaus tugged my sleeve. "They came from there," he whispered in German, pointing toward a narrow gap between two collapsed floors, a slanted, jagged passage that once might've been a hallway. Now it was a hiding place, the kind only kids small enough to slip through would think to use.

I felt Gideon move closer behind me, the heat of him brushing my shoulder. "They hide there?" he asked quietly.

"Yes." My voice shook despite me. "The Trümmerkinder. They slip through the ruins like rats. They know every tunnel, every crawlspace, every cellar. They can get in places I can't."

"And they came through here?" he asked Klaus.

Klaus nodded. "Bastian said... said we were lucky to have walls. He said they deserved it more. He took my chocolate. And... and he spit on our bed."

Gideon cursed under his breath, an American word I didn't want to translate, one that made me blush. A word I shouldn't have even known, but when you work in a bar... you learn quickly.

Axel flinched at the sound.

Gideon noticed. "I'm not angry at you," he said gently, kneeling to the boy's level. "I'm angry at them."

Axel blinked, confused. Nobody ever talked to him like that. He stood a little straighter. I wasn't sure he understood what Gideon said, but he understood the tone. I watched the exchange, and something warm curled low in my chest. Too warm. Too dangerous.

Gideon rose again. "Where are they now?"

Klaus shrugged. "They run. Fast."

"Show me where they hide," Gideon ordered.

I touched his arm, my fingers barely brushing the worn fabric of his jacket, but he froze as if it shocked him. "Gideon... don't hurt them."

"Why not?" His voice came out low, rough.

"Because they're children," I whispered.

He looked down at me, the shadows caught in his blue eyes until they turned almost black. "Children don't do this, Inga."

"They're hungry," I whispered. "Lost. Angry. They don't have any parents, no adults. They're homeless, and they know no rules but theirs. They're soldiers too, in their own way. Soldiers without anyone to tell them the war is over or who the enemy is."

He stared at me for a long moment, breathing hard, chest rising and falling like he was wrestling with something inside him. Something big. Something with claws.

Finally, he nodded once, jerkily. "Fine. I won't hurt them." But he added under his breath, so quiet I almost missed it, "Not unless they make me."

I didn't know why that sent a shiver down my spine.

"Come on then," I said softly, leading the way toward the broken hallway where the boys had slipped in earlier. "They stash food and blankets in the cellar beneath this section."

Gideon stepped right beside me, close enough that our arms brushed as we squeezed between two leaning walls. He didn't pull away, and neither did I.

The deeper we went, the darker it grew. Klaus clung to my fingers. Axel walked ahead like he knew every crack in the floor. Gideon's voice came from just behind me, low and steady. "If they hurt you... or Klaus..."

"I'm fine," I whispered.

"You're not," he said. "I've seen fine. This isn't it."

I didn't answer.

I couldn't.

Then Axel stopped suddenly. "Hier," he whispered, pointing at a narrow gap leading into a pitch-black cellar where the air smelled of damp earth and old fear. Gideon's hand brushed my back as he leaned forward.

I had no idea how he could possibly know it, but he snarled, "They're close."

The sound that came out of him didn't belong in a human throat. It wasn't loud—nothing that would echo or give us away—but it vibrated through the air between us, low and warning, like the growl of a cornered animal. My breath hitched. I didn't know what to think, only that something inside me reacted to it in a way that was equal parts fear and... something else. Something warm. Something that made my knees go weak.

How did he *know* they were close? How could he *sense* it? Before I could ask, he stepped in front of me, blocking the narrow gap with his body.

"Stay behind me," he murmured.

His voice was different, rough gravel instead of words. I found myself obeying without thinking. Axel nodded anxiously, his thin shoulders trembling. Klaus clutched my hand, squeezing tight. I felt him shaking too.

Gideon crouched, studying the dark opening the way a wolf studies a den, calculating, listening, waiting. The cellar was nothing but a jagged slit between fallen beams and cracked concrete, barely wide enough for a small child. Definitely not big enough for a grown man.

"Do they come out through here?" Gideon asked, eyes fixed on the dark.

I translated for Axel, who nodded vigorously. "They fit. You don't."

"It's how they disappear," Klaus whispered to me in German.

I translated for Gideon, and he swore under his breath. The air inside the cellar was damp and cold, carrying the faintest whisper of breath, small, uneven, like someone holding very still. My skin crawled. I hated cellars. Too many bad memories. Too many things the Soviets had dragged into darkness, never to walk out again.

Gideon leaned closer, one hand braced against the wall.

"There are at least three," he said softly. "One breathing hard. One whispering. One trying not to make noise."

I stared.

"H-how can you hear that?" I whispered.

He didn't answer. His jaw flexed. His nostrils flared slightly. And for one impossible second—a heartbeat so fast I nearly doubted it—I thought I saw something flare in his eyes. A glint of gold. Hot. Alive.

He blinked, and it was gone.

Before I could process it, a faint scuffling came from the dark. A shuffle of shoes on stone. A muttered curse.

"They're coming," Axel hissed.

Gideon lifted a hand toward me without turning. It wasn't a command. It was a barrier. A shield. He didn't have to say a word; I knew he meant *stay back*.

My pulse thundered in my ears.

Klaus squeezed my fingers. "Inga," he whispered, "warum—"

"Shh," I breathed in German. "Stay close."

Gideon shifted his weight, his muscles coiling tight beneath his jacket. He looked like he belonged in this darkness more than the boys did. Like the shadows recognized him.

A lanky figure squeezed through the gap first, thirteen, maybe fourteen, face smeared with grime, eyes sharp with suspicion and hunger. Then another. And behind them—barely visible—a smaller boy, hiding, watching.

I locked eyes with the one in front.

Bastian.

I knew it immediately.

The posture.

The coldness.

The way the other boys hovered behind him like he was their general.

His gaze flicked to Axel. Then to Klaus. Then to me.

Then, finally, to Gideon.

His jaw tightened.

"What do you want?" he spat in rough German.

Gideon didn't speak the language, but he understood the tone. He stepped forward, calm but impossibly imposing, nearly blocking the entire entryway with his body.

I swallowed and quickly translated. Bastian's eyes narrowed. He stood taller, shoulders lifting, trying to seem bigger than he was. Trying to seem like someone fearsome and important.

"You stole my brother's chocolate," I said quietly. "You broke our things. You frightened him."

Bastian shrugged, careless. "We need it more."

"You took it from a six-year-old," I snapped before I could stop myself.

Gideon's hand twitched, as if he were holding something inside with sheer force.

"Then he shouldn't have had it," Bastian said. "Kids like him don't get sweets unless they're willing to—"

He didn't finish. Because Gideon moved. Not fast. Not violent. Just… forward. One. A single step.

And every boy froze.

It wasn't strength that stopped them. Or size. It was something else, something in the air, heavy and electric. Like the space around him had changed, thickened, become charged with a pressure I could feel in my teeth.

Bastian swallowed.

"I don't want trouble," he muttered.

I knew Gideon didn't understand, yet he answered, low, each word steady as stone. "Then don't make any."

I translated, voice shaking.

Bastian's glare flicked between us, calculating. Then he spat to the side and jerked his head.

"Come on," he snapped at the others.

They slipped past us, vanishing into another tunnel of rubble like ghosts in the night. When they were gone, the tension snapped like a rope. I let out a breath I'd been holding.

Gideon straightened slowly, rolling his shoulders, breathing deeper than normal, forcing himself to calm down. Almost as if he were dragging a fierce beast back into its cage. I stared at him, unable to look away.

"What... what was that?" I whispered.

He didn't answer right away. Instead, he looked at Axel, then at Klaus, his gaze moving over them with a strange intensity, checking every scratch, every tremble, as if cataloging the harm done and the harm he would never allow again.

Then he straightened slowly, like he'd been holding his breath too long.

His hand rose halfway, as if to rake through his hair, but stopped, clenching instead.

A muscle jumped in his jaw. For a heartbeat, he didn't look like a pilot. Or a soldier. Or the man who'd walked me home.

There was something *feral* in the edges of him—a heat, a tension, a coiled readiness that made the space around us hum.

His eyes weren't just blue now. They were burning. Focused.

Like he was seeing more than any normal man could.

It stole my breath.

I didn't know what scared me more, the boys hiding in the rubble or the way Gideon seemed built to face a much darker enemy.

"Inga..." he said, his voice was rough, barely steady.

He wasn't angry now.

He wasn't even furious.

He was shaken.

And somehow, that terrified me more.

He dragged in a breath and finally met my eyes fully. "It's not okay," he said quietly. "Any of this."

His voice cracked something inside me. And I nodded, because it was all I could do.

"Let's get you all out of here," he murmured. "Before it gets more dangerous."

I didn't ask how he knew it was about to get more dangerous.

I just followed him—and walked through the ruins without fear for the first time in years.

Berlin — July 11 thru 16, 1948

THE MEMORY of her *apartment* wouldn't leave me alone.
Every time I closed my eyes, I saw it: three half-walls, a
roof patched with scraps, cardboard where glass
should've been. A mattress that had no business being
called a bed. Bare beams that would lose an argument
with the next strong wind.

Nobody should live like that. Certainly not a woman like
her. And sure as *hell* not kids.

For days afterward, I flew my routes and tried to shake it.
Tempelhof to Fassberg, Fassberg back to Tempelhof,
flour in, mail out. Engines, checklists, the endless rhythm
of the airlift. I told myself I was doing enough. I helped
drop hundreds of tons of food on this city every week.
That was my job. That was my responsibility.

But the image of Klaus's too-thin arms and Axel's limp
kept crawling back into my head like smoke. I'd come

from a tiny town in Montana. My little sister, Molly, used to complain if we didn't have second helpings of pie. I'd give anything to hear her whine about dessert now. I should write. I should call. Every night I thought it. Every morning I didn't.

Instead, I found myself standing in front of the PX.

It was ridiculous. I knew that. The PX was meant for us, American personnel, dependents, people with ID cards and paperwork. It was supposed to be a bubble of home in the middle of wreckage. Fluorescent lights, shelves, neat rows of goods that made no sense in a starving city: canned fruit, new socks, shaving cream, magazines, stacks of Hershey bars, nylons in crisp packets.

I walked in and felt the wrongness of it like a punch. Out there, kids were chewing on stale bread and boiling potatoes down to glue. In here, some lieutenant's wife was complaining that they were out of her favorite brand of lipstick.

It wasn't fair.

But I wasn't here for fair.

I picked up what I could carry without getting questions I didn't want to answer: two blankets, two pillows and cases—I thought a second, then added one of each for good measure—socks in a child's size and a size up, a couple of plain dresses that might fit Inga—serviceable, nothing fancy— undershirts and shorts for boys, a hammer and a box of nails, and lastly, some essentials, like soap. Real, good-smelling soap. Then I doubled back for whatever food I could smuggle out of the mess. Hamburger patties wrapped in paper, a few bread rolls, an apple or two pilfered from a crate, some boiled potatoes that wouldn't be missed.

Every piece I picked up, my dragon stirred. He liked this. Providing. Hoarding for someone other than me. It was an instinct older than war: bring back meat to the den, keep the young alive.

The soldier in me muttered about regulations. About boundaries. The man in me didn't care. At least not about that. What I did worry about was Inga. She'd be angry if I just turned up and dumped charity on her doorstep. I knew that in my bones. She was a proud woman. She wore her dignity like armor, because it was the one thing nobody could take from her. If I showed up while she was home, she'd probably throw half of it back in my face.

So I didn't show up when she was home.

I waited.

I knew roughly when she left for Die Ecke, late afternoon, coat pulled tight, hair pinned back, shoulders squared like she was going into battle. I watched from a distance once, just to be sure. Then, when the shadows stretched long and the city started lighting its candles and coal stoves, I made my move.

Klaus answered my knock. His eyes went round.

"Hallo," I said, feeling stupid. "Klaus. Hi."

He didn't understand the words, but he understood *me*.
His whole face lit up.

"Flieger!" he chirped—*pilot*—and stepped aside to let
me in.

Axel was there too, sitting on a crate, one leg stretched
out, hands folded like he was afraid to touch anything.
He stared at the bundle in my arms as if it might
explode.

"Hey," I murmured, lowering my voice like I was in a
church. "I brought you something."

Klaus bounced. "Was ist das?"

I didn't have the words, so I let the action speak. Blankets
first. Spread over the mattress that was nothing but sad
springs and thin cloth. The pillows next. I shoved it
under the sheet and patted it, then mimed sleeping.
Klaus laughed.

Then the food. I unwrapped the hamburgers, and the
smell hit the room like a bomb, a good one, for once.
Meat, fat, salt. Their eyes went comically wide.

"Holy hell," I whispered. "You really haven't eaten
anything like this in a while, have you?"

They didn't need translation. They needed permission. I
nodded. "Go on."

They descended like wolf pups, small, polite wolf pups

who still looked at me every three seconds to make sure it was really okay.

Watching them devour those burgers did something to me. It wasn't just hunger; it was the disbelief in their eyes, their expressions that got to me. It was the joy and confusion and this fragile, wild *hope* that maybe the world hadn't forgotten them entirely.

My throat burned again.

When they were done, Klaus leaned back, rubbing his stomach like an old man after Sunday dinner. "So gut," he sighed reverently.

"Tomorrow," I said, tapping his chest lightly, then my own, "we do this again, okay?"

He bobbed his head like one of those toy dogs people stick in car windows. Axel watched me differently. Not with hero worship. With wary curiosity. He understood more English than he let on.

I pointed at the blankets, then mimed cold, shivering, then warm. "Better?" I asked.

He nodded. "Better," he echoed carefully, pronouncing the *t*s hard.

I didn't stay long. Staying felt careless. Inga could come back without warning, or someone could see me arrive loaded down with gifts and leave empty-handed. That kind of thing didn't go unnoticed.

Berlin lived on rumor now. And the wrong story could cost someone everything.

'Still, the next night, I did it again.

Inga went to work. I waited a while, then went back to the ruin with another armful: clothes this time. Socks, shirts, and a sweater that might fit Klaus if he rolled the sleeves. A dress for Inga, blue, simple, with a little pattern. I folded it carefully and tucked it under the blanket where she slept. It felt like crossing a line I couldn't name.

Handing them more food, I asked, "Klaus—what did Inga say?"

He frowned, thinking, then rattled off a stream of German. I caught about every tenth word.

"Zornig..."—angry.

"Dankbar..."—grateful.

"Nicht brauchen..." —doesn't need.

"Gut."—good.

I understood enough to smirk and feel some guilt, then Axel jumped in; his English was halting, but purposeful. "She... not happy. But... happy," he said. "She... eh..." He spun a finger beside his head. "She say you are..." He frowned. "Stur. Ah... stubborn."

I huffed out a laugh. Yeah. That tracked.

Klaus tried to give me back one of the blankets. He pressed it into my hand and shook his head vigorously.

"Inga says…" Axel struggled, then settled on, "Too much."

I put the blanket back into Klaus's arms and closed his fingers around it. "Tell her," I said slowly, "that it makes me feel better. Me. Not her."

Axel translated. Klaus considered that with grave seriousness, then nodded once, as if he was willing to allow me this one strange American need.

We kept it up for a week.

I fixed what I could in the ruin—reinforced a leaning beam with a stray board, nailed a few planks over a dangerous gap, and more by the side of the bed. I couldn't make it safe, not really. But I could make it *less* lethal.

Twice, I ran into Bastian and his pack at the edge of the courtyard. The second time, he squared his shoulders like he wanted to prove something.

"Leave them alone," I warned in English, stepping in close enough that he had to tilt his head back to meet my eyes.

He didn't understand the words, but he understood the intent. And if he didn't at first, the dragon rumbling in my chest translated well enough. His bravado wilted. He muttered something under his breath and pulled his boys away.

The whole time, I avoided Die Ecke as if it were enemy territory. I didn't trust myself not to walk in and stare at her like a fool. I told myself it was better this way. Let her be angry. Let her be grateful. Let her never know how close I was to losing control of the careful distance I'd built for myself.

At night, I lay on my cot in McNair and stared at the ceiling.

I thought about home. About my parents and Molly sitting at a table that probably felt too big without me there. About my father pretending not to worry. About my mother sighing into space.

I thought about Molly, probably herding cows, or maybe riding in a rodeo by now, just to show off and protest the fact that she was a girl. I should write. I should call. Tell them I was still breathing. Tell them about a city that refused to die and a girl who refused to bend.

Instead, I thought about *her*.

About the way she'd looked at me in that alley, terror and trust mixed together. About the glimpse of her soul I'd seen when Axel and Klaus shared their chocolate. About the way saying her name in my head made something in me settle and light up all at once.

It wasn't smart.

It wasn't safe.

It wasn't anything I needed.

But wanting had never cared about need.

One afternoon, after a long, rough shift in low cloud cover, I came off duty and crossed the yard outside the billets. The sun was already slanting low, turning the broken edges of the city into sharp silhouettes. The lantern by the main gate flickered on early, casting a warm circle of light on the cobblestones outside the fence.

There were people drifting past, German couples walking arm in arm, a few GIs heading toward the tram, a girl laughing as a soldier spun her in a clumsy swing step. They kissed openly. Hugged. Like the war hadn't happened. Like the world wasn't balanced on the edge of another one.

I was still half in my head when I saw her. She stood just beyond the lantern light, hands knotted in front of her, looking… uncomfortable. Like she didn't know what she was doing there. Like she might bolt any second.

For a moment, I thought I was imagining her. I'd done it often enough. Then she turned her head, saw me, and something flared in her eyes.

She moved. Not just walked, she *lunged*.

"You!" she snapped, her voice cut through the clatter and chatter like a shot.

My heart stuttered.

I stopped just inside the gate—like the barrier would keep me safe from her wrath—fingers curling around the strap of my flight bag, the dragon lifting its head in my chest, alert.

This was it.

The week of sneaking, of bringing food and blankets and clothes, of patching her walls in secret, it had come due.

And I had no idea if she was about to thank me…or tear me apart.

Inga

Berlin — July 16, 1948, Friday, early afternoon

ALL WEEK, I lived with a war inside my chest, as if I hadn't had enough of that already. Gratitude on one side. Fury on the other.

Hope sharpened its claws between my ribs, and fear knelt on its neck. Every night I came home to something new Gideon had left behind: a blanket, a pillow, a sweater for Klaus, a bar of soap that smelled like roses. Left quietly, without witnesses or pride, like a man leaving offerings at a shrine he doubted he deserved to approach.

And every night at Die Ecke, I wondered if he'd walk through the door. I didn't know if I wanted him to so that I could rip his head off or—God help me—kiss him.

The infuriating part was that I couldn't tell what I felt anymore.

Klaus and Axel were fed. Really fed. Hamburgers, even cold and congealed, tasted like heaven. Then there had been that... pizza he brought. A strange American thing

—cheese, tomato, herbs—tasting like something from another world. And the spaghetti. I had licked the bowl when nobody was looking.

A girl was supposed to have pride. Mine was… wavering. And that made me angry. At him. At myself. At everything. Worse, I couldn't tell if what grew inside me when I thought of him was real… or gratitude masquerading as affection.

Gideon Griffin—Captain Gideon Griffin, with his impossible shoulders and too-blue eyes—was dangerous. Not the way the Russians were, but still dangerous. He meddled. He cared. He made me feel things I didn't want to feel.

That was how men like him trapped women like me. Not by demanding payment up front. No. By making you dependent. By giving you a glimpse of what life *could* be if the world were kind. He made Klaus smile. Made Axel feel seen. He patched our walls. Brought food. Brought warmth.

And now?

Now, surely he would want something.

A price.

A piece of me.

I'd thought about selling myself before. Too many times. When Klaus shivered from hunger. When my own body trembled with weakness. When my fingers searched for one last potato in an empty sack.

But every time, Mama's voice pulled me back from the brink. *Nicht so, mein Mädchen*—not this way, little girl.

So I hadn't done it.

Not even for Klaus.

Definitely not for me.

But now?

This infuriating American wasn't asking for anything. He was *making* me *want* something first. That was worse.

So I waited for him.

Every day after that first night, before my shift, I stood outside the American gate as couples passed me: German girls on the arms of soldiers, laughing, well-fed, their hair curled, their dresses new, their stockings un-torn and silky. Some were kissing openly, pressed against lamp posts, their mouths hungry or happy, I couldn't tell which —maybe both.

I knew what they paid.

I knew exactly what they'd given to earn that food, that clothing, that affection.

But God help me, they looked… happy.

That happiness felt like a punch in the stomach.

As I waited under the lantern—flickering against the gathering dusk—a stupid song wormed into my mind and refused to leave.

"Unter der Laterne... bei der Kaserne...

steht eine Lili Marleen..."

—Under the lantern, by the barracks gate, waits a Lili Marleen...

An *Ohrenwurm*—an earworm. The worst kind. It was cruelly fitting, because I *was* standing under a lantern, by the barracks gate, waiting for a soldier I had no business wanting.

When I finally saw him, the breath left my lungs. He was unmistakable, even in uniform among a sea of uniforms. The way he walked, straight-backed, sure, like he was born with purpose hammered into his bones. The way he filled out that bomber jacket, broad shoulders blocking the lantern glow behind him, leaving him haloed in warm gold.

My stomach fluttered first.

My heart followed.

"Deine Schritte kennt sie...

deinen schönen Gang"—*"She knows your footsteps... your lovely gait."*

Oh, this was ridiculous. Both him and the stupid song.

He didn't see me at first. Which was good. Because my lips tingled at the thought of him kissing me, and I needed that madness to stop. Before I did something stupid. Before he asked for his price, and I had no defenses left.

Then his head turned. His eyes found me. And he stopped.

Of course, he didn't walk to me.

He stayed behind the gate.

Coward.

Coward, or careful?

I couldn't decide which would hurt more. So I let my fury carry me.

"You!" I snapped, marching toward the iron bars.

His eyebrows lifted. "Inga—"

"What gives you the right?" I hissed, too loud, too wild, too raw. "You think you can just barge into my life? Into my home? Overpower little boys? Force your way into our space like you own it?"

His jaw tightened. "I didn't—"

"And then—then—you give us things we could never have otherwise. You think I don't know what that means? What men like you want?" My voice cracked, and I hated it, hated that he made me feel fragile. "Tell me what the price is, Captain."

"Inga—"

"No!" I nearly shouted. "Say it. What do you want? Because I'll tell you right now—flyboy—I'll never sleep with you. I'll never have sex with you. So whatever game you're playing—stop it."

He stared at me as if I'd slapped him.

Then his voice came out strangled. "You think I did all that so you'd have sex with me?"

"What else would you want?" I hissed. "What else do men ever want?"

His eyes flashed. First, there was hurt, then anger, then something hotter. "Has it ever occurred to you," he asked, in a low and lethal voice, "that someone might just do something kind because they *care*?"

My heart slammed against my ribs. Care? Nobody cared. That was the point. Understanding that was how you survived.

I shook my head violently. "Nobody does anything for free. Not now. Not here."

His anger sharpened. "Maybe where you stand."

"Yes. Here. In this city."

"Inga," he growled, "not the entire world is built on tit for tat."

"Mine is." I snapped.

He reached through the gate. Before I could step back, his hand closed around my waist, not harsh, not painful, but firm, drawing me close until the cold iron bars pressed between us, until our noses nearly touched. My hand moved instinctively up, my palm rested on his chest, and for a brief moment, I thought his skin under the shirt felt funny. Like scales... he must have had something in his pocket. My breath hitched. He smelled like cold wind and engine oil and something warm beneath it, something that made my knees give.

"Captain!" a GI barked from somewhere behind him.

He ignored it.

My pulse thundered.

I wanted him to kiss me—God, I wanted it—if only so I could hate him for it.

No, I was lying. I wanted him to kiss me because I wanted him.

I hated that more.

"If that is what you think of me," he said quietly, "you don't know me at all."

He let me go. The loss of his heat felt like a slap.

"Exactly," I hissed, forcing my voice steady. "I don't. And I don't want to."

He clenched his jaw. "You're impossible."

"Leave us alone!" I shouted, turning away before he could see the tears gathering. Then I walked off.

Fast. Too fast. Hoping he wouldn't follow. Dreading that he might not.

He didn't.

A tear slipped down my cheek, hot and humiliating. *Stupid girl*, I told myself. *Stupid, stupid girl.*

At the club, I kept looking toward the door, waiting for him to show, hating myself for it. He never came. His friends did. They watched me with wary curiosity, probably wondering how much of myself I had given to the captain.

Nobody touched me.

The tips were good.

And I hated all of it.

By the time I walked home, my throat was tight, and my feet were numb. I just wanted to crawl into my—new and warm—blanket and pretend none of this had ever happened.

But when I stepped inside the ruin, I froze. Klaus and Axel were sitting on—a rug. A real rug. Warm and soft and patterned. Covering the cold concrete. That wasn't all, though; they were playing a game, one of those American board games with bright colors and little pieces.

Chutes and Ladders, Klaus told me proudly, though he said it wrong and it came out "Shoots-and-Leddahs."

They had snacks.

Snacks!

Little crackers shaped like fish from a bright-red box.

They looked… fed. Safe. Happy.

Like two well-fed cats on a hearth rug instead of war ghosts in the ruins.

Klaus ran to me and hugged my waist. "Inga! Look! Look what Gideon brought!"

My heart stuttered painfully. On the crate was an MRE pouch, the instructions in English. Klaus demonstrated proudly how to heat it with the little chemical pack. I wanted to refuse it, but my stomach betrayed me with a loud, desperate growl.

"It's for you," Klaus said, pressing it into my hands. "All for you."

Despite myself, I tore it open. The rich smell of beef stew hit me like a wave. I ate. I devoured. I moaned. And then I saw more. By what once had been the kitchen, sat a loaf of bread. A jar of peanut butter. A whole jar of jelly. Grape jelly. I nearly fell to my knees.

I had given Klaus the last spoon of jelly I'd saved for his birthday the other day, and he'd been so happy. Now there was a whole jar. I pressed my hand to my mouth, breathing shakily. I nearly hated Gideon for this.

For making me feel so weak.

So grateful.

So overwhelmed.

But mostly…

I hated that a part of me wanted him here. Wanted to

tell him I was sorry. Wanted to know why he cared. Wanted to know if he hurt like this, too.

My eyes burned.

"Inga?" Klaus asked softly, touching my knee. "Happy?"

I forced a smile through tears. "Yes," I whispered. "I'm… happy."

But the truth was messier.

I was furious.

Relieved.

Confused.

Lonely.

And aching for a man I'd just told to leave me alone.

It hurt. It hurt so much I wanted to scream. Instead, I curled up on the new rug, blanket over my shoulders, Klaus tucked into one side, Axel on the other. Safe. Warm. Fed. And watched them play. And pretended for one night that there had been no war. That this wasn't a ruin but a home.

My mind was in turmoil. He must have brought all this while I was at work, like he had done every night this week. After I told him to leave us alone. After! The tears were threatening seriously now. It took a herculean effort, but I swallowed them back down. The boys were so happy, I didn't want to ruin it. I had ruined enough tonight.

What was I supposed to do now?

Gideon

Berlin — July 17, 1948, Saturday

I'D BEEN ANGRY BEFORE. War angry. Pilot angry. Losing-my-brothers angry.

But none of that held a candle to the fury I felt when Inga spat those words at me through the gate.

I'll never sleep with you. I'll never have sex with you.

Like that's what I wanted.

Well, you do, my conscience nagged.

That wasn't the point, and that wasn't why I was doing these things.

Like I was some bastard lined up at her door with ration cards and demands. *No, you're not that guy*, I assured myself.

I'd never been insulted like that, not even by Germans during the war, and hell, I'd dropped bombs on them. My blood had gone white-hot. My vision had tunneled, a growl had crawled up my throat, and if there hadn't been a gate between us, I don't know what I would've done.

Probably kissed her and proved her right.

It had taken some time, but eventually I cooled off. Enough for the first rational thoughts to enter my head. Slowly, the truth started to creep in. *She* doesn't *know you*, that much was true.

I swooped in like some kind of hero, dragon shifter, soldier, protector, whatever the hell I thought I was, and expected her to just… fall? Trust me? Because I brought food? Because I fixed a few planks of wood? Because I scared off some kids?

Christ.

I'd walked her home twice. Maybe three times if I counted the alley night. But every time had ended with me playing the big savior. Big shoulders. Big bravery. Big ego.

Not once did I give her space to actually know me. Not Gideon the man.

Just Gideon the rescuer. So whose fault was her misunderstanding?

Mine.

That truth had sat like a stone in my stomach. Made it impossible not to think about the other parts of what she'd said: *What is the price I'll have to pay?*

The idea that she'd thought I'd demand her body—that I'd take everything she had left—It hollowed me out.

The dragon went silent. Even he didn't know how to answer that. So instead of sulking or drinking myself numb with Carter, I'd done what I'd been doing all week. I went to see the kids. When I showed up with another bundle—bread, fruit, powdered milk, a mess-hall sandwich—Klaus's eyes lit up. Axel nodded once, his version of thanks. Their faith in me felt like a weight and a blessing.

That night, while the boys sat cross-legged on the rug—I still couldn't believe we'd gotten a rug into that ruin—I crouched and asked, slowly, "Klaus—Inga. Lieblingsblumen? Favorite flowers?"

Klaus blinked.

Axel blinked.

They exchanged confused glances.

"Blumen?" I repeated, miming holding a bouquet.

Klaus furrowed his brows. "Blumen? Wofür?"

Axel translated in his shy half-English. "Why… flowers?"

It hit me then. There weren't many flowers left in Berlin. The city had burned, starved, frozen. Nature had barely kept up. Flowers were one of the luxuries no one had the right to expect.

And still, I wanted to bring her some. I swallowed. "Eh… never mind."

This morning, I couldn't sit still. I paced. I shaved twice because I botched the first one. I pulled on civilian clothes—jeans, a faded shirt, a jacket that wasn't military issue—and hoped I looked less like a flying uniform and more like a man.

Then I went to find flowers. It took three hours and a long walk to the French sector. I paid too much. I didn't care. The bouquet wasn't big, just a handful of wilted daisies, two pale roses, and a sprig of something green, but it was all the city had.

By noon, my palms were sweating around the stems. When I reached her ruin, I hesitated. My heart kicked like it wanted out of my chest. I knocked on the makeshift door. I felt more anxious than I had flying over Germany dropping bombs.

A rustle.

A pause.

Then she opened it.

Saw me and froze.

Her eyes—brown like forest earth—went wide, flicking from my face to the flowers and back again. Her lips parted slightly. She didn't breathe for a full three seconds. I swallowed. Hard.

"I'm sorry," I said.

Two words. Not enough. But they were everything I had.

She didn't take the flowers, but she didn't slam the door or scream at me like last night.

Progress?

She just stared.

I saw the war on her face, the mistrust, the exhaustion, the brittle strength. The hope she tried to crush before I could see it. Every wound from the last few years lived in her eyes. I held the bouquet out a little more, like a shield, like a peace offering. "Please. Let me buy you lunch. Let me explain. Let me... fix what I broke."

She closed her eyes briefly, like she was fighting herself. When she opened them again, they shone strangely.

"And why," she whispered, voice trembling despite her stubborn posture, "would I do that?"

I breathed in, then answered honestly, "Because I would really, really like to get to know you, and I would really like for you to know me too."

Silence.

A long, tight silence.

Her gaze dropped to the flowers. Her throat worked. Her fingers twitched—just barely—toward the bouquet. Then she looked back up, and her voice came out hoarse, "You're... impossible."

I didn't dare grin, but I smiled, "Probably."

She let out a breath that trembled at the end. Then—
slowly, cautiously, like approaching a wounded animal—
she reached for the flowers. Her fingers brushed mine.
Sparks ignited. Real, physical sparks that shot up my
arm. She felt it too—her flush told on her, so did her
widening eyes.

"Lunch," she whispered, almost to herself. "We can...
talk."

Relief nearly knocked me off my feet. I held out my
hand, careful not to let it appear too eager or, God
forbid, grabby. "Come with me?"

She hesitated, but only for a few seconds. Before she took
my hand, though, she remembered. "Hold on, the
flowers."

I waited at the threshold, like I had never entered her
apartment before, until I heard the boys giggle. Of
course, they had stood right there, watching. I made a
face at them, and they giggled some more.

"Oh, for crying out loud, Gideon, come on in," Inga
called.

The boys giggled even harder as they watched me take
one measured, careful step after another as I entered. I
ducked under the low beam and stepped fully into the
room, the boys' eyes bright with mischief as if I'd just
walked into a sacred place where grown men didn't
belong. Maybe I didn't.

Inga moved across the patched floorboards with a strange combination of grace and weariness, the flowers cradled in her hands as if they were made of spun sugar and breath. She reached the little makeshift table—once a cabinet, now missing a door—and picked up an old tin can. Someone had scrubbed it clean ages ago. The label was long gone. She dipped it into the metal bucket beside the wall.

I frowned. The water inside was clear. Cold. Fresh. That meant she'd fetched it… from the pump halfway down the street, because there wasn't any running water here. She had carried it through the rubble. Up a slope of broken masonry and shattered stairwells. Every day. Probably twice a day. For months—no, years.

No wonder she was skittish. No wonder she mistrusted kindness. No wonder she'd assumed I wanted something in exchange. This city had taken a girl who deserved a soft, safe home and turned her into a warrior.

She filled the tin halfway, testing the weight, then lowered the flowers into it. They sagged a little, but their color brightened against the dull metal.

She turned and caught me watching. Her chin lifted—pride reasserting itself like a shield—but her eyes… her eyes softened, just a fraction.

"You can stop staring," she murmured. "It's just water."

Just water. Just a tin. Just a girl surviving in a place that should have killed her.

But to me, it felt like watching her light a candle in the ruins. I didn't move closer, not yet. The boys were still watching, whispering to each other in rapid-fire German, and Inga's cheeks warmed as she shot them a warning glare. They straightened instantly, the way kids do when they don't want to ruin a grown-up's fragile mood.

She brushed her palms against her skirt and finally approached me again. I couldn't look away. Couldn't breathe right. Couldn't pretend a single thing about this woman left me unaffected.

"I really am sorry," I said quietly. "For last night... for everything."

"Me too." Her voice was barely above a whisper. "And thank you. For the flowers."

The words sounded like they cost her something, not money, but vulnerability. I tucked that away into the place inside me I didn't let anyone near. The place she'd started to carve space into. She glanced toward the boys. "Klaus, Axel. Behave. I'll be back soon."

Axel nodded like this was the most serious mission of his life. Klaus beamed as if he were sending his sister off to a dance.

Then she stepped toward me. Right up to me. Close enough that I could smell the faint scent of the soap I'd brought her a few days ago. Close enough I could see the freckles across her nose I hadn't noticed before. Close enough that if I leaned forward an inch—

No.

Not yet.

Not now.

"Ready?" I asked.

She didn't take my hand this time. But she didn't pull away either when I took hers.

"I suppose," she tried—and failed—not to sound flustered. I pushed the door's makeshift panel aside and held it for her as she stepped out into the daylight. Right then, right in that moment, watching her square her shoulders against the world outside, I made myself a quiet promise: I would find out when someone had last done something kind for her. I would learn everything she didn't want to say. Every scar she hid behind sharp words. Every fear she carried alone. Every dream she'd buried under rubble.

I hadn't been lying. I really did want to get to know her. And God help me,

I wanted her to know me, too.

She turned back, catching me staring again, and her lips twitched. "Gideon," she said softly, a hint of warning, a hint of something else.

"Don't make me regret this."

I swallowed. "I won't," I said, and meant it more than anything I'd meant in a long, long time.

"Lunch?" she asked.

"Lunch," I said.

And together—awkward, hopeful, terrified—we walked out into the fragile daylight.

Berlin — July 17, 1948, Saturday

I TOLD myself I wouldn't care if he never came back. That I'd be fine.

That I didn't need him. That everything he had done—the food, the blankets, the clothes—had been a trick, a lure, a wolf's invitation dressed in kindness.

But the truth? The ugly, aching truth? When I opened that door and found Gideon standing there with a bouquet of flowers clenched awkwardly in his big hands, my heart nearly folded in on itself.

He came back. He apologized. Suddenly, something bright—something I thought had died inside me years ago—fluttered weakly to life. It terrified me.

I took the flowers because I didn't know what else to do with my hands. It had been so long since I had seen flowers, real flowers that go into a vase. Mother always had flowers around the house, well, before... every Sunday, she would go to the flower shop and buy bouquets. Some she would take to my grandma, some for our house. She had always bought the most expensive, exotic ones, but they didn't compare to what Gideon brought me. They were beautiful in the way only rare, impossible things are beautiful: colorful, fragile, smelling faintly like hope. I put them in an old tin with water I'd fetched that morning, lugging the bucket over broken stairs and rubble like I'd done a thousand times before.

Gideon watched me closely, making me feel like every little thing I did mattered, which in turn made me tremble, because it had been so long since someone had watched me in a protective way.

For some reason, I didn't want him to see how hard life had been. But he saw it anyway. He always seemed to see too much. When I finally turned back to him, I expected awkward silence or some forced politeness.

Instead, he held out his hand and said, "Come with me?"

Like it was simple.

It wasn't.

But God, I wanted it to be.

So, I took his hand and allowed myself to be led instead of doing the leading. We walked a few blocks back to where the city was rebuilding itself, where life was beginning to restart as if the war had never happened. He took me to a restaurant. A *real restaurant*.

I'd walked past it before, its windows fogged with warmth, with life, with everything the ruins around it didn't have. GIs brought their German girlfriends here. Sometimes, French or English soldiers, too. Women in pretty dresses, in brand-new nylons, laughing as if the world wasn't broken at the edges. I had never imagined stepping inside.

My breath caught the moment Gideon opened the door for me, and I was hit with the warmth and light. The sound of clinking glasses, the light tinkle of laughter. My gaze flicked over the white tablecloths and thick candles.

The aroma of food mingled with the smell of perfume and cologne. Another thing I hadn't encountered in years.

The food smelled so rich it made my head spin; so much, I swayed. Gideon's hand was instantly at my back, steady and gentle. "You okay?"

I nodded too fast. "Just… overwhelmed."

He pulled out a chair for me like a gentleman from a storybook. I felt more out of place than I ever had in my life. Memories of going to these kinds of places rushed me. *Inga, don't spill the juice. Inga, sit straight. Inga, don't grab the bread.* My mother's phantom voice was in my head, along with very distorted images of her and Father. It had been so long, I barely remembered what they looked like.

Thankfully, the server appeared. His raised eyebrows were enough to dispel my trip down memory lane. I didn't blame him. Gideon and I, we looked wrong together. Me, in my patched dress and scuffed shoes.

Gideon, in his clean civilian clothes that still couldn't hide the way he carried himself like a soldier.

"Wine?" the server asked.

My eyes widened. I shook my head so hard my curls tugged at the pins. "No… water. Just water. Please."

"Still or sparkling?" he asked.

I didn't even know sparkling water still existed. "Still," I whispered.

Gideon smiled at me, warm, reassuring. He ordered a beer for himself.

When the server brought menus, I froze again. The prices—God. The cheapest thing was already an unthinkable amount. Enough to feed Klaus and Axel for a week.

"Gideon," I hissed under my breath. "This costs a fortune."

He shrugged easily. "Don't worry about it."

"I am worrying."

He leaned forward, resting his forearms on the table. "Then don't. Please. Let me do this for you."

The way he said it… softly, almost pleading… I felt my resistance wavering. After a short internal debate, I pointed to the simplest dish. "I'll have this."

Gideon shook his head and took the menu gently from my hands. "No. What's your favorite?"

"I don't have favorites," I lied.

He tilted his head, and I couldn't help it. Every time my parents took me to a restaurant, I had the same thing: "Wiener Schnitzel with pommes frites," I breathed.

Gideon smiled, "I have no idea what that is, but judging by your expression, it must be delicious. I'll have the same."

The tension eased out of my shoulders like steam. The waiter returned with our drink orders, took our food requests, and brought a basket filled with bread rolls. When Gideon lifted the napkin thrown over the basket, I nearly cried.

Real rolls with a hard crust. I could already taste how soft and yeasty it would be on the inside. The smell hit me, just like the revelation that they were still warm.

And butter.

Actual butter.

I tore one open, and inhaled—the yeasty, warm, sweetness. My vision blurred. I tried to hide how the first bite made me moan softly, but Gideon heard it.

He laughed quietly. "Feels good, doesn't it?"

I nodded helplessly.

He took a bite himself and blinked. "Damn. This is good."

"You've never had German bread before?" I asked, shocked.

"Nope. We've got white bread back home. Soft as pillows but no real flavor. This?" He gestured with the half-eaten roll. "This is something else."

We both laughed, and just like that, the heaviness lifted. And we began to talk. He asked about my childhood.

"It was good," I said slowly. "Before the war. Before everything changed. My father was an architect. He refused to work for… for the people in power. So he lost his job. We lost our home."

Gideon listened—really listened—not with pity, but with something like interest. "I didn't know any German refused the Reich."

I nodded, "Not many dared, but not everyone voted for him."

"Father was drafted quickly," I added. "At first, there were postcards, Reichenberg, Karlsbad, Prague… all these pretty places he swore he'd take us someday. Then he was wounded and came home for a few weeks." I feel a sad smile creep over my lips at the memory of it. "That was when Klaus was *conceived*. After that, the cards came from farther east… Kraków, Warsaw, Minsk. And then nothing. They just stopped."

"I'm sorry," he said softly.

I nodded once. Then, mercifully, he shifted the topic. "Montana," he said, answering an earlier question. "The land of big skies and wide-open spaces. There are cattle everywhere. You ever been chased by a cow?"

I blinked. I was a city brat. Through and through.

"No?" He laughed. "You're lucky. They're mean as hell."

I burst out laughing, more born from gladness to stop talking about my family than real amusement, but it lightened the atmosphere enough so I could enjoy myself again. He told me about his family ranch. About his father, who could lasso anything that moved. His mother, who made pies so good he once ate three of them and threw up behind the barn. His sister, who tried to ride a horse backward at age five because it *looked easier that way."*

I laughed so hard my sides hurt. Earning me a stern glance from a woman across from me. I didn't care. I hadn't laughed like that in years.

Maybe ever.

When the food came—piping hot pommes frites and a large Wiener Schnitzel, so large, it didn't fully fit on the plate. I felt dizzy again. Gideon pointed at the pommes frites.

"French fries," he drew his brows together as if he had made the discovery of the year, and I laughed.

"We call it pommes for short," I explained, tapping my finger against one to gauge how hot it was.

"And this?" He pointed at the breaded, fried meat.

"Could be anything," I winked, "It's supposed to be veal, but..." I shrugged conspiratorially, "sometimes, it's made from pork, beef, chicken..." I left it dangling there, watching him grin.

He moved his knife back and forward, "You almost had me." He cut off a piece and ate it. "Definitely veal," he proclaimed.

I snickered, then sobered and took my first bite of a real Schnitzel in years. I closed my eyes and allowed the oily breadcrumbs to dissolve in my mouth. I moaned when I started to chew. "So good."

"Good." Gideon watched me intently with a strange expression on his face that I couldn't place; it looked almost pained.

"What?" I asked with my mouth full, forgetting my manners.

"You," his eyes darkened, "I could watch you for days."

Heat rose into my cheeks, and I looked down. "Don't."

"Don't what?"

"Don't be too nice to me."

He reached across the table and placed his thumb underneath my chin, "You deserve nice. Hell, you deserve more than nice, Inga. Let me help you."

With the taste of veal in my mouth, and the aroma of yeasty bread in the warm air, it was all too easy to return his gaze, to lower my defenses. And suddenly I wanted this. I wanted someone to take care of me. To be nice to me.

"Okay."

"Okay?" He looked shocked.

I couldn't help but laugh. "Okay. You may be nice to me."

"Alright." As if to make sure I didn't rescind, he focused on his food, cut another bite, and placed it in his mouth. God, this man was actually sexy eating. My blush deepened. I had no idea where that thought came from. It seemed that by lowering my defenses, I had opened the floodgates.

Our conversation slowed as the food soothed something deep inside me, hunger, yes, but something spiritual too. An ache I hadn't known I carried until it began to fade.

And all the while, Gideon watched me, as if seeing me happy made him happy too.

Our lunch was topped off with a slice of real cheesecake, and this time, Gideon openly admitted that this was the best cheesecake he'd ever had. I couldn't help it, but I chuckled, "Maybe one day I'll make you some cheesecake. One that will leave this one in the dust."

He finished what was left of mine, wiped his mouth with a napkin, leaned back, and shocked both of us by saying, "Darlin', even if it is only half as good as this one, I'll marry you."

Berlin — July 17, 1948, Saturday

I WALKED her to work afterward. Her steps were light—almost floating—like the good food had filled her bones with something weightier than calories. Something closer to hope. She kept glancing at me from the corner of her eye, almost shy, almost glowing, and every time she did, something in my chest tightened until breathing felt like a goddamn luxury.

At the bar's back entrance, she paused. The lunchtime crowds bustled past us, cars rattled over the cobblestones, GIs laughed too loudly, music drifted from an open window. But she didn't look at any of it.

She looked at me.

Right at me.

"I had a wonderful time," she said softly, with that hint of accent I had come to crave. "Yeah," I answered, my voice rougher than I meant it to be. "Me too."

For a second, it felt like the world slowed down just for us, like the ruins stood still, like the war had never happened, like she might let me kiss her right there under that sun-faded awning.

But then she smiled, a small, beautiful, uncertain thing, and slipped inside.

I stood there for another full minute like an idiot, grinning. Warm. Too warm.

And then the memory hit me like a punch.

Darlin', even if it's only half as good, I'll marry you.

What the hell had I been thinking?

Except…

I hadn't been drunk.

I hadn't been joking.

And the worst part?

I liked the thought more than I had any right to.

I walked back through the American sector in a haze, the city's ruins passing by in gray fragments. But for once, the destruction didn't bury me. For once, the nightmares weren't crowding behind my eyes. All I saw was her, her smile, her fingers brushing mine, the way her face softened when she took that first bite of bread like it was salvation.

By the time I reached the billet, my heart was doing a slow, stupid somersault.

The evening routine went by like a dream. I showered, declined Carter's invitation to go to a new bar someone had discovered in the Tiergarten, and went to bed. My mind was going in circles. The craziness of what I had said replayed in my head over and over, but the longer I thought about it, the less crazy it sounded. I would be able to take care of her. Her, her brother, and his friend. The army would provide housing. She could make that cheesecake. She could go to the PX and buy things. Pretty things.

You've only known her for a few weeks, my mind cautioned, but my heart and the dragon in me said it was enough. I had never felt about anybody like this before. I was sure she was *the one*.

Well, we'll never know. Fat chance of me getting my hands on ten eggs, sugar, and a kilo of cream cheese, Inga had laughed my offhanded proposal off. If only she knew that at the PX, ten eggs were nothing. The *quark*—whatever the hell that was—would be harder to come by.

With those thoughts rolling around inside my head, sleep wasn't coming, and when I looked at my watch, I realized what time it was in Montana. Ranch time. My father would already be awake. He was always awake before dawn. Soon, he would be out, feeding the cattle, checking fences, yelling at my little brother to saddle the damn horse properly. I've been delaying this call for weeks. The war was over, but with the situation in Berlin, I knew my family was still worried sick over me, and I wasn't making it easier by not calling.

I headed to the CQ desk—Charge of Quarters—the little room right off the hallway where a bored sergeant kept watch, logged who came and went, monitored the phones, and tried not to fall asleep.

Sergeant Dwyer was on duty, reading a three-day-old newspaper. He looked up as I approached.

"Need the line, Captain?" he asked, chewing on a toothpick.

"Yeah," I said. "If it's free."

"Private Jenkins is finishing up with his girl in Milwaukee," Dwyer smirked. "He's been whispering sweet nothings for twenty minutes. God help us all."

I leaned against the wall, pretending not to hear the lovesick babbling drifting down the hall. When Jenkins finally hung up, blushing and glowing like he'd been kissed through the damn wires, Dwyer waved me forward.

"All yours, Sir."

I dialed home.

The line crackled. Popped. Hissed.

Then—

"Griffin Ranch," came my father's voice, deep and steady as a mountain.

My chest clenched.

"Dad," I said. "It's me."

A startled pause, then warmth flooded the line. "Gideon! Boy, we thought you'd forgotten you had a family."

Before I could respond, I heard another receiver click on. "Oh heavens, Gideon? Gideon, sweetheart, is that you?" My mother.

Of course she was listening in. I smiled so hard my cheekbones hurt. "Hey, Ma."

There were questions, a dozen of them—

Are you eating?

Are you safe?

Are you sleeping?

Is Berlin as terrible as they say?

Are you taking care of yourself?

Are you warm enough?

Do you need more socks?

I answered them all, as best I could.

And then... I couldn't help myself.

"I met someone," I said softly.

Dead silence on both extensions.

Then my mother gasped. "Oh my Lord—"

And my father let out a low, amused grunt. "Knew it."

"She's German," I added.

My mother squeaked. My father let out a slow whistle.

"Well," Dad said finally, "war's over. A heart goes where it damn well pleases."

"What's she like?" Mom demanded. "Is she kind? Is she pretty? Does she bring out the best in you? Gideon Joseph Griffin, you answer me!"

I rubbed the back of my neck. "She's... incredible. Strong. Smarter than me. Braver than me. Fierce as hell. And funny, when she lets herself be."

"Ah," Dad said knowingly. "One of those."

Mom whispered, "I want to know everything."

I don't know what pushed me to say it. Maybe the ache in my chest. Maybe the sound of Inga's laugh, still echoing in my skull. Maybe the way my father had gone quiet in that knowing, almost amused way he had whenever life cornered me into something important.

But whatever the reason, before we wrapped up the call, I said quietly, "Hey, Dad?"

"Yeah, son?"

"How'd you know?" My voice dropped even lower. "With Mom. How'd you know she was... the one?"

Mom made a delighted, muffled shriek on the other end. Dad cleared his throat, the way he did when he was trying not to get sentimental.

"Well now," he said. "That's a hell of a question."

Another pause, and I gave him time to collect himself, listening to my mom's heavy breathing from her pressing a handkerchief against her lips—I could just see it in my mind's eye—to prevent us from hearing her excited giggles. As if…

Finally, Dad collected his thoughts, "I guess I knew when bein' around her made the worst parts of me a little quieter."

I sank onto the edge of the small wooden bench by the CQ desk. Dad continued, in a voice warm and steady as a heartbeat. "Your mother… she didn't make my troubles vanish. She just made 'em less loud. Like when you move a skittish horse from a stormy field to a quiet pasture. Same storm's blowin', but suddenly, you can breathe again."

I closed my eyes.

He kept going.

"And when she laughed? Son, I swear to God the world made sense for a minute."

This time, Mom couldn't suppress a soft chuckle.

"And when she looked at me, I felt like the man I was supposed to be. Not the fool I was at twenty."

Something in my chest twisted.

"So that's how I knew," Dad finished. "When life felt… easier with her. Brighter. Like she was somethin' I didn't know I'd been missin' until she walked right into me one lucky day."

Mom whispered, "He still looks at me that way, you know."

Dad coughed loudly. "Woman, you're gonna embarrass the boy."

But I wasn't embarrassed. I was struck still. Because every word he said—

each damn one, hit me like a truth I'd been circling without admitting.

I swallowed hard. "Thanks, Dad."

"You treat that girl right," he said. "If she's anything like your mother, she'll keep you on your toes."

I laughed under my breath. "Oh, she does."

"Then good," he said simply. "She's already done you some good, I can hear it."

He wasn't wrong. "Tell us more about her," my mother demanded.

I told them a little, not about the rubble, or the hunger, or the danger, just enough for them to picture her. Enough to let me say her name out loud, like it meant something. "Inga."

It felt like a promise when I said it.

Dad sighed. "Well, son… sounds like you're a goner."

Maybe I was. We talked a little longer, about Montana, about my sister, about the stubborn mare that still hated everyone except Mom.

Then Dad checked the time and said he had to feed the cattle before the sun went up.

"We love you," my mother said fiercely.

"Get some rest," Dad added.

"Write more," Mom insisted.

"Don't get shot down," Dad grumbled.

"I won't," I promised, even though in Berlin no promise like that meant anything.

We hung up.

I walked back to my room with a feeling I hadn't had in years.

Warm.

Content.

Alive.

I stretched out on my cot, listening to the echo of their voices, the memory of Inga's laughter, and the steady, impossible beat of something new unfurling inside me.

For once... sleep came easy.

And when it did, I dreamed of her.

Inga

Berlin — July 20, 1948, Tuesday

I HADN'T SEEN Gideon in three days. Not at the bar. Not passing through the street. Not hovering awkwardly outside the alley pretending he wasn't waiting for me.

Nothing.

But the boys had.

Every evening while I worked, Gideon brought them food. A pot of stew one night. Two hamburgers wrapped in paper the next. A whole tin of peaches the night after that. They never came hungry to meet me after my shift, not anymore.

Axel giggled whenever he said Gideon's name, as if he carried a secret too big for his small body. "He says," Axel whispered one evening, eyes bright, "that when he's got a day off, he's going to take you on a *real* date."

My heart tightened in a way that should've worried me.

A date.

Me.

The idea sent heat curling low in my stomach whenever I thought about it, made the corners of my mouth lift even when I tried to force them down. I wanted that more than I'd let myself want anything in a long time.

But before I could wonder more about it, Klaus shouted from across the rubble.

"Inga!"

I turned, then froze. Axel was leading a little girl through the broken doorway of what we generously called our home. She couldn't have been older than Klaus. Six. Maybe seven. A tangle of dirt-blond hair hung over her face, her eyes huge and startled like a wild animal brought into a cage. Her arm hung at a strange angle.

I knew immediately it was broken.

"Oh God." I crouched in front of her. "Hello," I whispered gently. "I'm Inga, what's your name?"

She blinked. Her lips parted. "Hilde," she breathed, in a voice thinner than paper.

That was all she knew. That was all *anyone* knew. Axel swallowed hard and explained in his small, solemn voice. "Bastian and the others... they chased her. She fell through a hole. I got her out."

I stared at the crooked limb and swallowed the rising bile down.

Trümmerkinder were everywhere now, orphans, half-orphans, feral children raised by the ruins themselves. They stole to eat, slept in cellars or burnt-out cars, followed older boys who ruled the rubble like kings. The war had ended, but for them it had never stopped.

Hilde trembled, watching me with the wide, blind trust of someone with nothing left to lose. My throat closed. "Oh, sweetheart..." I whispered, brushing a leaf out of her hair. "You poor thing."

But then panic slammed into me. What was I going to do? I couldn't afford a doctor. I couldn't leave her alone. And I had to be at *Die Ecke* in less than an hour.

"Klaus," I said, trying to keep the fear from my voice, "go find Elke. Ask if she can take my shift tonight. Tell her it's important. Very important."

Klaus nodded instantly and sprinted out through the rubble. I watched him dodge a rusted pipe and the jagged cement blocks he knew by heart. When he was out of sight, I lifted Hilde carefully—as carefully as I could—but she still whimpered, burying her face in my shoulder. She was tiny. Too tiny. Lighter than she should've been, like half her bones were missing.

Axel hovered at my elbow, uncertain. "She followed us," he said. "Maybe she thought... maybe she thought we would help her."

I kissed Hilde's temple. "You did the right thing bringing her here."

"But what do we do now?" Axel whispered.

I had no answer.

Not one.

Because every option I had was wrong.

Take her to the Jugendamt—youth care?

They would scoop her up like lost luggage and send her to one of those giant children's homes, where three kids shared a bed, and no one remembered your name. She'd disappear into the system, swallowed whole. Maybe sent to the countryside. Maybe not sent anywhere at all. Just… stuck.

A hospital?

We couldn't pay. And even if they treated her, they'd report her immediately. No papers. No parents. Gone.

The church orphanage down the street?

Overcrowded, strict, cold. I'd seen the line of thin faces staring out the windows like ghosts. Hilde would wither there. Her spirit would crumble.

A black-market doctor?

Maybe.

But where would I find one? And how could I trust someone whose hands traded in desperation? None of the paths were safe for her. None led anywhere but to a terrible outcome. This had been my worst nightmare for Klaus, and now for Axel too. This girl was a stranger to me, but she was just a kid and already pulling on all my heartstrings and protective instincts.

And God help me... I couldn't choose any of those options for her. Not for this tiny, trembling scrap of a girl who already looked like life had eaten half of her. I held her a little closer. Her small fingers clutched my blouse as if she'd been waiting her whole life for someone to hold on to.

Axel looked up at me, waiting for a miracle I didn't have. Hopelessness hit me like a punch to the lungs. I could barely keep Klaus and Axel fed. Barely keep a roof over our heads—if it even counted as a roof. Barely keep myself sane.

How was I supposed to take on another child? How was anyone supposed to? But then Hilde whimpered softly against my neck. And suddenly the answer didn't matter. Because the world had failed her. I just couldn't be the next person to do that.

I swallowed hard. "We take care of her," I said.

My voice didn't shake, but my heart did.

Axel's eyes went wide.

"Us?" he breathed.

"Yes, us," I whispered. "Just like we take care of each other."

He nodded, a little proud, a little scared. I sat Hilde on the mattress, smoothing her hair back gently. Not for the first time since Gideon had vanished into the sky for three long days, I wished he were here, but this time, it had nothing to do with girlish dreams. And not because he could rescue me, either, but because I didn't know what to do. And because some foolish, dangerous part of my heart believed he would.

Klaus came skidding back through the rubble, cheeks flushed, panting hard. "Elke says she will take your shift!" he announced triumphantly. "She said she wants the extra cigarettes anyway."

Relief washed through me so fast it nearly knocked me over. Bless Elke.

Bless her shameless hustle and soft heart underneath it all.

Hilde whimpered then, a small, thin sound that made every hair on my arms stand up. I pressed my cheek to her tangled hair. "It's alright," I whispered. "I know it hurts. I know."

Klaus dug frantically through the little box where we kept our precious stash, things Gideon had brought on nights before. He pulled out crackers, half a chocolate bar, and a tiny tin of something that might have been Spam.

He opened a packet of those dry American crackers, broke one in half, and set it in Hilde's good hand as if it were sacred.

She sniffed it, unsure, like a frightened animal, then nibbled. I didn't breathe until she took the first bite and then ate like she hadn't eaten in days.

Maybe she hadn't.

I wiped her face with a damp cloth. The dirt lifted away to reveal a child underneath, and a bruise on her cheek I hadn't seen yet. My throat tightened.

"Axel," I murmured, "heat some water."

He did, with a seriousness unusual for him, feeding scraps of wood and paper into the little tin stove. I washed Hilde carefully, murmuring to her, trying to keep her calm. She flinched each time I came near her broken arm.

"I'm so sorry," I whispered. "I'll make it better soon. I promise."

Then I took one of Klaus's shirts—too small for him now anyway—and cut it into strips. My hands shook as I fashioned a makeshift sling. It wasn't perfect. It might not even be good, but as I wrapped Hilde's sling around her tiny shoulder, a thought crept in, a soft, terrifying, persistent thought.

If I could help her… if I could help Axel… Maybe I could help all of them.

The Trümmerkinder. Children nobody claimed. Children nobody loved.

As I tied the knot behind her neck, Hilde sagged into me, exhausted. Her eyelids lowered, and she seemed to be falling asleep until a knock startled her awake and sent my heart stuttering. God help me, I didn't realize how much I had been hoping for that knock.

I nodded at Klaus and Axel. "Go. Open it."

They darted toward the door, pushing aside the patched boards. Gideon stepped inside. And for a second, everything in me stopped. He filled the space like he belonged there—leather jacket unbuttoned, hair windswept from flying. He carried a flat box that smelled unmistakably like pizza, the American kind the boys now worshipped.

His eyes landed on me, "Inga!" he breathed.

The way he said my name—relief, worry, something too big to name—made my knees go weak. He crossed the room in three strides, like he was going to kiss me. My heart picked up in anticipation. I wanted him to, so much. His hands lifted... stopped... then hovered uselessly in the air as he reined himself back.

He swallowed hard. "I... I didn't expect—"

His eyes fell on Hilde, and his entire demeanor changed. "What—who—?" He crouched beside her instantly, eyes sharp. "Inga, what happened?"

I told him everything. The fall. The gang of boys. The broken arm. Her having no one, nowhere. Her being one more Trümmerkind swallowed by a city that had no mercy left.

"She needs a hospital," he said immediately.

"I can't," I whispered.

He looked at me sharply. "Can't?"

I explained about the options and how bad any of them were, because they would all lead back to Hilde being taken to an orphanage.

Gideon's jaw tensed.

He looked at Hilde again, at the way she shrank from the world, and something hardened in him.

"Okay," he said softly. "Then we won't do that."

He stood, thinking fast—pacing once, twice—raking a hand through his hair. Then his eyes lit with an idea.

"I know someone," he said. "On base. A medic. He owes me a favor."

I stared at him.

"But… she has no papers. No guardian. No—"

"She doesn't need any of that," he said firmly. "Not where I'm taking her. The base clinic has a back entrance, and the night shift doesn't ask questions if you're with someone in uniform."

Axel gasped. Klaus looked awed. Hilde just blinked, dazed. And me? My breath caught. He was the miracle I had been praying for. "You would do that?" I whispered.

"Of course," he said simply. "For you, for her. It's the decent thing to do."

Heat climbed my throat. He held his arms out.

"Let me take her," he murmured.

I transferred Hilde carefully into his embrace. She weighed almost nothing. The sling held, but barely. Gideon adjusted it instinctively, as if he'd carried wounded children before.

Klaus grabbed my coat. Axel snatched the dirty stuffed animal he brought home one day. I wrapped Hilde in one of the new blankets Gideon had brought days ago. Then we stepped out into the night, into the ruins.

Inga

Berlin — July 20, 1948, Tuesday night

GETTING HILDE to the hospital was the right thing—of course it was—but the closer we got to the American sector, the more my heart hammered against my ribs. Berlin didn't like it when people crossed invisible lines. And for a German to get near the barracks was a thick red one.

Gideon carried Hilde against his chest, wrapped in his jacket, her tiny face tucked under his chin. Klaus walked close by my side. Axel stayed on my other flank, stiff and alert like a guard dog half his size. We moved through the darkened street, still lit in places by lanterns and makeshift fires smoldering in oil drums.

Halfway there, Gideon's hand slid to my back, gentle but firm. "Stay close," he said quietly.

"I am," I whispered, scanning the ruins out of habit.

"No—closer." His voice dropped even lower. "Someone's behind us."

A bolt of panic shot through me. I followed his line of sight. A figure stood half hidden between the shattered columns of an old post building. Not moving. Just... watching.

My stomach tightened. "Probably Bastian. He was angry that we interfered. He doesn't forget."

"That's not a kid," Gideon murmured. "Too big. Too still."

Cold settled at the base of my spine. A grown man watching children from the shadows... nothing good ever followed that.

I grabbed Klaus's hand. "Don't look back. Just walk."

We'd just passed by the edge of a ruined square when raised voices cracked the air, sharp, panicked, French. Three French soldiers were pressed against a wall, weapons drawn but hands shaking, while six Russians loomed over them, drunk or eager for trouble or both.

Gideon stopped dead. "Keep going," he told me.

I stared at him. "Gideon—"

"Go," he said again, placing Hilde carefully into my arms. "I'll catch up."

I didn't move. And neither did the boys.

Axel shook his head. "No."

Klaus planted his feet. "We stay with you."

Gideon cursed softly. "I don't have time to argue."

"We're not leaving," I said, breath tight. "Not while you—"

He gritted his teeth so hard I heard it. His eyes flared, and I could have sworn I saw gold glinting in them. This was the third time I'd noticed it, and a shiver ran through me. Not in a bad way, though. He turned toward the Russians. He didn't walk. He stalked—filled with a power I'd never seen contained in a single body.

The French soldiers looked up, desperate hope flickering. The Russians spun, one laughed, one spat, one raised a fist. And Gideon moved.

Fast.

Too fast to follow.

One Russian went down immediately; he hit the ground so hard the sound cracked like a broken tree limb. Another lunged, and Gideon blocked him with an arm that didn't budge an inch. He twisted, fluid as water, and the man flew backward into rubble.

A third tried to draw a knife. Gideon's boot kicked it out of his hand and sent him sprawling. Another Russian tried to swing his rifle, Gideon stepped in, yanked it from him like plucking a twig, and threw the weapon so far over his shoulder, I never saw where it landed.

The last two hesitated, trading uncertain looks. Gideon cracked his neck, like he was just getting started, and they ran.

Just like that.

The boys didn't breathe.

Neither did I.

The French looked obviously uncomfortable; they mumbled some Mercis and took off too.

When he came back to us, some wild lightning still flickering behind his eyes, he looked almost... embarrassed. Klaus was the first to speak.

"Wow, how did you do that?" he blurted—in English.

Gideon stopped short. "You speak English now?"

Axel puffed his chest. "I taught him."

Klaus nodded proudly. "How did you do it?"

Gideon glanced at me, then crouched so he was eye-level with them. "Training," he said. "And being really stubborn."

"Can you teach us?" Klaus asked.

Gideon's smile softened. "Yeah, kid. I can teach you."

My chest ached.

He hailed a cab—an actual cab—and the boys' eyes went huge. Even Hilde perked up, staring at the fading black paint like it was a magic carriage. The driver gave us a look, unimpressed at the sight of three ragged German kids, one of whom was half-awake, wearing a makeshift sling, and being carried by an equally ragged woman. But the moment he saw Gideon's uniform, he straightened.

"McNair?" the driver asked.

"Yeah," Gideon said. "And step on it."

Klaus pressed his nose to the window, watching the city shift from ruins to the more intact American zone. Axel whispered under his breath, counting the moving cars like each one was a miracle. Hilde curled deeper into my arms, safe for the first time in who knew how long.

I leaned toward Gideon. "You didn't have to do that back there."

"Yes," he said simply, "I did."

We drove through Checkpoint Bravo; GIs waved us on, barely glancing at the kids. The cab rolled into McNair Barracks, and the boys' jaws dropped. To them, it must have looked like a fortress of shining glass. Bright lights. Tall buildings. Soldiers in crisp uniforms. A jeep roared by. Men laughed. Order. Structure. Normalcy.

Everything our side of the city didn't have.

"Wow," Klaus breathed.

Axel stared at the big stone entrance as if it were a castle gate. "This is where you live?"

Gideon shrugged. "Sort of. It's just barracks."

"Just?" I whispered, stunned. "This… this is beautiful."

He looked at me, and for a moment, his expression turned soft and vulnerable. As if he were seeing the barracks through my eyes and realizing how bleak Berlin looked in comparison.

Inside, he smuggled us through a staff door, nodding at a sleepy soldier at the desk who barely noticed. The hospital wing was warmer, cleaner, and brighter than anything the kids had ever seen.

Hilde was treated quickly. A real doctor set her arm properly, wrapped it carefully, and even gave her a lollipop from a bowl on the counter. Hilde stared at it like it was a ruby. Then her whole face lit up with the most beatific smile I had ever seen. My throat tightened.

When the doctor stepped away, Gideon leaned against the wall beside me. Close. Too close. Close enough that I felt the heat from his body, causing the inside of my stomach to flutter with unknown sensations. My skin turned hypersensitive in anticipation of a touch, a brush, any kind of contact.

"You need to be careful," he warned me quietly.

"I am always careful," I murmured.

"Not careful enough." His voice hardened. "The Russians are pushing harder every day. They want a spark. One spark. Any spark. And today…"

He shook his head. "Today could've been it."

I nodded. I knew. You had to be blind and deaf not to know what was going on in the city. We were locked in like animals in a cage. Any way out was through the Russian sector, and I doubted they would let us leave on the other side. Even I knew that Berlin had been a race. A prize. The highest trophy, and Russia was pissed off that they had to share it. There is only gold for Russia, no silver, no bronze. I had heard stories about the Russian sector, how the people there were nothing more than prisoners. They weren't allowed out at all. The entire city was in a chokehold.

"Do you have family in West Germany?" Gideon asked me suddenly. "Anyone who could take you? Anyone safe?"

"No," I whispered. "I told you. This is my home."

"A dangerous home."

I lifted my chin. "I'm not leaving. I won't abandon Klaus. Or Axel. Or Hilde. Or the others like them."

His jaw ticked. Stubborn challenging stubborn.

"You're impossible," he said.

"You're not my boss," I shot back.

We stared at each other. Something softened first in him. Then in me. From across the clinic, Hilde held out her candy and whispered, "Inga."

The way she said my name... it made all the fear worth it.

Gideon let out a slow breath. "Come on," he murmured. "Let's get you all home."

Home.

Not rubble.

Home.

Berlin — July 21, 1948, Wednesday

JAMISON'S OFFICE was usually spotless. It was one of the things I admired about him: tight ship, tight uniform, tight rules. The kind of man who kept his pencils in a straight line and his boots polished even when Berlin was falling apart outside.

But today?

It looked like hell.

Two overstuffed inboxes sagged under classified folders. A cold cup of coffee sat forgotten near the edge of the desk, and a greasy ring stained the blotter. Three maps of Berlin were pinned to the wall, one with so many red X's it looked like a battlefield. Another had colored pins marking air corridors. A third had hastily drawn arrows, scribbles, and notes in thick black marker.

The window behind him was cracked open to let out the cigarette smoke, but all it let in was gray light and the distant grinding of jackhammers as Trümmerfrauen smashed at rubble piles down the street.

Jamison looked worse than the office.

His uniform was impeccable, yes, but there were deep lines carved under his eyes. His face was pale, a shade lighter than his collar, from too many days locked inside, and there was just the faintest tremor in his hands as he sorted through a stack of papers.

He didn't look like an officer. He looked like a man holding back a landslide with his bare hands. When he finally noticed me, he waved me inside without looking up. "Griffin. Close the door. Sit."

I did. A moment passed—him reading, me waiting—before he glanced up over the file.

"So," he said dryly, "any more *incidents* that never happened?"

I huffed a humorless laugh. "Not since the last ones."

He raised a brow. "Clarify."

I leaned back in the chair. "Two Soviet fighters stalked me on approach this morning."

His jaw tightened. "How close?"

"Close enough to see the pilot's cigarette dangling out his window."

Jamison muttered something vicious under his breath. "Did they cross the corridor boundary?"

"No. They stayed just outside. Watching."

"Harassment," he said. "Deliberate. They want a reaction."

I nodded. "They won't get one."

Jamison gave me a weary look. "They'll get something eventually. This city is a damn mousetrap, and Stalin's shaking it to see who flicks the cheese."

I didn't answer. There was nothing to say. Silence stretched a moment; the only sound was the distant jackhammer rhythm outside.

"Alright," he sighed finally. "What do you need, Griffin?"

I swallowed. "I want to get married."

Jamison blinked. Once. Twice.

"Married," he repeated, as if I'd spoken in Russian.

"Yes, sir."

He exhaled, not annoyed, just stunned. Then he opened a drawer and pulled out a stack of forms so thick it could stop a bullet. "Fiancée visa. Sponsorship. Background checks. Double background checks. Civilian affidavits. Moral conduct certificate. Sector clearance."

He stacked the pages like a house of cards. "And you'll need a chaplain willing to sign."

I blinked. "That's… a lot."

"This," he said, tapping the mountain of forms, "*is* a lot. But you asked."

I stared down at the pages, heart pounding with something halfway between terror and anticipation.

"How long?" I asked.

"If everything goes right? Two weeks."

It didn't take him long to realize my disappointment. He didn't know why I was in such a haste, didn't know how much I wanted to get Inga and the kids out of those ruins. Still, he threw me a breadcrumb. "If everything goes *very* right? One."

One week. My stomach did a strange, swooping thing. Jamison watched me carefully. "This girl—she must be something."

"She is," I said, voice rougher than intended.

Jamison exhaled and leaned back in his chair. The springs groaned under the weight of a man carrying too many secrets. "Then don't screw it up, Captain. Berlin eats good things first."

I hesitated at the door. "Sir," I asked, "if I *don't see* more... incidents—"

"You tell me," he said immediately. "No one else. Not Carter, not your squadron, *not* the press. Me."

Even if you have to pretend it never happened, his eyes seemed to say.

"Yes, sir."

"Good." He waved me off, already reaching for another crisis folder. "Now get out of my office before something explodes in the British sector and ruins my hour."

As I stepped into the hallway, the floor trembled faintly. Somewhere far away, a dud bomb had gone off, another reminder that Berlin still burned beneath the rubble. As if it had been summoned by Jamison's words.

I clutched the paperwork to my chest.

For the first time in months, I felt like I was moving toward something good.

Suddenly, Berlin glittered in a way I hadn't noticed before. It was still broken, still gray, still coughing dust into the sky... but it felt different. Lighter. Hopeful. Because I had a future now. A direction. A plan.

I stopped by the bank and withdrew a large amount of money. I wasn't going to go cheap on this ring. Then I spent thirty minutes hunting down a jeweler in the American sector, a store with glass so clean it looked like magic and chrome fittings that caught the sunlight in sharp, white flares. I pushed open the door, and a bell chimed with a soft, polite note that felt strangely out of place in Berlin. Inside, the air smelled faintly of polish and lemon, and the display cases glowed under warm electric lamps. For a moment, I forgot the rubble outside. The hunger. The tension. The Russians.

In here, the world was intact.

The jeweler appeared from the back room like he'd been conjured, gray hair slicked, mustache neatly trimmed, suit pressed to perfection. He looked old enough to have lived through three wars and stubborn enough to survive a fourth.

"Guten Tag," he said. "How may I assist you, Captain?"

"I'm looking for an engagement ring," I said, feeling the words strike somewhere deep in my chest. "A good one."

His eyes sharpened. "For a German girl?"

"Yes."

He studied me for a moment, as if measuring not just my rank, but my intentions. Then he nodded once and motioned me toward the far counter.

"You will want something... traditional. Not ostentatious." He lowered his voice. "But meaningful."

I followed him to a case separate from the others, its contents hidden beneath a velvet drape. When he lifted the cloth, light struck gold. There were rings, dozens of them. But my gaze went to one immediately.

A ring that didn't shine, it glowed.

The jeweler noticed. "Ah," he murmured, "that one is... special."

It was gold, warm and soft in color, shaped into delicate vines and leaves that curled protectively around a round-cut diamond. The design wasn't modern; it was timeless. Almost mythic. Like something a forest spirit might wear.

Two tiny diamonds flanked the center stone like droplets of morning dew. I swallowed.

"That center stone," the jeweler said quietly, "is just over one carat. Very rare these days."

I reached out, barely letting my fingertips brush the band. Heat sparked from the metal straight into my ribcage, settling somewhere dangerously close to my heart.

"It's perfect," I said.

"It is exquisite," he replied. "A piece like this... it speaks of devotion. Of choosing someone fully."

Exactly how I felt. I lifted the ring carefully, feeling its weight, not heavy, just enough to mean something. Would she even believe this was for her? Would she accept it? Would she cry? Would she smile?

God, I hoped so.

"Is this the one you want, Captain?" the jeweler asked gently.

"If it doesn't fit," I swallowed. It had to fit; it just had to. It was her. Perfect.

"Then bring it back here, and I'll resize it, for free." The man smiled warmly.

I nodded, determined. "Yes. That's one."

He closed the box gently and slid it toward me on the

counter. "The price is… ah." He hesitated. "Let us say it is not inexpensive. One thousand dollars, Captain."

I didn't blink. If he was watching my face for shock, I didn't give him any. I had been prepared to pay a lot more for the ring. I pulled my billfold from my inner pocket and placed crisp bills—American bills—on the counter.

The jeweler's eyes widened almost imperceptibly. No German civilian had seen that much money in one place since the war began. Most Americans hadn't either.

He cleared his throat. "You… pay in full?"

"Yes," I said. "In full."

He stared at me a moment longer, as if trying to place me, rank, family, origins, anything that could explain a pilot in dusty boots casually dropping more than most Berliners made in a year.

But he didn't ask.

Instead, he bowed his head. "Take good care of her, Captain."

"I will," I murmured.

It wasn't a promise. It was a vow. "Then let me polish it for you."

As he worked, I imagined sliding it onto her hand. Inga, who had nothing.

Inga, who had survived everything. Inga, whose eyes had been empty until she looked at me. She deserved something beautiful. She deserved something permanent. She deserved something that felt like hope.

And this ring… felt like a promise carved into gold.

When the jeweler was done, he placed it in a velvet-lined box and folded the lid shut with reverence. I slipped the box into my jacket pocket, feeling its warmth settle over my heart. Then I stepped back into Berlin—into dust, ruins, danger—into the world that looked so different now. Because in my pocket was the future I wanted. And I was going to give it to her.

I bought toys next: a carved wooden horse for Klaus, a set of bright tin cars for Axel, a cloth doll with yellow yarn hair for Hilde.

Candy too. Chocolate, licorice, gum.

I felt ridiculous, like Santa Claus in July, but I didn't care. I wanted to give them everything.

Outside, Berlin throbbed with rebuilding energy: Jackhammers rattled like bones shaking. Trümmerfrauen passed bricks down long chains of hands, faces streaked with dust and determination. Children darted between ruins like feral cats. Speaking of cats—

Two stray dogs trotted across the street in front of me, ribs showing, tails wagging anyway. A cat watched from the skeleton of a third-floor window, green eyes bright above the crumbled ledge.

This city refused to die. And so did everything in it. Including me.

I was halfway back to McNair when Carter fell in beside me.

"Lot of packages you got there, Griff," he drawled, nodding to the bag under my arm. "Christmas come early?"

I rolled my eyes. "Got something for the kids."

"Ah."

His smirk flickered. "You spend an awful lot of time with that girl and her... brood."

My jaw tightened. "They're good kids."

"Sure," Carter said. "But you know how this goes. A German girl smiles at you, acts helpless, tells you she needs you—"

I stopped walking and felt the cold wash over me. "Careful," I warned.

He either didn't notice or he didn't care.

"I'm just saying," he continued, shrugging. "These girls know Americans'll marry 'em if they play the part right. Ticket out of the rubble. I've seen guys get trapped. Pregnancies. Blackmail. *Oh, Lieutenant, I can't possibly survive without you*—"

The dragon slammed against my ribs so hard I saw gold flash in the corners of my vision. I stepped closer, my tone a warning snarl, "Don't."

My voice sounded strange, low and dangerous.

I watched Carter's smile die, "Griff, I'm trying to help you—"

"No," I growled. "You're trying to poison something good because you don't understand it."

His head moved slowly from side to side, a look of incredulity flitting over his features, "You actually thinking of marrying her?"

I nodded once. I didn't owe him an explanation; he wasn't a friend. My only friend in this place died a few hundred feet above Berlin, years ago. Normal humans weren't my friends. Still, in an effort to keep it civil, I said, "Yeah. I am."

Carter stared at me like I'd confessed murder. "Jesus, man," he breathed. "You're serious."

I walked away. I didn't trust myself to stay.

I'd barely turned the next corner when a figure stepped out of an alleyway. The man in the gray suit. The CIA agent. He smiled like a wolf. Little did he know that my dragon would swallow him whole if he stood in my way. "Captain Griffin. Been looking for you."

A chill moved down my spine. "I'm off-duty."

"But your other half," he said quietly, "never is."

That froze me. He couldn't possibly know.

"What are you talking about?" I said carefully.

He stepped into my space, voice soft but razor-sharp. "The dragon, Captain. The one you're barely keeping leashed."

Said dragon tried its hardest to come through my chest and devour the man threatening us. Heat rippled under my skin. I scanned the street, empty except for dust and a distant jackhammer.

"You're out of your damn mind," I snarled.

He smirked. He stepped closer—too close—and lowered his voice. "You think we don't know what you are, Captain?"

My spine went rigid. "Back. Off."

His smile cut like a knife. "Saxony. April '45. Ring any bells?"

Ice slid down my ribs. "Don't," I warned, not liking the images creeping up inside me.

"Two German fighter aces filed identical reports about an American plane."

He tapped his temple. "*Your* plane."

My breath locked.

"They swore—swore under oath—you leaned out your cockpit window and spewed fire at the Messerschmitt that shot your friend down."

My heart slammed against my ribs hard enough to bruise. I fought the urge to close my eyes. I could almost smell the smoke from Mark's plane as it spiraled down. Down, down, down. The cockpit was in flames; he never had a chance to get out.

"Funny thing?" the CIA man went on. "Your crew chief filed something similar. Said he saw your cockpit glow like a furnace. Said the heat coming off you warped metal."

"That's bullshit," I snapped, but I was sure my eyes flared.

He studied me with a predator's patience. "Is it?"

A pulse of heat shot up my throat, unwelcome, instinctive.

I swallowed it hard. "Those were combat hallucinations," I ground out. "Fog of war. Grief. People saw what they wanted to see."

He shook his head slowly. "No, Captain. People saw what they *feared* they saw."

My hands curled into fists.

"Mark Avery died that day," he said softly. "You think we don't know how close you were? You think we don't track anomalies when soldiers snap?"

I stepped forward, barely keeping the dragon under my skin.

"Say his name again," I growled, "and see what happens."

The man didn't flinch. Not even a blink. "We don't need you to admit anything," he murmured. "We already have the reports. All we need… is your cooperation."

"What do you want?" I ground out.

"Oh, yes." He flashed teeth. "We want you to work for us. Quietly. Covertly. You could walk into the Soviet sector like a ghost. Fly over it. Burn the truth out of the sky."

"No," I said instantly.

"You want to marry that girl." His smile sharpened. "I can help with that."

My blood went cold. "You stay away from her."

He raised his hands. "Hey, now. I'm offering a trade. You give us intelligence on Soviet positions, on troop movements, on who's defecting. And in exchange…" He tapped his temple. "We keep your secret. And your girl gets every form she needs approved… or I can delay it indefinitely."

The dragon roared inside me. Hot, blistering, violent. I clenched my fists so hard my nails nearly cut skin.

"If you ever show up near her," I kept my voice low and restrained the fire that wanted to torch this bastard, "I will end you."

"That's what I'm counting on," he whispered. "Your

instincts. Your… abilities." He put his hand on my shoulder. "You need us, Captain. And we need you."

"No," I repeated, shaking him off. "For your sake, walk away."

For a heartbeat, we stood there, the dragon inside me snarling, the CIA man's ambition cracking like ice, Berlin trembling beneath our feet from another bomb some unfortunate soul had stepped on.

He stepped back first. "Sooner or later," he said, "you'll realize we're on the same side."

He turned and disappeared into the alley.

I knew one thing for certain: if he came close to Inga, I would turn him into a pile of ash. No matter what oath I had sworn on my final initiation. I tightened my grip on the ring box in my pocket. I'd buy her safety myself if I had to.

I'd take her and the kids out of this city with my own two hands.

And if anyone tried to stop me—

the dragon would not be held back.

Berlin — July 21, 1948, Wednesday night

THE PAPERWORK WEIGHED HEAVIER in my pocket than a service pistol. It should have made me feel triumphant. I had a ring. I had a plan. For the first time since the war, the future felt like something I could choose instead of something I survived.

But the truth burrowed under that excitement like a splinter. I hadn't told Inga the truth. Not about the war. Not about my family. Not about the dragon. Hell, I hadn't even asked her to marry me.

I stood under the lantern outside Die Ecke, the warm yellow glow pooling in a circle on the cobblestones. Berlin had finally stopped pretending it was still winter. The air was warmer tonight, soft, carrying faint scents of wet earth, coal dust, and something sweet from a nearby bakery trying to get by with American flour.

A soft summer breeze lifted the edges of loose papers on the street, carried laughter from inside the bar, and cooled the back of my neck. My dragon didn't care about breezes. It cared about her.

You cannot mate without revealing your fire, it hissed inside me. *You cannot choose her without letting her choose you.*

I clenched my fists in my jacket pockets. What would she say? What would she do?

Would she scream?

Would she run?

Would she look at me like I was a monster wearing a man's skin?

Could I live through that?

The lantern flickered. Somewhere down the street, the low growl of an American jeep rolling over cobblestones reached me. A late-night patrol, making sure the streets stayed safe. Berlin never slept. Not really. It clawed its way back to life day by day, brick by brick.

And so had she.

She'd been clawing her way back long before I met her.

I saw her through the doorway before she stepped out, hair pinned up but unraveling, wisps curling around her neck. Her dress was clean but worn, mended so many times the seams told stories. Her shoes were scuffed, too thin for the streets she walked. But she had a glow tonight. A softness at the edges of her exhaustion. One strand of hair fell across her cheek, and she brushed it back with a tired, delicate motion that made my chest ache.

She stepped out of the doorway, blinked into the lantern light... and then saw me. Her whole face changed.

Her smile was small at first, surprised, shy, blooming slow enough to break me wide open. Then it brightened into something warm and tender, the kind of smile a man would spend his life trying to earn again.

That was it.

That smile did me in.

She didn't run. She didn't flinch. She didn't cling to fear the way so many people did in this broken city. She just looked at me like I was someone she wanted to see. Something inside me surged forward without permission, dragon, man, or both, I didn't know. I stepped into her space, slid an arm around her waist, and lifted her effortlessly, her feet leaving the cobblestones as if she weighed nothing at all.

She gasped, just faintly, her hands flying to my shoulders. And then, I kissed her. Not rushed. Not hungry. Not claiming.

Tender.

God, so tender it almost hurt.

Her lips were soft, warm, tasting faintly of chocolate from the bar, faintly of something sweet and innocent I didn't have a name for. Her breath trembled against mine, and when she melted into the kiss—full-body, trusting, yielding—I knew instantly, instinctively: She'd never been kissed before.

The realization undid me.

My hands shook where they held her. My heart hammered against my ribs. The dragon inside me purred —a low, molten rumble that spread through my bones— not violent, not feral, but... content. At peace. Something I'd never felt.

When the kiss finally broke, she stayed close, her forehead brushing mine, her breath soft against my cheek.

"That was..." She laughed quietly, breathlessly. "That was the best thing that has happened to me in... a very long time."

Her eyes were luminous in the lantern glow. I set her down slowly, reluctantly. She smoothed her dress, tucked a strand of hair behind her ear, and her cheeks flushed the prettiest shade of rose I'd ever seen.

"Careful, fly boy," she teased softly, "I'm starting to get used to you picking me up."

I swallowed. Hard.

"I'll pick you up for the rest of your life," I said before I could stop myself, "if you let me."

Her breath caught. The lantern flickered between us like a heartbeat. People didn't kiss in public like this in Berlin, at least not decent people, not in front of a bar, not when propriety still clung to the world like a ghost of the old days. A pair of older women passing by paused, whispering in German I couldn't fully catch, but their tone said everything: scandalous, reckless, young, foolish, hopeful.

Inga's fingers brushed mine—just a whisper of touch— but my entire body lit up like a struck match. The air didn't smell like ash anymore. Not around her. Deep down in the marrow of my bones, in the quiet of my dragon's breath, I knew. My father had been right: When a man knows, he knows.

She was the one.

This wasn't the right place.

This wasn't the right time.

Berlin was broken, starving, dangerous.

I hadn't told her the biggest truth about myself.

But none of that mattered. Because when she smiled at me like that—small, hopeful, a little shy, a little daring— the world narrowed to her breath on my lips and the warmth of her hand still brushing my fingertips. My heart made the decision before my mind even caught up.

One moment, I was standing in front of her, still tasting her sweetness on my mouth. The next, I was dropping to one knee on the cobblestones.

Her breath hitched—a soft, startled sound—as I pulled the velvet box from my pocket. The lantern above us flickered, casting gold over her face as she clasped both hands to her mouth.

"Inga," I said, my voice low, rough, shaking more than I wanted, "I know this is sudden. Hell, it's more than sudden. I shouldn't feel this way yet." I looked up at her —really looked—at the girl who had survived bombs and hunger and loss and cruelty, who stitched her dresses and pieced her life together out of ruins and still managed to laugh with her little brother.

"But to hell with should," I whispered.

Her eyes filled instantly—bright, shimmering, breaking my heart cleanly in two.

"I love you," I confessed. The words landed in the quiet like a vow.

"More than I ever thought possible."

Her hands trembled; one tear escaped and slid down her cheek before she could wipe it away. I wanted to catch it with my thumb. I wanted to kiss it away. I wanted to take every tear she'd ever shed and bury them so deep they could never reach her again.

"I never thought I'd find someone like you," I continued, my voice cracking. "Someone warm, and strong, and giving—even when you don't have anything left to give."

She shook her head, but I kept going. "Someone who'd take in children who aren't hers. Who'd starve herself so they could eat. Who'd stand on broken streets with her chin high, even when she deserves so much more than this city has ever given her."

Her lips parted. A tiny, wounded sound escaped her, disbelief or hope or both.

"Inga," I said, realizing I didn't even know her last name but not caring one bit, opening the box to show her the ring that felt like it held all my breath inside it, "you deserve someone to take care of you." Her tears fell harder now, and her hands were trembling. "Let it be me."

She covered her mouth again, a sob shaking through her. Her knees gave out a little, like the weight of the moment was too much for her thin body to hold.

"Marry me," I whispered. "Let me love you. Let me take you out of this. Let me give you a life where you never have to be afraid again."

The ring glowed between us, gold and light and promise.

"I can't give you the world," I said softly. "But I swear I will build you one."

She stared at me like she couldn't breathe. Like she'd been hit by something bigger than hope. Bigger than fear. Bigger than everything this ruined city had taken from her.

"Inga…" My voice broke on her name. "Say yes."

Inga

Berlin — July 21, 1948, Wednesday night

TONIGHT HAD BEEN one of the worst. Before I stepped outside and saw him standing under the lantern, everything hurt: my feet, my shoulders, my pride. Die Ecke had been packed with airmen and soldiers from three different sectors, all loud, all restless, all hungry for distraction.

One English soldier slapped my backside so hard my eyes watered.

I spun and dumped a full mug of beer over his head, and my boss made me pay for the beer.

Then a French officer pulled me into his lap and pretended it was a joke when I shoved myself free. A Russian in civilian clothes tried to follow me to the supply room until Elke stepped in and told him a British MP was watching.

Drunk men sang off-key. Someone vomited in the corner.

A glass shattered when two Americans started a fistfight over a pack of cigarettes.

And I had to clean it all.

By eleven, my head throbbed. By midnight, my insides felt hollow and shaking. By closing, I wanted to curl up on the floor and disappear. So when I pushed open the door and stepped into the cool night air, I wasn't expecting a miracle. But there he was.

Gideon Griffin.

Standing under the lantern as if he'd been painted there by some generous dream. For one foolish second, the world softened. The noise faded. My heart stopped hurting.

A thought hit me uninvited, childish, reckless. *What if he were my boyfriend?*

What if this—this man with the gentle eyes and impossible shoulders and quiet strength—was really here for me? My stomach fluttered, betraying me completely. Because it wasn't just gratitude. It wasn't just what he'd done for Klaus, Axel, and Hilde.

It was him.

The way his presence settled me, steadied me, like I didn't have to hold up the sky alone.

A dangerous notion.

So dangerous.

He could leave Berlin tomorrow.

He could vanish like everything good in my life.

And I'd be standing in the ruins again, clutching nothing.

But God…

How I wanted to believe him. To believe this was more than a GI being kind for a week. More than attention. More than hunger dressed up as affection.

Then he kissed me. And something deep inside me cracked open like a frozen river breaking in spring. When he dropped to one knee—when I saw the velvet box—my entire world stopped. My heart screamed.

My mind screamed louder. *This isn't real,* it insisted. *You don't know him. You don't know anything about him. He's American. He'll leave you. He'll leave Klaus. He'll break you.*

But my heart—my stupid, desperate heart—beat so hard I thought I'd collapse.

Boom-boom-boom.

Gid-e-on.

Gid-e-on.

I didn't know anything about him. I knew that. But I also knew this: he had carried me out of danger. He had protected me when I froze. He had fed my brother, fed Axel, fed Hilde. He had patched our home. He had looked at me like I was worth something. When he hadn't needed to.

His voice shook as he spoke. And each word tore me further open: *Warm. Strong. Giving.*

The message was clear and oh-so-alluring: *Let me take care of you.*

No one had ever said anything like that to me. No one ever would again.

Tears streamed down my cheeks, hot and unstoppable, because for the first time since before the war, I felt like a girl in a fairy tale. Like maybe—just maybe—someone could choose me. Not out of need or hunger or cruelty.

But out of love.

Real love.

He said he loved me.

And I believed him.

I believed him in the way a starving person believes bread exists when they finally smell it fresh from an oven. In the way a lost child believes safety exists when someone holds out a hand. I wanted this to be real so badly it hurt.

"I..." My voice broke. My knees shook. "I don't know what to say."

My mind still screamed: *He's a stranger. Don't trust this. It will break you.*

But my heart whispered, trembling: *He sees you. He chooses you. This is real. Take it. Take it.*

And between them—between fear and longing, ruin and hope, past and future—I stood trembling, breathless, unable to look away from the man who had just given me the most beautiful moment of my life. My heart was beating so hard it hurt. My cheeks were wet. My whole body trembled as if I'd stepped into a dream where nothing made sense, but everything felt right.

I loved him.

The realization struck me, not softly, but like a beam of light through the wreckage of my life, sudden, fierce, blinding. I loved him. I loved the way he looked at me, the way he protected Klaus, the way he saw me even when I tried so hard to hide.

I wanted him. I wanted to rest. I wanted to lean. I wanted not to carry the world on my shoulders alone anymore. And if that made me weak, then fine.

If it made me foolish, then so be it.

If it hurt me later… well, everything in my life had already hurt. At least this—this love—felt warm and right. He stayed on one knee, chest rising and falling unevenly, eyes locked on mine like he was praying.

I took a breath that stuttered painfully in my chest. Then another. Then—

"Yes," I whispered.

His head jerked up.

"Yes?" he echoed, stunned.

"Y-yes," I laughed through tears. "Yes."

His face broke open, joy, disbelief, relief all crashing into each other, and then he surged to his feet, swept me into his arms, and crushed me against his chest with a sound that came from deep inside him, half-laugh, half-sob.

I wrapped my arms around his neck as he twirled me in a circle, lantern light and night sky spinning together. I squealed, and he laughed, and for the first time in years —maybe ever—I felt weightless. Like Berlin wasn't broken. Like I wasn't broken. Like love was something that could actually happen to people like me.

He kissed me again—joyful this time, smiling against my mouth—and I melted into it, let myself feel all of it: safety, desire, hope, home.

When he pulled back, breathless, he put the ring on my finger. It was just slightly too big, but the sight of it made my heart lurch.

"Oh—Gideon—" It caught the lantern light and scattered it like shattered starlight.

I stared. Speechless. "Oh no… this is… this is too much," I whispered. "I can't… this is… I've never—"

I didn't know much about jewels, but I remembered my mother's ring, small, delicate, half the size of this stone. She'd been so proud of it. Women used to lean close when she cleaned their flats, whispering their envy, their admiration. Even the wealthy Hausfrauen she'd worked for hadn't owned anything like this.

"I..." my voice faltered, "I don't understand. This must be... glass? Or paste? I'll have to be careful with it; I don't want to scratch—"

His hand cupped my cheek, thumb brushing a tear I hadn't realized was falling.

"It's real," he murmured. "Every bit of it. And you deserve more than this. A thousand times more."

I swallowed hard. The world tilted. The ring glittered like a dream I wasn't ready to wake from.

"Oh, Gideon... it's so beautiful. Thank you," I whispered.

He smiled—slow, bright, breathtakingly—and kissed my forehead.

"No," he said softly. "Thank *you*. You're making me the happiest man alive."

He pressed another kiss to my cheek, then pulled back, eyes gleaming with mischief and excitement.

"Now," he said, rubbing his hands together, "let's go see the children?" He grinned. "I have gifts."

We walked hand in hand through the warm night, and my fingers laced with his like they belonged there. Everything inside me felt new, tender, and trembling, and too big to fit in my chest. I kept touching the ring, afraid it would vanish if I blinked too long.

Gideon talked softly as we walked, his voice deep and

calm and so reassuring. His thumb brushed the back of my hand like he was memorizing me.

"I spoke with my commanding officer," he said. "The paperwork has already been started. Two weeks, tops."

I nearly stumbled. "Two… weeks?"

"If everything goes smoothly," he continued, completely unfazed, "you and the kids will have a real roof over your heads. Heat. Windows. A proper bed for every one of you."

Heat.

Windows.

Beds.

My throat closed.

"Government housing?" I whispered, hardly daring to imagine.

He hesitated just long enough for me to hear the truth in the silence. "They won't give it unless everything is approved," he said gently. "So if not—I'll hire a realtor."

I stopped walking. "A realtor?"

He smiled at me under the lantern light, soft and earnest. "Yes. To help us find a place. A good one. A safe one. Something big enough for all of us."

All of us. The words sank into me slowly, sweetly, terrifyingly. Warmth flooded my chest, and with it a wave of dizzy disbelief.

"You can't just do that," I whispered. "Gideon… that costs… so much."

He lifted our joined hands and kissed my fingertips. "I promised to take care of you. Let me."

A soft sound escaped me—half laugh, half sob—and he pulled me close, tucking me against him like I belonged there. And maybe I did. Maybe for the first time in my life, I belonged somewhere.

We rounded the corner toward my street—the ruins jagged and familiar—when a small, frantic figure darted out from the shadows. Axel.

His face was white with terror. "Inga!" he gasped, breath hitching. "Inga—sie haben Klaus—!"

My heart stopped.

"They took Klaus!" he cried in German, clutching my arm. "The Russians! Two soldiers — they came— they— they grabbed him—"

The world went silent. Everything, the warm night, the happiness, the ring on my finger, fell away like a dream snapping in half.

"What?" I whispered. "Nein… nein… Axel, no…"

"I was coming to Die Ecke—" he panted. "About an hour ago—they stormed our place—they took him— they put him in a car— they drove— that way—"

He pointed down the dark street. My knees buckled. The world tilted.

No. No, no, no, no.

Not Klaus. Not my brother. Not the last piece of my family. My breath left me in a single, sharp sob. It didn't make sense. None of it made sense. "Why?" I choked. "Why would they take him? He's just a little boy—he's harmless—why—?"

Gideon turned toward me, his jaw was clenched so tight I could see the muscle jump. "I don't know," he kept his voice low and dark and shaking with something danger-ous. "But I'll find out."

His eyes locked on mine, burning with fury and promise.

"I swear to you, Inga," he said, voice breaking on my name, "I'll find out why—and I'll get him back."

I folded into him then, collapsing against his chest as the world tilted and fell away. His arms caught me instantly, holding me up, holding me together.

When he was sure I could stand on my own, he dropped into a crouch in front of Axel, gripping his shoulders gently but firmly.

"Which way?" he demanded.

Axel pointed again, shaking so hard his teeth chattered. Gideon rose and turned to me. His expression—God—I had never seen anything like it. All humanity stripped away. All warmth gone.

Just deadly focus.

"Inga," he said, and my name in his voice nearly broke me. "I need you to be strong now."

"I— I can't—" My voice tore apart.

"You can," he said fiercely. "You have to. I need to know you'll be safe so I can go after him."

I grabbed his jacket with shaking fingers, clinging to him as if my life depended on it. "Please—" I choked. "Please bring him back. Please—he's all I have—"

Gideon wrapped his arms around me, fierce and protective, holding me against his chest like he could shield me from the world. "I swear," he murmured into my hair.

His voice shook, with fury, with fear, with something deeper. "I swear on my life, Inga—I'll bring him home."

I sobbed against him, my entire body shaking uncontrollably. Because happiness always had a price. And this time, the price was Klaus.

My Klaus.

My little brother.

My heart.

Gideon pulled back just far enough to look me in the eyes. "I'm going," he said. "Stay with Axel and Hilde. Go to your friend's house, Elke, is it?"

Numbly, I nodded. He put a wad of dollar notes into my hand, "Just in case. And here," he scribbled something on a piece of paper, "this is my dad's number. If I don't come back, call him. He'll help." He took my chin in his hand and tilted it up, "Don't go anywhere until I'm back."

I nodded, even though every part of me screamed not to let go of him. He brushed his thumb across my cheek one last time. Soft, loving, and heartbreaking.

Then he turned and ran into the night.

And I collapsed to my knees in the dirt, clutching Axel as he cried, the warm breeze turning cold around us, the ring on my finger too bright, too beautiful, too cruel. "Please," I whispered into the darkness. "Please bring him back to me."

Berlin — July 21, 1948, Wednesday night

As I DISAPPEARED into the dark, I refused to think about Klaus. If I let myself think about the boy too long, think about how small he was, how soft his hair still felt under my palm, how he'd smiled at me and held Inga's hand like she was his universe—I shook my head—I'd burn the city down.

So I didn't think. I moved.

I cut into the first alley past the corner, narrow and stinking of coal smoke, piss, and rotting brick. A stray dog bolted deeper into the shadows when it saw me, ribs sharp under its mangy coat. A cat stared down from a second-floor window with no glass, just a black rectangle cut into ruined stone.

This was a bad idea. Shifting in the city was always a bad idea. Too many eyes. Too many guns. Too much that could go wrong.

The dragon did not care.

They took our brood, he snarled. *They took our hatchling!*

He wasn't mine by blood, but that didn't matter. Klaus had crawled under my skin the day he'd waved at my plane below the air bridge, and something in the dragon had quietly marked him.

One of ours.

I pulled my jacket off, then my shirt, fingers moving fast, breath coming too hard. Boots, socks, trousers—folded them into a bundle the dragon could carry. The cobblestones were cool under my bare feet.

I closed my eyes and let the dragon uncoil the second I stopped holding him down. Heat began in my chest, low and deep, a coal that had been sitting banked all day suddenly cracked open. It spread along my ribs, down my spine, licking through my veins with molten fingers.

Bones stretched.

Joints popped.

The world tilted.

I clenched my teeth and rode it out, jaw grinding as my muscles bunched and twisted, tendons lengthening, skin tightening. Scales rippled up my arms, across my chest, down my legs in a wave of molten gold and bronze, catching the faint lantern light in a thousand tiny mirrors.

My hands curled, fingers lengthening, nails turning black and hard as iron. My shoulders wrenched backward, blades tearing free, unfolding into wings, vast, heavy, every movement a rush of air and muscle. My vision sharpened; the alley exploded into detail: every crack in the bricks, every shift in the shadows, the shimmer of heat from the sewer vent.

The pain was bright, clean, familiar. It felt like coming home.

When it passed, I was no longer standing; I was crouched low in the alley, massive and coiled, tail thrumming against stone, wings half-furled to avoid brushing the walls.

I exhaled.

A thin streamer of smoke curled out into the night. I picked up the bundle of my clothes with one talon. The dragon's eyes—my eyes—saw Berlin differently from above the ruins. Even hunched, my head brushed the second story. With care, I pressed claws into the stone and launched myself upward, wings unfurling in a heavy, thunderous beat.

For one second, my belly cleared the rooftop by inches. Then I was above it, wings catching a stray gust, rising into the hazy sky. The city spread beneath me like an open wound. Pale scars of half-cleared streets. Black craters where buildings once stood. The skeletal spire of the ruined church, a snapped finger pointing accusingly at the stars. A few pockets of life: a tram rattling along a repaired line, its windows casting a warm yellow glow; a single street musician playing a lonely accordion on a corner; a line of women carrying buckets from a pump, their washing lines strung between broken walls.

I pulled a deep breath into my lungs. Under the coal smoke and river stink and distant engine fumes, scents sharpened into layers. Warm metal from Tempelhof. Cold stone from the government quarter. Old blood from a bombed hospital that would never be rebuilt. Soot, urine, damp plaster.

No Klaus.

Not yet.

But the dragon could smell fear like a storm on the air. And underneath that, the sour tang of Soviet tobacco and cheap spirits, the reek of gasoline and leather from Russian trucks, the faint trace of the grease they used on their rifles.

They were everywhere. But the line between sectors had its own scent too. Three times I wheeled low over the boundary streets, muscles itching to dive, but I held back. If they saw a dragon in their air? That wouldn't just be a provocation.

That would be war.

Information first, I told myself. *Then fire.*

Reluctantly, I angled toward the American sector, toward a street I had always avoided. A requisitioned townhouse with darker windows than the others. Extra guards. Curtains that never opened fully.

The spook's nest.

I circled once, twice, then dropped low into an alley behind it, claws scraping brick as I pulled in wings and let the bones break backward into a man's shape again. The reverse shift was faster—less fight, more collapse—but it still stole my breath. When I could stand, I grabbed my clothes from the bundle and yanked them on with shaking hands. I didn't bother with the front door.

By the time I reached the corner, the scent was already there: ink, cold tobacco, soap too expensive for this city. The gray suit. I would have recognized it anywhere. I followed it.

He was under a broken gas lamp two blocks away, flame flickering weakly inside the glass like it didn't want to be alive. He stood with his back to me, lighting a cigarette with careful hands, talking to a man who looked like he'd be rather anywhere else than here with *him*.

I stepped into the alley, and the spook turned slightly. If he was surprised to see me, he didn't let on. I jerked my chin at the other man, and he was smart enough to recognize my interruption as a *get out of jail free card* and took off.

"You're going to tell me where the boy is," I told the spook.

He exhaled smoke and sighed, long-suffering. "You pilots," he said mildly. "So dramatic. Catch me up."

I closed the distance in three steps. Not fast. Not loud. Just inevitable. "Klaus," I clarified. "Six years old. He was taken tonight."

That got him to finally turn. Up close, his calm looked thinner. His eyes flicked once—left, right—measuring exits. The dragon stirred under my skin, pleased.

"You're asking about matters you don't understand, Captain," he shook his head.

I leaned in close enough for him to feel the heat bleed off me. "Try me."

His eyes flickered slightly, then he shrugged. "Children disappear in Berlin every day."

He was right, I'd heard about the Russians *collecting* children and taking them into the east sector. Still, "Not like this. Not after you threatened her."

It took a good amount of self-control not to grab him by the throat and pin him against the wall. Every second wasted here was time Inga suffered not knowing, and Klaus... God knows what.

"They're usually taken in groups," I went on to make it clear I knew more than he thought I did. "Trucks. Promises. Klaus was targeted."

That's when I remembered the dark shadow a few nights ago when we were taking Hilde to the hospital. I should have listened to my instincts. I should have stopped and demanded what he wanted. I ran a hand through my hair. Too late. Fury weaved through me; it was getting harder to control by the moment. "Where," I repeated softly, "is Klaus?"

He studied me for a long moment, then smiled without humor. "You really would burn the city down for her, wouldn't you."

That wasn't a question.

"You've been interested in my services before," I said. "Now I'm interested in your information."

His smile sharpened. "Careful. That sounds like an offer."

I took another step. The gas lamp guttered. Steam hissed through my teeth.

"I'm not offering," I said. "I'm collecting."

"Now, let's talk about that. Tit for tat." He tried with a gleam in his eyes. He thought he had me.

We glared at each other. I allowed the dragon to shift through, carefully, just enough for the Spook to see the fire in my eyes. Finally, he spoke. "I didn't order to have the child taken, but my bet would be that he is alive." My lungs unlocked, my eyes narrowed, and he must have realized I wasn't in the mood for games, so he added, "With family."

The word didn't make any sense.

"Inga is his family," I growled.

He sighed. "His Father. He's with the Russians—high-ranking and untouchable."

My blood went ice-cold, my mind whirled. Inga said her father went missing in Russia. If he were alive... no, there wasn't time for any of that right now, I would find out the details later.

"Address," I demanded. "Now."

He shook his head once. "And what will you do for me if I give it to you?"

"I'll let you live."

We stared at each other again. He backed down first. But he tried, "If you cross that line, you can't uncross it. East Berlin is not your playground."

I smiled, slow and cold. "Let me worry about that."

The dragon surged. The lamp shattered. Glass rained down around us, and the flame went out with a hiss. In the sudden dark, he swallowed hard and gave me the address. I stepped back, already pulling away, already shedding skin and bone as I ran. Within moments, Berlin reeled beneath me as I rose, the city small and fragile and flammable.

I would bring Klaus home. And anyone who stood in my way would learn exactly what kind of monster they'd just provoked.

Inga

Berlin — July 21, 1948, Wednesday night

THE SCENT of boiled laundry and potatoes still lingered in Elke's flat, the scent that clung to every hallway in Berlin these days. Axel sat on the floor with Hilde, trying to feed her bits of chocolate Gideon had brought, but she only sucked them until they melted and smeared down her chin.

I couldn't sit. I couldn't breathe. I couldn't be still.

I kept pacing the narrow length of the room, hands twisting in my hair, my heart beating so hard it felt like I was bruising from the inside out.

"I can't just stay here," I cried for the fifth time, turning sharply at the wall. "I can't not do anything, not when Klaus—when—"

"You have to calm down," Elke insisted, trying to pull me into one of her mismatched kitchen chairs. "Gideon is an American pilot. He knows what to do."

Her voice was steady, but there was something else in it too, a brittle edge. Envy. She'd wanted this for years. A man in uniform. A way out.

"I still can't believe you're engaged to one," she murmured, half dreamy, half sulking. "An American, Inga. How in heaven's name did you manage that? You never even flirt with the soldiers."

I shot her a look. "I didn't *manage* anything," I snapped, too raw, and added "Gideon… saved me" to soften it.

Elke sighed dramatically and pressed a hand to her chest. "Oh, romance…"

She leaned back in her chair, eyes drifting toward the ceiling. "Trust me, I've tried to get saved like that, and all I got was a man who smelled like beer telling me *nice legs*."

Normally, I would have laughed. Tonight I couldn't. I knew she was just trying to relax me, to pass the time, and I loved her for it. But I was too restless. I didn't even have a chance to answer before a sharp knock rattled the door on its hinges. Elke jumped. Axel froze. Even Hilde let out a small squeak and hid behind his arm.

My heart thudded painfully.

Elke moved toward the door cautiously. "Who is it?"

"Russki," a man's voice answered through the wood. "I have message."

My blood turned to ice. Elke turned wide, terrified eyes on me. I shook my head; the words, "Don't open—" came out automatically, but I stopped myself. The Russians were the ones who, according to Axel, had taken Klaus. So if they were at Elke's door now, here… they had to know about Klaus. I stepped forward with my heart pulsing in my throat. "I'll take it."

The door creaked open just enough for a Russian soldier to stand in the gap. He was older than most, uniform rumpled, eyes sharp and unreadable. He held out a folded piece of paper.

"For you," he said in heavily accented German. "Inga Weber."

Every breath in my body stopped. I took the paper with trembling fingers. It was dirty around the edges, like it had been carried for hours. My name was written on the outside in a handwriting I hadn't seen in… God. Years. A lifetime ago.

My father's handwriting.

No.

No, it couldn't be.

I unfolded it with numb fingers.

· · ·

D*aughter,*

I know this must be a shock, but I'm alive and safe. Do not listen to anyone. They lied to us for years.

I need you to trust me and follow the man who brings this letter. He'll take you to me. And Klaus.

We can finally be a family again.

Vati

The room spun. My throat closed, and my vision blurred.

"He... he's alive?" I whispered, hardly hearing my own voice. "My father—alive? And he has Klaus?"

Elke snatched the letter from my hands. Her eyes flew across the page, then she looked up at me sharply.

"No," she said, shaking her head. "No, Inga. Don't believe this. This is what they do. Russians lie. They lure women. They lure—"

"I don't have a choice," I whispered. Because it was true. I didn't. I had to take the chance.

If my father was alive...

"Klaus," I forced out. "He has Klaus. I have to go."

Elke grabbed my wrist, panic rising. "Inga, you don't know this man! You don't know anything—"

"I know my father's handwriting," I argued stubbornly, but my voice trembled. "I have to go. I have to see them. Even if it's a lie. Even if it's a trap. I have to know."

Elke stared, helpless and horrified. I reached into my coat pocket and pressed the money Gideon had given me—money I'd never even dreamed of touching—into her palm.

Her eyes went wide. "Inga, what is this?"

"Take care of the children," I whispered. "Please. Feed them. Keep them safe."

"Inga, don't do this," she begged. "Don't go. What about Gideon? What about—"

Pain ripped through my chest.

"I'll come back," I promised.

I didn't believe it. But I said it anyway.

Because I needed to believe that somehow, someway, everything wouldn't fall apart again. I turned to Axel and Hilde. Axel shot to his feet, pale and shaking. Hilde clung to his arm, eyes huge.

"I'll be back," I whispered to them. "Stay with Elke. Don't leave the flat."

Then I stepped outside. The Russian soldier was waiting patiently beside a gleaming black limousine, polished so brightly it reflected the ruin around it like a twisted mirror. My stomach dropped.

"Please," he said simply, opening the door. "Come. Your father waits."

I looked back at the ruins, at the only home I had left, and then stepped inside the car. The door shut with a soft thud. The world outside disappeared as the limousine rolled toward Checkpoint Charlie, toward the East, toward whatever waited for me behind those walls.

The limousine glided silently through the sleepy, early-morning streets, its wheels whispering over cracked cobblestones. Berlin felt unreal, too quiet after the panic, after Klaus… I pressed my forehead to the cool glass as the world slid by.

People were already lining up with ration cards in their hands, shuffling their feet, blowing into cold fingers even though summer had touched the air. A few women had small children wrapped in blankets, leaning tiredly against their skirts. A baker's cart rattled past, the driver calling out the day's meager offerings.

And there—my heart squeezed—Old Manne, the man I'd waited beside so many mornings. He stood with his one arm tucked against his coat, staring ahead with that weary patience carved into all of us. I wanted to pound on the window and shout at him. Tell him I was engaged. Tell him Klaus was taken.

Tell him I was terrified.

But the car kept moving.

We passed the rebuilt blocks, new storefronts, smoothed stone facades, hopeful construction scaffolds catching the first pale light. West Berlin's stubborn determination glowed faintly, like a lantern refusing to go out.

But then—Checkpoint Charlie loomed ahead. A barrier. A border. A scar across the city.

American soldiers stood guard on one side, their uniforms neat, boots polished, rifles gleaming. Beyond them, past the striped barrier arm and the concrete teeth on the road, Eastern soldiers waited with blank expressions, weapons slung casually over their shoulders, as if violence were just another morning chore.

My stomach twisted.

The car rolled to a stop.

One of the American MPs stepped forward. He didn't look directly at me—didn't even try—but he peered into the car with suspicion, then glanced at the papers the Russian soldier handed over. His jaw tensed. His fingers twitched. For a moment, I thought he might pull me out, ask who I was, ask if I was here willingly. But whatever was on that paper—the Russian's pass—made his face fall still and cold. He stepped back.

The barrier rose.

And we crossed.

It felt like stepping through a mirror into a darker version of the world. The air itself seemed heavier. Even the light dimmed, as if the sun grew tired here. What small flickers of hope the cleared-out West held—the new bricks, the painted storefronts, the cautious smiles—died instantly. On the East side, rubble still swallowed entire blocks. Buildings leaned like burned matchsticks. Men trudged rather than walked. Women stared with hollow, hungry eyes. Even the children—if they could still be called that—moved like shadows, stiff and silent, as though the simple act of living required too much effort.

"Why... why does it look worse?" I whispered before I could stop myself.

The soldier didn't answer.

We drove deeper, past lines of people waiting outside distribution centers, past groups of men clearing debris with dull eyes. Everything was gray. Everything was exhausted. Everything looked... hopeless.

This had been my city, too. It still was.

But even I felt the difference. As if someone had reached into this quarter of Berlin and pulled the warmth out of it. My heart thudded painfully. Was Klaus here? Was he somewhere in this cold, lifeless place, alone and terrified?

The limo turned onto a quieter street, a street that didn't match the rest.

The rubble thinned. Sidewalks became smooth. The grime lessened.

We turned again, and my breath caught. A villa rose before us. A real villa. Four stories, pale stone washed clean, windows intact, a balcony with wrought iron

curling like lace. The garden—an actual garden—over-
flowed with trimmed hedges, roses, and an enormous
chestnut tree spreading its branches protectively
overhead.

I stared.

It looked like something from a fairy tale. Something
from before the war.

Something from the life my mother used to daydream
aloud while cleaning rich women's apartments.

My throat tightened painfully.

This wasn't right.

Nothing about this was right.

The car stopped at the foot of the steps. A man in a
pressed black suit—an actual butler—stepped forward
and opened the door with a gentle bow.

"Fräulein Weber," he said, as if he'd been expecting me
for years. "Please, follow me."

My legs shook as I stepped out. The garden soil was
fragrant, rich and alive, something I hadn't smelled in
years. It made my chest ache. Inside, the villa was even
more unreal. Plush carpets muffled every footstep.
Golden sconces flickered with warm lamplight. The walls
were lined with dark, polished wood, gleaming so clean I
could see my reflection in it.

Portraits hung from the walls, men in uniforms, women
in pearls, landscapes untouched by war. It felt like step-

ping into a dream. Into someone else's life. Into a memory I didn't belong to. The butler led me down a hallway where the air smelled faintly of lemon polish and soap, luxury scents. My heart punched against my ribs, too fast, too much. At the end of the hall, double doors stood open.

In the center of a sitting room—more beautiful than any place I had ever seen—stood a man.

Tall.

Pale, but well-fed.

Dressed in a perfectly tailored suit, shoes polished to a shine. His hair was thinner, his jaw sharper, but—my breath caught. My knees nearly buckled.

"Vati," I whispered.

He turned. And smiled.

"Inga," he breathed, stepping forward with open arms.

A sob broke from me before I even knew it was coming. I ran—sprinting across the carpet—and flung myself into his arms. He caught me easily, lifting me the way he used to when I was small, when the world was safe and warm and full of promise. I buried my face against his chest, inhaling the scent of soap and wool and the faintest trace of tobacco. For one moment—one precious, stolen moment—I let myself ignore every warning my instincts screamed. I let myself believe I was safe. That Klaus was safe. That my father had come back to me from the dead. I let myself be a daughter again.

"Vati," I sobbed. "Vati—Vati—oh God, you're alive."

His hand stroked the back of my head. "Yes, mein Mädchen," he murmured, voice warm and soothing. "I'm alive. I'm here."

I clung tighter. For just one heartbeat, I didn't question anything. I just held on. 'I was a child again, safe in my father's arms, his coat scratchy against my cheek, his chest warm and familiar. His hand stroked my hair exactly the way he used to, slow, soothing, gentle. Time didn't exist. The world fell away, all the fear and hunger and years of loneliness dissolving like dust on my tongue.

But then reality crept back in. Like cold water rising slowly around my ankles.

Klaus.

Where was Klaus?

I stiffened and pulled back just enough to look at him. His face, older, drawn, but well-fed, his cheeks fuller than mine had been in years, blurred through my tears. "Vati… where is Klaus?"

He smiled, soft and paternal, brushing a strand of hair from my forehead. "He's asleep, mein Engel—my angel. Safe. You'll see him soon."

Relief and panic twisted together in my chest. He cupped my face with both hands, tilting it up toward the light. "Let me look at you," he whispered, eyes shining. "Gott, you've grown. You're a junge Frau—young woman—

now… and so beautiful. My little girl. You look so much like your mother."

My throat tightened. Tears poured freely again. "I missed you," I sobbed. "I missed you so much."

"I know." He pulled me close, holding me with a strength that felt both comforting and frightening. "You were everything that kept me alive. Everything that helped me survive."

I clung to him, desperate and confused.

"What happened?" I whispered.

He sighed and guided me to sit on the edge of a velvet chaise. The room was too bright, too clean, too rich. My thin skirt felt like it didn't belong anywhere near it.

"I was wounded," he began. "In '43. Badly. The Red Army overran our position. I was taken prisoner with others. They dragged us east… to a camp." His eyes drifted to some far-off memory. His voice dropped. "It was… unspeakable, Inga. Cold beyond anything you could ever imagine. Days of hunger. Men dying beside me." He swallowed hard. "I didn't expect to live."

I squeezed his hand.

"But then one officer… one Russian officer… saw something in me." His lips curved with reverence and pride. "He learned I wasn't with the Party. That I'd refused to join. He protected me."

A shiver went down my spine. A premonition of what was to come.

"He taught me the values of communism," my father continued. "He showed me there was another way. A better way. One where all Germans could be lifted from the filth the Nazis dragged us into. He gave me a place... a purpose. A life." His eyes shone with fervor. "And now, here I am."

He straightened with quiet triumph. "A Senior Advisor to the Soviet Reconstruction Committee." He said it like a king announcing his coronation.

My stomach turned.

"We can be a family again," he proclaimed gently, taking my hands. "All of us. Safe. Protected. Together."

I tried to breathe. I tried to think. But none of this made sense.

"And Mutti?" I whispered. He froze for only a heartbeat, but long enough for me to see it. "You know... what happened?" I asked quietly. "The Russians..." I swallowed. "They took her. They—"

"Bedauerliche Opfer," he replied calmly.

The words struck like a slap. *Regrettable casualties.*

"What?" I whispered.

He sighed. "In war, things happen. Terrible things. But understand, Inga, what the Germans did to the Russian women..." He shook his head. "It's only natural—"

"Natural?" The word ripped out of me like fire. "Mutti was murdered!"

He didn't even flinch.

"Yes. And so were their mothers. Their sisters. Their daughters. The Red Army lost more than we can imagine. It is the nature of war that such violence—"

"No," I cried. "No, Vati, that is not natural! Nothing about that is—"

He raised a hand, not angrily, just firmly. "You will understand in time," he said. "You'll see the truth when you are no longer blinded by Western propaganda."

Propaganda.

The world spun.

"I want to see Klaus," I demanded sharply.

"Of course," he murmured. "Come."

He led me upstairs through halls that grew richer with every step, ornate runners, polished banisters, vases of flowers that shouldn't exist in Berlin anymore. At the top of the grand staircase, he turned left into a long corridor with tall windows overlooking the garden. We passed two doors before stopping at a third.

He opened it gently. Inside, in a soft bed beneath a quilted blanket, lay Klaus. My little brother. Fast asleep, his fist curled near his cheek, chest rising and falling steadily. Clean. Warm. Safe.

My knees nearly buckled.

"Oh..." I breathed, pressing a hand to my mouth. "Klaus..."

I stepped inside, tears streaming anew, the room blurring around him. Behind me, my father rested a gentle hand on my shoulder. "Everything will be wonderful now," he whispered. "You'll see."

But something deep inside me curled tight in warning. His tone was wrong.

Too practiced. Too smooth. As the early morning light hit the quilt, I realized: This wasn't the reunion of a family. This was the opening move of a trap.

My knees felt weak as we walked back down the staircase, Klaus' sleeping face still burned behind my eyes. Relief warred with dread in my chest, wild, frantic, crashing like two storms colliding. My father's hand remained gently on my back as if I might fall.

"Es ist viel—it's a lot," he murmured. "I know, my child. I know."

He guided me toward the sitting room again, the one that looked like something from a storybook where nothing bad ever happened. Only this wasn't a story-book. This was a nightmare wearing silk gloves. I swallowed hard. My voice shook as I forced the words out. "Can your driver take Klaus and me back now, and we—"

"Back?" His voice snapped like a whip.

I froze.

"This is your home," he said, soft but sharp. "Where you belong."

Something inside me shrank. Something else, a stubborn, terrified part, flared instead.

"To get our things," I explained quickly.

"What things could you possibly have?" he sneered, his lips curling. "Rags? Scraps? Trash from a bombed-out ruin? You don't need those old… burdens."

Old burdens. My breath stilled in my throat. I tried, "A bracelet. From Mutti. It's all we have left. And some toys for Klaus—"

"I will get you new things," he said briskly. "Better things. Everything you could ever want."

"I want to go back," I insisted. My voice cracked like thin ice. "Tonight. Please. Just for our things."

His expression hardened. The warmth vanished like someone had blown out a candle.

"No," he said. "You're not going anywhere."

A cold shudder ran down my spine. "Vati, please—"

"Komm," he interrupted, gently gripping my arm. "Du bist müde—you're tired. You need rest. We will talk tomorrow."

"No," I breathed, pulling my arm free. "I need to talk to Gideon."

That got his full attention.

"Gideon?" he repeated sharply.

"My fiancé," I said, standing straighter than I felt. "I need to let him know I'm safe."

His face twisted. "Fiancé?" he spat. "An American?" He said it like a curse. "Good God, Mädchen!" he thundered. "Do you have any idea how this will look? How people will talk? How the Party will see it? You will break up with him immediately."

"I will not!" My voice tore out of me, raw.

His eyes narrowed, sharp, calculating, predatory, draining all the blood from my face. He wasn't asking. This was an order.

"No American," he snapped, "will drag my daughter into disgrace."

Something inside me cracked. "Klaus!" I yelled, turning toward the stairs. "Klaus, wake up! Let's go home— Klaus—"

My father didn't grab me. He didn't need to. Because as I stood in the doorway shouting for my brother, reality hit with a force that knocked the air from my lungs. We weren't leaving this place. Not if he didn't want us to. I had no money. No papers. No identity in the East. No right to cross a border guarded by armed men. The villa was a gilded cage. My knees gave out. I pressed a hand to the wall to keep from collapsing to the floor.

Gideon.

Oh God—Gideon.

Would I ever see him again?

My heart splintered, piece by piece, the way buildings had split during the firestorms. I clutched my mother's memory to my chest like a shield and whispered, voice broken, "Gideon, what have I done?"

East Berlin — July 22, 1948, Thursday night

I WANTED to go after Klaus the moment I left the Spook, but if I didn't show up for duty, Jamison would have no choice but to call the MPs and report me AWOL. It would mean a city-wide search. And once that started, everything unraveled. I'd end up in the brig, maybe worse. Desertion in this powder keg of a city wasn't something they took lightly.

Of course, no cell could hold the dragon. But letting him loose—*here*, now—would mean exposure. Questions. Hands reaching for things they didn't understand. I couldn't risk that. Not yet. Not when Klaus was still out there.

No. The smart move was to wait. To endure. To wait for the end of my shift and let darkness fall again. It was the hardest order I'd ever followed.

So I stole clothes from a line strung between two half-standing buildings and made it back to the barracks in time for my shift, I wasn't the first, and I wouldn't be the last GI to show up like that. A few smirks followed me down the corridor. Raised eyebrows. A chuckle or two.

No one asked questions. In Berlin, you learned quickly not to.

I changed back into my uniform, button by button, fingers clumsy, hands still faintly shaking. Not from the shift. From the effort it took to keep the dragon leashed.

Thankfully, no Yaks harassed us that day. I wasn't sure I could have stopped myself from burning them out of the sky if they had. The dragon kept lifting his head at every engine sound, tasting the air, daring me to give him permission.

Soon, I promised him silently. Soon.

He paced under my skin, coils tight, wings scraping the inside of my ribs. He wanted blood. He wanted Klaus. He wanted the man who thought he could reach across borders and histories and take what wasn't his. Every snap of a button felt like another lock on a cage that was already buckling.

I told myself to breathe. To finish the shift. To keep my head down. But the moment it ended, I didn't go back to the barracks. I went to see Inga first. I needed to. I needed to tell her that I knew where Klaus was, that he was alive, that I would bring him back. I needed to be the one to tell her about her father, before someone else did it wrong, before fear got there first. I needed to see her face, to hear her voice, to reassure myself that at least this much was still intact.

So I cut west through streets still half-lit, half-ruined, my boots finding the same paths they always did. Rubble and shadow and the echo of my own steps. Elke's building leaned like it had given up on standing straight, but there was light in the window. That eased something tight and painful in my chest.

Elke opened the door just a crack. Her face told me everything before she spoke. "You're too late," she said, and her voice broke on the words, like saying them softly might change what they meant.

The dragon surged in anticipation, sensing blood, sensing loss.

Elke told me about the Russian. About the knock at the door. About the letter. About Inga's father, a name dragged back from the past like a weapon. She told me how polite the man had been. How calm. How there hadn't been shouting, just certainty. She said Inga went with him.

The dragon slammed against my ribs, a roar clawing up my throat, hot and feral and desperate to tear the world apart until it gave her back. For a second I thought I might let it happen, that I might tear free right there in Elke's doorway and damn the consequences.

I swallowed it down until my jaw ached, until my teeth ground together hard enough to hurt.

Inga was gone.

"When?" I asked, though my voice barely sounded like my own.

"Last night," Elke said. "Only an hour or two after you left."

The dragon went very still. That was worse.

He paced under my skin, furious, coils tight, wings scraping the inside of my ribs. He wanted blood. He wanted Klaus. He wanted *Inga*.

As much as it tore at me, I told myself they were safe for now. If her father had gone through the trouble of finding them—of taking them—he wouldn't harm them. Not yet. Dragons were good at patience when the hunt required it, even if every instinct screamed otherwise.

I knew where Gerhard Weber lived—the CIA bastard had given me the address. "*High-ranking and untouchable,* he'd warned. Ridiculous.

Nothing was untouchable to a dragon.

When the last patrol rolled past the alley behind Elke's house I hid in, I stripped and let the shift take me. Bones cracked. Heat flooded my veins. Claws punched through my skin. My spine arched, and wings burst into existence with a rush of air that rattled loose stones.

I rose—silent, heavy, and deadly—into the night sky. Below me, the border gleamed like a scar across the city.

Checkpoint Charlie.

Surrounded by barbed wire and watchtowers swarming with men with guns they thought meant something. I skimmed above them in the dark, a shadow on a darker sky.

No one looked up.

They never did.

Weber's villa rose like a palace in the middle of ruin. A mirage in the middle of a desert. I made out several guards posted at the gate and door.

My dragon snarled.

Prey.

I dropped low, gliding between broken chimneys until I reached the tree line behind the garden. Then I folded my wings tight and descended into the shadows. The first guard didn't even have time to scream.

One clawed sweep—silent and precise—and he slumped into the hydrangeas. Alive but unconscious. The dragon wanted to finish the kill, but the man in me warned that casualties would raise too many red flags, could ignite the powder keg that was Berlin, and I wasn't about to burn down the city or start WWIII. Not yet. Not if I could help it. But I would if they forced me to. I'd do anything for Inga and the kids. Including turning the world to ashes.

One by one, I removed them: the guards at the back entrance, the men patrolling the grounds, the watchman with a rifle too large for his shaking hands. No alarms rang out, no blood that mattered was spilled.

Dragons were made for war.

But we could be quiet when we needed to be.

I slunk to a tall, ornate window framed by velvet curtains. I still needed to find out how many guards were inside to make this clean. I peered inside at a warm dining room glowing with lamplight. Beyond that, voices floated faintly—calm, polite, wrong.

I crept to the next window.

Where I froze. There—in a parlor of silk and gold—sat Inga, Klaus, and a man I assumed was their father. It might have looked idyllic to anyone else. But I knew Inga. I knew Klaus. What I saw in their eyes made the dragon inside me bare his teeth. Inga sat rigid, her hands were folded so tightly her knuckles were white. Klaus perched beside her, too stiff, too silent. His eyes darted to the door every few seconds like he was waiting to bolt.

Gerhard sat opposite them, smiling with the smug confidence of a man who believed he owned everything in the room, including them.

My blood boiled. Nobody keeps my people from me. All thoughts of making it *clean* were gone, the dragon inside me thrust forward, his instincts overrode any rational thought the man might have been still capable of. One powerful leap—

a snap of wings—

a crash of glass—

I smashed through the window in a storm of claws and firelit eyes, shards raining across the floor.

Screams erupted.

Gerhard stumbled backward, knocking over a table. Two guards burst in with rifles. I roared—a sound that shook the walls—and batted one rifle aside like a toy. Flames curled from my teeth, scorching the rug but sparing the men. They dropped their weapons and fled in terror. Three seconds later, the parlor was empty of everyone but four people:

Inga.

Klaus.

Gerhard.

And me.

I shifted before I knew I was doing it. The terror in Inga's eyes was too much to bear. My bones snapped back, my wings collapsed, and my claws shrank back into fingers. Within seconds, I was kneeling on the shattered floor, glass cutting into my knees, breath heaving.

"Inga," I gasped, "don't be scared. I'm sorry—I'm so sorry—I should have told you what—"

"Gideon!" Her scream wasn't of fear. It was relief.

She ran to me, threw herself into my arms with the force of a crashing wave, burying her face against my neck.

"Gideon, you came," she cried, shaking. "You came. I love you. I love you so much."

I clutched her against me, one hand in her hair, one around her waist. Everything in me—man and dragon—lit up like fire in dry grass.

"Inga," I whispered into her skin, "I'd tear this whole damn city apart for you."

Klaus hovered at first, wide-eyed and trembling from head to toe, but then he rushed forward and pressed himself against my side. I pulled him in, too, my heart ripped open from the deep love I felt from both of them.

Behind us, Gerhard shrieked.

"Du… du Teufel! You MONSTER! You will NOT take my daughter!"

Inga turned, her eyes were blazing with something fierce and broken and finally awakened.

"'He's not a monster," her voice was low and calm, her chin lifted, pointing at him. "You are."

Gerhard recoiled like she'd struck him. I stood, pulling Inga and Klaus behind me.

"We're leaving," I said.

"You'll never make it out," he hissed. "The guards—"

"Are unconscious," I growled.

His face drained of color.

I guided Inga and Klaus outside, into the moonlit garden. Inga clung to my hand like it was the only thing keeping her from drowning.

"Gideon," she whispered, voice quivering. "How... how are we going to get out of here?"

I turned to her fully. "Do you trust me?"

She swallowed. Then nodded. "With my life. With Klaus's. Always."

My heart broke and healed at the same time. I couldn't resist any longer; I pressed my lips to her forehead, wanting to kiss her into oblivion, but this would have to do for now. "Good."

Then I stepped back. Wings tore from my shoulders in a burst of firelit shadow, and scales rippled over my skin as the dragon surged forward. Inga didn't scream—didn't even flinch—she only watched, her expression a blend of awe, terror, and... belief.

When I lowered myself to the ground, wings tucked, back broad and warm with gold scales shimmering under the moon, she understood.

"Cool!" I heard Klaus exclaim.

She helped him climb onto my back, settling him between her arms. He trembled, but excitement flickered beneath the fear.

"He's warm!" he whispered.

Inga climbed carefully behind him, pressing close, hands gripping the ridge of scales along my neck as if she'd done this all her life.

"I'm here," she murmured. "I won't let go."

The dragon rumbled, pleased, possessive, and most of all, relieved that she was safe and with me.

I launched upward. The villa shrank below us, and the East Sector passed beneath our wings in a blur of ruined streets. The night air rushed around us, cool and wild.

Klaus let out a whoop of pure delight.

Inga's laughter—shaky, breathless, disbelieving—followed like music.

And for the first time in my life, with the woman I loved and the child I would die to protect clinging to my back, I felt whole.

A dragon.

A man.

A protector.

A mate.

Inga

Berlin — July 22, 1948, Thursday night

I KEPT RUNNING through the same impossible questions. How do I get out? How do I get Klaus out? How do I reach Gideon?

I had no answers to any of them.

The villa was a palace, yes—but it was also a prison.

There was a phone downstairs, a black rotary thing on a delicate little table in the hallway, but even if I could sneak to it, even if I could dial... I didn't know Gideon's number. Elke didn't have a phone. Die Ecke had one, but I didn't know what to ask the operator for. I didn't know anything.

I hadn't seen any way to leave the villa yet, without an escort. I didn't have papers or money. I had no freedom. Every possibility dried up before it even formed.

So I sat stiffly on a velvet sofa beside Klaus, pretending to sip tea while my father smiled his polished smile. Everything about the room gleamed: polished floors, expensive drapes, silver trays. Everything in me shriveled.

Klaus leaned into my side without seeming to notice he was doing it, and I threaded my fingers through his. They were cold and a little sticky.

"Are you tired, Klaus?" my father asked gently.

Klaus didn't answer. This man was a stranger to him. He had no memories of our father—had never met him, before today— and that was probably a blessing for him, because for me, it added to the torture of seeing my miraculously-returned-from-the-dead father in front of me, yet not. He was nothing but a bad caricature of the man I knew and called Vati once upon a time.

Klaus stared at the door, squeezing my heart, because he knew. He understood more than any six-year-old should.

My father kept talking about how *wonderful* life would be now, how we'd never want for anything again, how we'd all live here as *a model family*, how I would learn *proper values*. How I would forget the *lies of the West*.

I pretended to listen. Inside, I was screaming.

And then—

Something shifted. There was no warning other than maybe a slight change in the air, a ripple of… heat, a strange prickling sensation that rolled over my skin, like the atmosphere in the room had thickened. I straightened.

Klaus felt it too—his fingers tightened around mine.

My father kept talking, oblivious.

"Vati," I said suddenly, cutting him off. "Do you hear—?"

The words died as the window behind him darkened. Not by a cloud or shadow. With something alive. Something vast. For a split second, my brain refused to understand what I was seeing: a hulking shape, bronze-gold scales catching faint moonlight, wings unfurling in a terrifying silhouette—

A dragon.

A DRAGON!

A scream ripped out of my throat before I could stop it, and I yanked Klaus against me as the window exploded inward. Glass rained like frozen stars.

The whole room shook.

The dragon landed in the parlor in a thunder of muscle and heat, filling the space like a living storm. The air around him shimmered with warmth, not burning my skin warm, but washing over me like a heartbeat.

Klaus buried his face in my side. My father stumbled back with a shriek. "GOTT IM HIMMEL—!"

Two guards burst in with rifles raised. The dragon roared. A sound that rattled my bones but didn't frighten me. Not like it should have. Not like it frightened the others. Because as that roar rolled through me, something strange and impossible happened. Recognition hit me. Recognition that came on a deep, primal level. It came from a flash of those eyes. Those golden eyes. The way they were burning. Fierce and familiar: Gideon's eyes.

My breath stopped, and my heart flipped.

That's him.

The thought wasn't logical, it wasn't even possible or sane, and yet, I knew.

Everything in me knew.

The dragon lunged, sweeping the rifles aside with one massive claw without hurting the men. Their terror won out, and they bolted.

As I stared at the dragon, his form rippled, shifted. It looked like it collapsed inward. Bones snapped, wings folded, scales dissolved into skin, heat became breath, and then Gideon knelt in the shattered glass, buck naked, panting, eyes blazing with the same fierce gold I had seen glimpses of before.

My hands flew to my mouth. "Gideon," I whispered.

He looked up at me.

"Inga," he gasped. "Don't be scared. I'm sorry—I'm so sorry—I should have told you what I—"

I didn't let him finish. "GIDEON!"

I launched myself at him so fast we both nearly toppled

backward. My arms wrapped around his neck, my face pressed to his shoulder, and tears spilled hot and wild.

"You came," I cried. "You came. I love you—I love you so much—"

His arms locked around me, one hand dug in my hair, the other crushed me to his chest like he never wanted to let me go again, like he needed me close to reassure himself I was real and here.

"Inga," he whispered in a broken voice. "I'd tear this whole damn city apart for you."

His words *should* have scared me. Hell, everything about this should have scared me. But it didn't.

Maybe I'd used up all my fear years ago, in those long nights crouched in the shelter with my mother while the bombs fell like the sky was breaking open. Some nights they were distant, a dull thud that rattled the lantern glass.

Sometimes they were so close, the world *exploded*, plaster rained down on us like dirty snow, the earth heaving under our feet as if it wanted to swallow us whole.

That had been fear. Real fear. The kind that crawls into your bones and stays there forever. The kind that makes your body tremble and shake more than any chills ever could. I remembered clinging to my mother, fingers digging into her coat, certain she could hold the ceiling up with her bare hands if she had to. Certain she could keep me safe. Certain she would survive.

I'd been wrong.

But standing before Gideon now… That old terror didn't rise. Not even close. Nothing about him—his words, his fire, his fury—made me want to run.

Because every line of his body, every breath he took, told me one truth: He would burn the world down for *me*. And for some insane, impossible reason, that was the most comforting thing I had ever felt. No one had ever protected me. No one had ever chosen me. No one had ever stood between me and danger.

In his presence, for the first time since the war began, I felt something I barely recognized: Safe.

Safe in the way only someone who has survived too many close calls can understand. Safe in the way that feels like stepping into warm light after years of crawling through an icy tundra. Safe in the way that made my entire body finally, *finally* exhale.

Klaus hovered behind me. He was trembling at first, but slowly, shyly, he stepped forward. Gideon reached out a hand, and Klaus ran into him too, burying his face in Gideon's chest as Gideon wrapped both of us close.

My heart nearly burst. Behind us, my father shrieked.

"DU TEUFEL! You monster! You will NOT take my daughter!"

I turned my head toward him, my eyes burning with unshed tears, my voice shaking with fury and clarity. "'He's not a monster," I said softly. "You are."

The rage that crossed his face... I'll never forget it.

Gideon rose, pulling Klaus and me with him. "We're leaving," he stated.

"You'll never make it out," my father hissed. "The guards—"

"Are unconscious," Gideon growled.

My father went pale, but he didn't try to stop us. Maybe he couldn't. Maybe he finally saw what real strength looked like.

Outside, the garden glowed pale under the moon. I grabbed Gideon's hand. "Gideon, how... how are we going to get out of here?"

He turned to me fully. "Do you trust me?"

A shiver ran through me, not of fear, but of certainty. "Yes," I whispered. "With my life. With Klaus."

His expression softened. Then he stepped back. And the man I loved exploded into golden flame and wings and scales. I gasped, stumbling backward with Klaus as the dragon lowered himself to the ground, enormous but... gentle. His eye was level with mine, bright gold, warm, waiting.

Then I understood. He wanted us to climb on.

"Komm," I whispered to Klaus. "He won't let us fall."

Klaus pressed against me. He was still trembling, but I could tell he was thrilled too.

"Cool!" he exclaimed.

When he climbed onto Gideon's back, he let out a tiny laugh. I climbed on behind him, gripping the ridges of scales along Gideon's neck. The warmth of his dragon form seeped into my bones.

Without warning, he launched into the sky. I clung to Klaus, who let out a whoop of pure joy, high and bright, echoing over the rooftops. Wind roared past us, cool and wild. The ground fell away. And I felt free. So incredibly free, I let out a shriek of pure, undiluted joy! Nothing I had ever experienced before in my life compared to this feeling of flying, of sitting on... the man I loved... feeling his warmth between my legs, it was... obscene. Arousing in a strange way that I didn't have words for. And comforting, all at once.

The villa shrank into a toy house. The city opened beneath us in all its broken, wounded beauty. A laugh escaped me—shaky, breathless, disbelieving.

I was riding a dragon.

I was riding Gideon.

The man I loved.

The man who had come for me.

The man who was taking me home.

The wind carried Klaus's laughter, my own, and the dragon's deep rumble of happiness.

And for the first time in years—Years!—I felt free.

If the flight had felt like a dream, the landing jolted me back to reality. Gideon dropped into the ruins behind an old factory, wings folding in with the fluid grace of something ancient. Klaus and I slid off his back as he lowered himself, and I steadied myself against the cool bricks as he shifted shape again. Scales vanished, wings tucked into nothing, and suddenly he was just Gideon—stark-butt naked, breathless, beautiful. Klaus giggled, "Er is nackend—he's naked."

Gideon blushed, actually blushed, and grabbed his uniform, which he must have stashed, pulling it on quickly, urgency replacing every gentle moment we'd shared in the sky.

"We need to get the others," he said. "Now."

I nodded. His hand found mine, warm and grounding, and we hurried through the dim streets to Elke's building. My heart nearly burst when Axel flung the door open the second we knocked.

"You're back!" he gasped, voice breaking. "And you… you found Klaus!"

Before I could answer, Hilde peeked out from behind him, wide-eyed and smudged and so heartbreakingly small. Then she darted forward, grabbing the hem of my dress like she was afraid I might vanish again.

"We're going someplace safe," Gideon told them. "All of us."

Elke stared at him like he was a fairy tale stepping into her flat, like she wasn't sure he was real.

"You're the American," she whispered. "The... fiancé."

Her eyes flicked between us, confused and hopeful and a little jealous.

"I'll keep everyone safe," Gideon said gently. "Thank you for watching them."

She nodded, stunned. But not too stunned to ask, "Do you have... a friend by any chance?"

Gideon gave her a small smile, but he didn't answer other than to wave goodbye and usher us outside again—me, Klaus, Axel, and Hilde—all following Gideon like he was some kind of guardian angel in a leather jacket.

We took a taxi and crossed into Charlottenburg, the heart of the British sector. The devastation thinned here, still present, of course, but the buildings stood straighter, the sidewalks clearer. Shops along the Kurfürstendamm had lights again. A tram rattled by. A café with boarded windows had a handwritten sign promising *Kaffee-Ersatz* tomorrow morning.

The taxi stopped. Gideon helped us out, and my eyes fell on a sign, *Hotel am Zoo*.

A real hotel. With intact windows that glowed warm, golden light across the street. With polished brass fittings. With a doorman in an immaculate coat, opening the door for two well-dressed women who looked like they belonged in another world entirely.

My breath broke.

"Gideon," I whispered, grabbing his sleeve, "we can't go in there. People like us—this is for diplomats, officers, rich people, not—"

"You're with me," he said softly.

Those three words nearly undid me.

Inside, the lobby glittered. Marble floors reflected light from crystal chandeliers. The scent of polish and clean linen wrapped around me like a memory of childhood, before hunger, before fear, before everything fell apart.

Hilde hid behind my skirt, overwhelmed. Axel stared open-mouthed, and Klaus's hand trembled in mine.

Gideon walked to the desk like he belonged there. Like he'd done it a hundred times before.

"Suite, please," he told the clerk.

The man blinked at the three children, and at me in my patched dress, then looked back at Gideon's confident expression and American uniform.

"Yes, sir," he said quickly. "A large suite."

Keys and money changed hands, the clerk nodded quietly, and a bellboy appeared from out of nowhere, leading us toward a pair of metal doors, where he pressed a brass button. I jumped a little when the doors slid open with a soft, mechanical sigh.

Inside was a tiny room lined with polished brass and mirrored panels. A velvet mat softened the floor. Warm light glowed from a little domed lamp overhead.

An elevator.

A real elevator.

I hadn't stepped into one since before the war, since the days when Mutti used to take me to clean apartments in the upscale district, and I'd watch the doors open and close with wide-eyed fascination.

Klaus tugged on my sleeve, staring inside as if it were the gateway to another world.

"Inga," he whispered, "is… is it safe?" His voice wavered.

Axel hovered behind him, trying to look brave, but his eyes were darting around like a cornered animal. Hilde pressed her face against my skirt, terrified and curious all at once.

"It's safe," I assured them softly, though a little knot had formed in my own stomach. "It's just… a lift. A machine that takes us up."

A machine that worked. Here. In this city. In this life.

I swallowed an inappropriate giggle down.

Gideon gestured us forward. "It's okay. I promise."

The bellboy smiled politely, holding the accordion grate open. Klaus stepped in first—cautiously—then gasped when his reflection appeared in the mirrored walls. Axel followed, eyes even wider. Hilde shuffled in with tiny, hesitant steps.

I stepped in last.

The air inside smelled faintly of metal and something sweet, perfume, many different perfumes. A smell I associated with people who had never known hunger. The bellboy slid the grate shut, then the outer doors, and with a soft jolt, the elevator began to rise. Klaus grabbed my hand. Axel gripped the railing so tightly his knuckles went white. Hilde's eyes got huge, her mouth forming a perfect *O*.

My own heart thudded. Not with fear, exactly... with something else: wonder, memory, and the shock of comfort after a decade of nothing but survival.

The elevator hummed, climbing steadily. Light shimmered on the polished brass. Our reflections moved with us, four lost souls caught in a golden box, rising higher and higher, as if we were being lifted out of our old lives entirely.

"Inga," Klaus whispered, "we're flying. Again."

This time I let the giggle out—it was a small, incredulous sound—because in a way, he was right.

"It feels like magic," Axel said softly, his voice reverent.

Hilde reached out and touched the mirror, her fingers trembling as she watched her own reflection do the same. Something tightened in my chest. This wasn't just an elevator. This wasn't just a lift in a fancy hotel. This was the first moment—the very first—where I realized Gideon hadn't just rescued us.

He was giving us a new world.

A world with warmth and light and elevators and hope. The elevator came to a gentle stop. A soft chime sounded. The bellboy opened the doors. Warm golden light spilled in again, guiding us forward.

The bellboy led us toward another set of double doors, and when he opened them, more warm air rushed at me, and for a brief instant, I was transported back in time— back to when my father still worked at the firm, when Christmas meant tinsel instead of terror, when we could afford to dream.

The suite was... indescribable. High ceilings with crown molding like lace.

A chandelier dripping with crystal droplets. A sofa uphol- stered in deep emerald velvet. Carpets thick enough to drown your toes in.

Tentatively, the kids moved forward and put their toes on the carpet. Hilde giggled, and Axel jumped up and down. Klaus took his shoes and socks off and whooped. "It's like stepping on a cloud."

The other two followed his example. Gideon took my hand, and together we watched the mesmerized kids as they explored a room the likes of which they had never seen before.

A silver fruit bowl and tiny paper-wrapped mints stood on a big wooden table, and the kids rushed forward, like kids did on Christmas night. Just a foot before they reached the table, they stopped and, in unison, stared at Gideon and me. He squeezed my hand and waved them on, "Take what you like."

The children didn't need any further encouragement. Like starving animals, they fell over the fruit and mints.

The bellboy cleared his throat gently, the sound delicate, so he didn't interrupt the children's frenzy. "If you'll follow me, Fräulein… sir?"

Gideon gave him a nod. "Lead the way."

Klaus, Axel, and Hilde were too busy stuffing grapes and mints into their mouths—and pockets—to notice us stepping away. I didn't think I'd ever seen children eat fruit with such reverence, as if every bite might disappear if they didn't hold on to it. Only Gideon and I followed the bellboy deeper into the suite.

He opened a door on the right.

"This is the first bedroom," he announced softly.

I stepped inside and stopped cold. A bed. A real bed. Large, bright white, with pillows piled like clouds and a comforter so thick it looked sinful. A wardrobe with polished brass handles gleamed in the corner. A small writing desk with a lamp sat against the wall, and the light wasn't flickering or dim; it shone steady and warm.

My breath caught. Not because I hadn't seen luxury today—I had. My father's villa had been filled with polished wood, gleaming floors, and rooms designed to impress. But *this* was different.

This room didn't feel like it was trying to prove something. It didn't loom over me with its perfection. It didn't press down on my ribs with velvet cages and gilded walls. It simply… existed.

Warm.

Clean.

Safe.

Untouched by the war in a way that felt gentle instead of threatening. The bellboy motioned to a second door farther down. "And here is the master bedroom, sir."

This one was even grander. A king-sized bed. Heavy velvet drapes. A balcony with wrought iron railings looking down over the Ku'damm. Another wardrobe. Another chandelier, smaller but still shimmering.

My fingertips brushed the banister on the balcony door. It was cold and smooth and perfect. A life I'd never thought I would see again.

The bellboy continued. "There is also a smaller water closet by the entryway, and—" He paused dramatically, then opened a third door. "—the main bath."

I gasped. It wasn't just a bathtub. It was palatial. Porcelain, deep enough to drown in. Two brass faucets. A rack with tiny glass bottles of bath salts and soap in shapes I hadn't seen since childhood. White towels stacked high like folded snow. A mirrored cabinet gleamed so brightly it reflected my stunned face with painful clarity.

"Oh… oh," I whispered, hand over my mouth. "It's… beautiful."

The bellboy didn't blink at my reaction. Maybe he was used to people like me, people who had gone without too long. He simply bowed his head. "If you need anything else, the front desk is available at all hours."

Gideon handed him some cigarettes, and the bellboy left. The door clicked shut behind him.

Silence settled like a blanket.

Only the faint noises of children in the other room could be heard. Hilde giggling, Axel saying, "Try this one!" and Klaus crunching into an apple, floated faintly through the suite.

I stood frozen in the bathroom doorway, unable to move. Gideon stepped behind me so quietly I didn't notice until his warm hand slid gently into mine.

"What do you think?" he asked softly.

My throat tightened. "I—I don't remember… anything like this. Not since before the war. Before… everything."

He squeezed my fingers. "I wanted you to feel safe," he murmured. "All of you."

My eyes blurred. "I don't even know how to... be in a place like this anymore," I whispered.

"You don't have to know," he said, turning me gently to face him. "You only have to rest."

His thumb brushed across the back of my hand, slow and reassuring. "And tonight," he added, voice low, "you finally can."

A tear slipped down my cheek before I could catch it. I wasn't crying over the bathtub. Or the beds. Or the carpets. Or the stupid fruits. I was crying because for the first time in years, I wasn't surviving.

I was being cared for.

I stepped forward, and my fingers brushed the tub, "My God," I whispered. "I haven't... not since before the war... not even a warm wash..."

The kids must have finished the fruits, because Hilde wandered in behind me and gasped so loudly she scared herself.

"You all go first," I said, choking on emotion.

Gideon placed a gentle hand on my back.

Klaus' eyes were huge. "But... the water?"

I knelt and kissed his forehead. "There's enough hot water for all of us. Running water. Hot water. All night."

Klaus blinked rapidly, overwhelmed. Axel hovered by the door, uncertain.

"Hilde first," I said, "she's the smallest."

Gideon helped them one by one, running warm water, adding soap bubbles, wrapping Hilde in a giant towel afterward like she was royalty, ever careful of her broken arm that was set in a cast. Axel's giggle echoed off the tiles; Klaus splashed so hard I thought we'd flood the place.

And the whole time, Gideon moved with a quiet tenderness that made my chest ache. Finally, the children were warm and clean and wrapped in blankets on the large bed in the other room, dozing under the soft glow of a table lamp.

It was my turn.

Gideon stood by the bathroom door, looking suddenly shy. "There's a lock; take all the time you need."

He stepped away to give me privacy. The moment the bathroom door clicked shut behind me, the world hushed. For a long time, I simply stood there in the steam, staring at the porcelain tub as if it might vanish if I blinked. Then I turned the brass faucet, watching in awe as steaming water poured out, steady, abundant, effortless.

Hot water.

My breath trembled.

I sank into the tub slowly, almost reverently, the heat wrapped around me like a blanket I hadn't been allowed to touch for years. It stung at first; my skin wasn't used to warmth, but then a soft moan escaped me as the ache in my bones loosened.

Warm. So warm.

The soap smelled faintly floral, rich and creamy. I lathered it over my arms and watched gray water swirl away from my skin, the kind of filth you didn't even notice anymore until it was gone.

For a few minutes, I didn't think at all.

I just *felt*.

Felt the water.

Felt the heat.

Felt the softness of the towel at my back.

Felt alive.

But gradually, like a tide creeping back to shore, my thoughts returned. The last forty-eight hours unraveled in my mind like a reel of film:

Gideon's voice—*I love you.*

His knee hitting the cobblestones.

The ring.

I lifted my hand out of the water and stared at it. The diamond caught the lamplight overhead and threw tiny stars across the tiled wall. It was so beautiful. So impossibly beautiful.

I turned my fingers, watching the sparkles dance.

"Is this really mine?" I whispered to myself.

The ring felt heavy and delicate all at once, like a promise I was terrified to hold. Then my chest tightened.

Klaus.

Axel's terrified face as he'd told me the Russians had dragged him away.

My father's letter.

Him standing in the villa doorway like a resurrected ghost. Alive! After all these years. Then the suffocating realization that *he* hadn't come back to us; he had become something else entirely. My Vati had died long ago in Russia.

My breath caught.

The water lapped gently at my collarbones. What had he called my mother's death? *Bedauerliche Opfer*—Regrettable casualties?

I clenched my jaw, heat prickling behind my eyes. How could the man who had tucked me into bed and taught me how to draw flowers say that? How could he sit in luxury while children starved in the street?

A shiver ran through me despite the warmth.

And then—

Gideon.

My heart softened.

Gideon, shifting in a burst of heat and light, scales shimmering like hammered gold. His eyes—those same gold-flecked eyes—looking at me from a dragon's face. I squeezed my eyes shut, letting the water lap over my shoulders. That should have terrified me. It should have made me scream.

Or question my sanity.

But instead…

I had known. The moment I saw him—saw *it*—I had recognized him. Not with logic. Not with reason. With something older, deeper, instinctive.

"Gideon," I whispered, the name trembling on my lips like a prayer.

I placed my hand over my heart, feeling its frantic rhythm. This was real.

All of it.

The ring glinting on my finger.

The warmth of the water.

The children sleeping in the next room.

The dragon who had crashed through a window to save me.

The man who had flown us over the ruined city like a guardian made of fire and wings.

I wasn't insane. I wasn't dreaming. This was real.

And if dragons existed—

If love like this could exist—

If a life beyond fear, beyond hunger, beyond rubble could exist—

Then maybe I could believe in something again. I leaned back, letting my head rest against the rim of the tub, tears trailing softly into the steam. Everything hurt. Everything healed. Everything was possible.

"I don't know how I got here," I whispered to myself, voice cracking. "But Gott, I'm glad I did."

The water held me gently, like an embrace. The ring flashed again.

And somewhere beyond the bathroom door, I heard Gideon's low voice soothing Klaus, and I knew: My world had changed.

Forever.

Berlin — July 23, 1948, Friday morning

THE SUN barely scraped the sky when I woke. For the second time in weeks, maybe months, I'd actually slept. Deeply. No fire. No engines screaming. No visions of wings tearing or metal burning.

Just breathing.

It was amazing what a comfort it was to know she was safe under the same roof. I pushed myself upright and rubbed a hand over my face. The suite was dim and warm; the curtains were drawn. I could hear the kids breathing softly from the other room—small, steady breaths like little anchors holding this moment down. I had given them the other bedroom and slept on the couch.

I felt like a creeper when I entered the master bedroom where Inga was asleep, curled on her side on the edge of the bed, hair spilling over the pillow like chestnut silk. She looked... peaceful. The kind of peaceful I hadn't seen on her before. The kind of peaceful someone only has when no one is hunting them anymore.

God, I loved her.

Next, I moved carefully to the room where the kids slept. All three were curled up on the bed. Hilde was on the side to protect her arm. Klaus splayed like a starfish on the other side, and Axel lay across the foot of the bed.

I smiled. They'd eaten themselves into unconsciousness. Room service had come and gone to our room all night. I laughed to myself at the thought that the kids' stomachs were bottomless pits. Who would have thought that I would take so much enjoyment out of feeding them?

I picked up the hotel phone and ordered breakfast. "Everything you have," I told the desk clerk. "And extras of it."

The man didn't even question it. He must have already been warned about us. By the time the knock came, and the trays rolled in—eggs, bacon, real butter, fresh rolls, marmalade, fruit, porridge, sausages—the suite smelled like an actual morning, not war and dust.

I went to wake her.

She stirred when I touched her shoulder gently, eyelashes fluttering. Her eyes opened, slow and soft, still warm with sleep. For a second, she looked confused. But when she saw me, the most beatific smile I had ever seen crossed her features. You'd think she saw an angel, not a dragon like me.

"Gideon?" she whispered.

"Breakfast is here," I said. "Come eat. You'll need strength for today."

She sat up, pulling the blanket around her shoulders.

"Did you sleep?" she asked.

"For once," I said. "Yeah."

She smiled, small but genuine. I held out my hand. "Come on. Before the kids devour everything."

She slid her hand into mine, her fingers small and cold and perfect. As she stepped closer, the hotel robe slipped off one shoulder, exposing a line of smooth skin that made my throat tighten.

She noticed my stare. Her cheeks flushed a soft, warm pink. I reached up and brushed the fallen hair behind her ear, my thumb grazing her cheek. Her breath hitched— just once—and it felt like that single sound branded itself into my chest.

"Inga…" I murmured.

She looked up at me with those wide, trusting eyes, and something inside me snapped loose. I bent down and kissed her. Not like yesterday, this kiss was deeper. Hotter. It conveyed all the desire and pent-up emotions I had for her. It was a slow, hungry kiss that tasted like the start of something dangerous and sacred all at once.

Her hand slid to the back of my neck, and her fingers threaded through my hair. She pressed closer, chest to chest, mouth opening under mine like she'd been waiting her whole life to breathe this way.

Heat roared through me. Through *him*, too, the dragon stirred under my skin, purred at the feel of her, the scent of her, the softness of her body against mine.

If the kids hadn't been asleep only a few feet away, I would've lifted her into my arms and... I broke the kiss before I lost control, resting my forehead to hers.

"I have to go in," I forced out. "They'll have the roster posted. I don't know yet how many hours I'll be flying today."

Her eyes flickered with worry.

I cupped her cheek. "Hey. Look at me."

She swallowed. "What if you don't come back tonight?"

"I will," I said, voice firm. "Some days I fly twelve hours, some days two. Some days, I get grounded because the engines decide to hate me. But I will always come back. To you. To all of you."

Her fingers curled around my wrist. "You promise?"

"With everything I am."

She kissed me again—quick, soft, warm—and whispered, "Be safe."

I kissed her forehead, then her ring, then stepped back before I could drag her into my arms again.

"I'll be back as soon as I can," I said. "Order what you want. What the kids want. Clothes, shoes—hell, order the whole damn store. Whatever you need, you get."

I grabbed my jacket, shrugged it on, and headed for the door. Right before I stepped out, I looked back. She was still standing there in the morning light, hair messy and lips flushed from my kiss, wrapped in a bathrobe and looking at me like she'd finally found a place to rest her heart.

It nearly wrecked me.

"Love you," I said before I could stop myself.

Her breath caught. "I love you too."

I closed the door gently behind me and headed toward Tempelhof. The roster was waiting. Engines were waiting. The sky was waiting.

But everything in me was already flying back to her.

I hailed another cab to get back to the barracks, my head still buzzing with the memory of Inga's kiss.

God, her kiss.

I felt it on my mouth even now, warm and soft, hesitant and bold all at once. Enough to undo me. Enough to make me think about a future I'd never allowed myself to imagine.

By the time I reached the barracks, the sky was turning orange. The shift change whistle hadn't blown yet, so the place was quiet. I showered fast, letting hot water pound the knots out of my shoulders. I scrubbed glass and dust out of my hair and pulled on a fresh uniform.

When I stepped into the common room, Carter was waiting with a cup of bad coffee and an expression that meant trouble.

"Well, well," he drawled as I passed. "Look who's glowing like a kid at Christmas. What'd you do, Griff? Pick up one of them German girls last night?"

I didn't respond. He kept going.

"Bet she was grateful, huh?" Carter grinned. "Those Fräuleins will do *anything* for an American uniform. Hell, half of 'em are begging for—"

I dropped my duffel bag, grabbed his collar, and slammed him against the wall so hard the tin mug in his hand clattered to the floor.

His eyes went huge.

"Watch your mouth," I snarled. "You talk about her like that again, and we'll see how grateful you are for a trip to the infirmary."

"J—Jesus, Griffin—" he sputtered. "I didn't mean—"

"I don't care what you meant."

I let him go, and he slid down the wall, dazed.

"Don't talk about Inga," I said, voice low and deadly. "Ever."

He nodded frantically, and I walked away without looking back. I didn't trust myself not to slam my fist into him again.

I only made it ten steps toward the flight board before a shadow slid into my path. Gray suit. Cold eyes. The CIA man.

"Captain Griffin," he said, adjusting his tie. "How's our little... domestic situation?"

My jaw ticked.

"Say one more thing about my family," I said quietly, "and I'll throw you through a wall."

"Family?" he echoed, raising an eyebrow. "Already so attached? You do move quickly—"

A thread of heat slipped up my throat. Steam curled from my nostrils, causing his expression to falter. Unfortunately, he didn't back down.

"I'm here to remind you," he said, "that dragons—yes, it's time to quit dancing around the truth, we both know what you are—pose a national interest. And East Berlin is a volatile situation. We want your cooperation."

"I don't give a damn what you want."

"And," he continued as if I hadn't spoken, "we expect you to report any incidents—like those leading to a certain Soviet *visit* you survived—before acting alone again."

I stepped into his space, close enough for him to smell the heat coming off my skin. "You listen to me. You will fast-track the marriage forms. All of them. I want the paper-work done today."

"That takes weeks—"

"You will get them done NOW."

He scoffed. "We don't respond to threats."

I let the dragon slip.

Just a little.

My eyes flared gold. Heat shimmered between us. Smoke curled from my nose in two precise bursts. The man's face drained of color.

"Watch me," I growled.

His breath hitched. "Captain—"

"You will also expedite the housing assignment. Large quarters. For a family." He opened his mouth, but I kept going. "And you will leave us alone. Completely. No surveillance. No *interest*. No tests."

"This isn't how—"

"Do you know who one of my father's close friends is?" I asked softly.

He blinked.

"Senator Burton K. Wheeler."

That hit him like a punch.

Montana.

West.

Power.

Legacy.

Connections stretching into places men like him feared.

"He visited our ranch every summer while I was growing up," I continued. "He taught me how to shoot. He plays poker with my father. And he will be VERY interested to learn that the Office of Policy Coordination has been harassing his friend's son, and his future daughter-in-law, in violation of *every* regulation you pretend to follow."

The OPC man swallowed. Hard.

"And that," I added, letting my eyes flicker gold again, "is the *human* part of my threat."

His knees almost buckled. "I'll… see what I can do," he whispered.

"You'll do exactly what I told you," I corrected. "Or I won't need to burn your office down. I'll just make a phone call."

He nodded shakily.

"And stay away from my family," I said. "If you come near them, I won't show you the polite version of what I am."

I walked past him, leaving him pale and sweating in the middle of the hallway.

The walk to the roster board should have calmed me, but it didn't. Between Carter and the OPC guy, my blood was flowing like lava. Hot and thick. At the roster board, my flight time was posted.

Six hours of continuous lift runs.

Then two hours downtime.

During which I would make some phone calls, because I knew Inga wouldn't do as I asked, and even if she did, she wouldn't buy nearly as much as she and the kids needed.

The next four hours after that of flying, I could handle too. Yes, it would be a long day, but I could handle anything now.

Because I had someone to come home to.

I touched the dog tags under my uniform, thinking of her, of warm bathwater, of her soft lips against mine, of her whispering *I love you* in the morning light.

"I'll be back, sweetheart," I murmured to myself as I headed for the plane. "And nothing on this earth will keep me from you."

Inga

Berlin — July 23, 1948, Friday night

I DIDN'T EVEN HEAR the first knock. I was brushing Klaus's hair—it was still fluffy and soft from last night's bath—when a polite tap sounded at the suite door.

Axel, sitting cross-legged on the carpet with a half-eaten apple, froze, while Hilde dove under the table.

"Don't worry," I said, even though my heart jumped too. "It's just the hotel staff."

I opened the door carefully and nearly fainted. Two women stood there, each holding an armful of fabric swatches and measuring tapes around their necks. Behind them, a man waited with polished wooden boxes and a leather tool kit.

"Fräulein Weber?" one of the women asked. "Captain Griffin arranged fittings. Clothes for you and the children."

My jaw dropped. "I—he—what?"

"Shall we begin?" she asked with a professional smile.

Before I could protest, the three of them filed into the suite and transformed it into something between a boutique and a miracle. Within an hour, both boys had several pairs of trousers and shirts, and a pair of sturdy shoes each. Hilde had two dresses that made her twirl and clap her hands, as well as shoes. And I... I had dresses. So many, I didn't know how I would ever wear them. Whenever I tried to protest, the ladies told me this was at the *Captain's orders* and that they wouldn't do their job if they listened to me.

When the seamstress fastened the last button, I nearly burst into tears. And Gideon wasn't even here.

I thought that was the end of it. But I was wrong, not even an hour later, another knock came. Two hotel staff members wheeled in books, a whole stack of them, then toys. Puzzles, games, a doll and dollhouse. And...

A train set.

An entire metal train with tracks and switches and a little station house that lit up. Little people who stood, miniature trees, cars...

Klaus froze mid-step. Axel's jaw dropped. Hilde made a noise I didn't know children could make, half squeal, half gasp, full of wonder.

"For us?" Klaus whispered.

"Yes," I said softly. "For you."

They didn't move at first, as if afraid it would vanish. Then Axel whispered, "This is better than Christmas," and they descended on the train set like tiny engineers possessed by joy. Their laughter filled the suite. Pure. Bright. Unbroken by hunger.

I allowed myself to simply *watch* them be children.

Food kept coming too.

Plates of warm rolls. Cold meats. Jars of preserves. Cakes left discreetly by the staff. Hot soup. Fresh fruit. Someone knocked again with pastries. Then someone else with a tray of milk bottles.

I didn't understand any of it.

All I knew was that every minute felt like another piece of the future I never dared to imagine. I had no idea how Gideon could afford any of this, but I had to trust him. He hadn't let me down yet, and I had promised myself I would enjoy this. No matter what followed, this was just a time to be happy.

By early evening, the kids were full and pink-cheeked, the suite warm with lamps and steam from the kettle the kitchen kept bringing up. I wanted everything perfect for when Gideon came *home.*

I arranged the dining table the way I remembered my mother doing, carefully placing silverware and unfolding cloth napkins. I smoothed the tablecloth a dozen times. I adjusted a chair. Lit the little candle in the center.

Then I found the bellboy on his way down the hall. When he looked up, I pressed two of Gideon's cigarettes into his palm.

"Please… when Captain Griffin returns, tell the kitchen immediately. I want them to bring dinner up fresh and hot." I leaned closer. "And don't tell him I bribed you."

The boy smiled sheepishly. "Yes, Fräulein."

I exhaled.

Now all I could do was wait.

More hours passed. I felt disoriented. I didn't know what to do with this happiness or with myself when I had nothing to do or worry about. It was a strange new world for me. The children napped, woke, played with the train, and napped again. I looked at the books, started reading one, then another when I couldn't remember a word I had read.

I kept glancing at the door every few minutes. Every sound in the hallway made my heart race. Then finally— finally—a knock. Followed by a familiar voice. "Inga?"

I nearly flew to the door. When I opened it, there he was. Windblown from the tarmac. His uniform was rumpled in places, his hair a mess. Exhaustion poured from every line of his body.

And yet—

He smiled like dawn when he saw me.

"You're home," I whispered.

Home.

What a strange word to say to a man I'd known for only a few weeks. But it felt right. He stepped inside and froze when he saw the table, the children clean and smiling and tumbling toward him.

"Gideon!" Klaus yelled. "Look! Look what we have!"

Axel grabbed his hand.

Hilde showed him her doll and hugged him. I swear I saw tears in his eyes. Klaus pointed at the train. They spoke over each other, a chaotic joy he seemed ready to collapse under. Then all three of them wrapped around his legs like he was Christmas, Easter, and their birthdays combined.

Gideon blinked fast—too fast—and knelt, gathering all three into his arms at once.

"Thank you," I whispered from behind him. "For… all of this. For everything."

He looked up at me, his jaw was tight with emotion, and stood. I don't know what he was going to say, because just then another knock came, and several hotel employees entered, pushing carts with silver-domed plates ahead of them.

"Dinner?" he asked softly.

I nodded.

We sat like a family. We ate like a family. We laughed like a family.

For the first time in years, for the first time since bombs fell and my father disappeared and the world ended, I felt my heart put itself back together. After dessert, the train set called them again, the children pulled Gideon to the floor, and he went—willingly—switching tracks and pretending to crash trains. Klaus giggled hysterically the entire time. Then Hilde talked him into playing with her and her dollhouse, and I thought my heart would melt right there on the spot.

Later that night, the kids took warm baths, yawning through the steam. Hilde fell asleep with the towel still wrapped around her head. Axel didn't make it through pulling on his new pajamas. Klaus clung to Gideon's neck until his eyes finally fluttered closed, and Gideon carried him to bed like he weighed nothing. I tucked them in, one by one, smoothing hair, whispering soft goodnights, letting my heart stretch and ache with all the love inside it.

And every time I looked up… he was there. Gideon, standing in the doorway. Warm. Tall. Safe. Watching me like I was something holy.

My heart pounded like it was trying to break free. Because all day—every moment, every breath—one thought had been circling me like a hawk. One thought I didn't want to face, yet couldn't escape. I wanted him. Not just his help. Not just his kindness. Not just his protection.

Him.

His mouth. His hands. His heat. His steady, unshakeable presence that made the world finally feel like it wasn't ending. After he left this morning…

after that kiss… after his hands held my face so gently… something inside me had woken up. I kept trying to ignore it during the fittings, but in moments when the seamstress tugged fabric at my waist or brushed against my skin, something inside me fluttered and tightened. My body felt strange, too warm, oddly sensitive. Like something deep in me had been waiting too long and was suddenly starving.

Was that arousal?

I didn't know.

I'd only ever known fear around men. Fear and desperation and the knowledge that everything could be taken from me at any moment.

But with Gideon?

There was no fear.

Only…want.

And now that the children were finally asleep, their small breaths soft and steady in the dark, I stepped out into the sitting room where Gideon waited. Getting ready to make his bed on the couch. He looked up the moment I entered. His eyes softened like they always did when they fell on me. And the world tilted.

"Hey," he said quietly.

"Hey," I whispered.

He stepped toward me. "Everything okay?"

I nodded. Then shook my head. Then nodded again.

He smiled faintly. "Which one?"

"All of them," I said helplessly.

He chuckled under his breath, then sobered when he saw my hands trembling. I swallowed hard. "My mind… my body…" I whispered, cheeks burning. "They feel strange. Different. Ever since this morning. Ever since your kiss." His breath caught. "And I don't know what it means. I've never—" My voice cracked. "I've never wanted anything like this. Anyone like this."

Gideon took a slow step toward me, then another. He stopped close enough that I felt his warmth brush against my skin. "You don't owe me anything," he said softly. "Not ever."

"I know." And I did. Deep down, I truly did. And this wasn't about paying back or anything like that; this was about what *I* wanted. "But I want…" My voice trembled again as I was unable to finish the sentence. I swallowed hard and pulled up all my courage. "I want to be yours. Completely. Not because I have to. Not because I'm desperate. Not because I'm trying to pay you back." I lifted my hand to his chest, feeling the solid heat of him beneath my palm. "But because I love you. Because I trust you. Because I want this."

His breath left him in a hard, shaky exhale. "Inga," he murmured, "you have no idea what you're doing to me."

I stepped closer, closing the last inch between us. "Tell me," I whispered. "Tell me what you did today."

He cupped my cheek, thumb brushing lightly against my skin. "I fast-tracked the marriage forms," he said. "Housing, too. Everything we need."

My throat tightened. "We're going to be married," I whispered. "Soon."

He nodded, eyes turning molten. "If you still want me."

My voice was small and shy but certain. "I want you tonight, Gideon, and I'll want you tomorrow. And the day after that. And for as long as the world lets me keep you."

He sucked in a breath like the words physically hit him. "Inga…" he whispered.

I rose onto my toes, slid my hand around the back of his neck, and pulled him down into a kiss that shook both of us. Heat surged between us, warm and deep and infinite. His arms came around me, lifting me effortlessly, holding me as if I were something precious and beloved.

I buried my face in his neck and breathed him in. "Take me to bed," I whispered.

He froze only for a heartbeat before he carried me toward the bedroom, his forehead pressed to mine, his breath uneven.

"I'll be careful," he promised.

"I know," I whispered. "That's why I want you."

He set me down with care, so the bed frame barely creaked, and knelt to level his gaze with mine. I tried to remember how to breathe. His hands, warm and broad, bracketed my face like I was something rare. I wanted to make a joke, to laugh off the nervous quake in my legs, but I couldn't find any words.

Not that he gave me time to search. Gideon kissed me with something between prayer and hunger, soft, then firm, his mouth coaxing mine open, our breaths mingling until my lungs ached in a new, delicious way. No one had ever touched me like this before, not even in dreams. Every caress was a new word in a language I'd never learned.

His fingers found my hair, traced the nape of my neck, and moved to unclasp the row of pearl buttons on my blouse. He fumbled the top one, cursed softly, and that small clumsiness made him suddenly, heartbreakingly real. My heart rattled in my chest, trying to beat free.

"It's okay," I whispered. "You don't have to be so careful." But I wanted him to be.

He shook his head with a little smile. "You deserve careful," he replied hoarsely.

Then he undressed me, one patient motion after another: my blouse, untucked and slid from my shoulders; the thin chemise, up over my head; the new skirt, unzipped and dropped. He tipped his head, as if viewing a painting he'd studied and never entirely figured out. His hands hovered at my hips, then rested there, gentle as feathers.

"You're perfect," he whispered, and I knew he believed it, even if I didn't.

He kissed me again, harder this time, and I arched into him, every nerve awake. When his mouth wandered down, along my throat, and over the hinge of my shoulder, I shivered all over, a glitchy circuit of need I didn't know how to fix. His breath was everywhere, in my hair, on my skin, and my entire body felt like it was listening for the next place he'd go.

He cupped my breast, his thumb moving in a soft, slow circle over the tip, and even that felt like a miracle, like something I wasn't allowed to want. I gasped despite myself. He just grinned into my skin and mapped a line lower, over my ribs, tracing the sharp edge of hunger that war had left behind.

He kissed my belly, lingered above the scar nobody saw, and I almost wept from being seen.

"Inga," he murmured, drawing out the name like it was the answer to some riddle, "tell me what you want."

I thought I'd choke on the honesty. "You," I mumbled, "just you."

He nodded. "Then you have me." He moved down further, reaching the point where nobody had ever touched me before. He breathed in, as though he could commit my scent to memory, and then—oh, Mother of God—he pressed his mouth to the place between my legs and kissed me there, slow and reverent.

I startled, nearly closing my knees around his ears. "No— Gideon—" I gasped, because this was not something I recognized, not something any of the women in the block had whispered about, even when no one else was listening.

"It's okay, Inga," he murmured, in a voice thick with worship and promise, every edge of the words vibrating against my skin as if they were a spell. "I swear. Let me show you how beautiful this can be."

I couldn't see him at first, my eyes squeezed shut, my jaw set hard against the embarrassment of being so exposed, but then his breath washed over me, warm and steady, and I forced myself to look. He knelt there as if in prayer, his broad shoulders bracketed between my thighs, hands splayed to either side, and for a wild, shattering moment, I understood why all those medieval paintings showed angels with swords and burning halos: there was some- thing holy in the hunger of his gaze, something that demanded surrender. And I gave it, helpless as a child, a little animal with no defenses left.

He didn't rush, didn't lunge or scrape or devour. Instead, he studied me, as though memorizing every trembling line, and only when my nerves had spun themselves into a sharp, unbearable thread did he lower his mouth and kiss me, soft at first, a feathering of lips, almost chaste. I didn't know what to do. My legs wanted to shut, to run, to fight, but his hands held me gently apart, just enough to say: *Stay. Trust me. I won't let you fall.*

The first time his tongue touched me, I made a sound—embarrassing, primal, nowhere close to a word. He went still, checking my face, searching. I met his eyes, and in the silence between heartbeats, I nodded. *Please*, I meant but couldn't say. *Please keep going. Please don't stop.*

He smiled, small and secret, then started kissing me here in earnest. Kissing and licking. I'd never known pleasure like this could exist. Every slow, deliberate movement was a question; every answer I gave him, a permission. He never hurried, never forced. Just mapped me with lips and tongue and breath, sometimes humming low in his chest, a sound that vibrated up through me, made the world only that frequency, that moment, that man.

And when his fingers joined, slipping inside with infinite caution, my whole body spasmed in shock. I was so tight, so unprepared, I almost told him to stop. Instead, he moved with me, waited, coaxed, teaching me how to want and how to be wanted. All the while, his mouth never left me, and the pressure built and built until I thought I'd shatter from it.

I had no idea what to expect, what would happen. But the sensations inside me kept building toward something. Something big. I sensed it. I began to tense in anticipation of it, whatever *it* was. My mind went blank, white heat and static, every muscle straining toward a pleasure I'd never thought belonged to me. I heard myself whimper, then cry out, and then I was *coming*—my body seizing up, then unraveling, every atom unspooling in his arms. I didn't know if it lasted seconds or centuries. All I knew was that I'd never felt anything so good, so pure, so much mine.

When it was over, he didn't leave. He pressed one last gentle kiss to my hipbone and then curled up beside me, his hand on my thigh, just resting there, as if to say: *You're safe. You're here. I'm not going anywhere.* The tears started then, slow and silly and impossible to explain, and he just brushed them away with the back of his fingers, humming something tuneless and kind.

I blinked, dazed. "You… what was that?"

He grinned, smug and shy at once. "Your first?"

"Yes," I said, everything hot and wet and trembling. "I didn't know it could be—like that."

He brushed my cheek. "If you ever want to stop, you just say."

I shook my head: no, never.

He shucked his shirt, folding it neatly, and then his undershirt, his belt, every barrier, until I saw the full expanse of him. He was beautiful, in a battered-soldier way: broad, muscled, covered in scars like a map tracing everywhere he'd been hurt and healed. His man part rose from a dark nest of hair, thick and proud, and I didn't feel fear, just awe. That he wanted me at all, that he wasn't ashamed to show it.

He kissed me again and, when I opened to him, he guided himself gently against me. I tensed. He paused, stroking my hair, kissing the tears from my cheeks before I even knew I was crying them.

"You're safe," he reminded me. "We go as slow as you need."

He pushed in, just the barest tip, and waited. My body ached around him, tight and not quite ready, but I wanted this, wanted him to be the first and last and only. He moved an inch at a time, coaxing my body open, kissing my jaw, my ear, every moan and whimper he made holy with his mouth. It hurt, but it didn't matter. The pain was clean, a line drawn under the past and a new, fierce hunger scrawled on top of it. The worst was over quickly, and when he was fully inside me, he just held me, breathing slowly, his hands rubbing circles between my shoulder blades.

"Inga," he whispered again, "look at me."

I did. His eyes were damp, almost shocked. "You're perfect," he breathed, and began to move, not hard, not fast, just a steady, rising tide that pulled waves of pleasure behind the pain.

I wrapped my arms around his back, claws digging in, and for the first time in my life, I wasn't afraid of what I felt. Only that it would stop.

"Is it..." I shuddered, unsure of the question.

He finished it for me, moving his hips just so. "It's good. You're making me crazy."

He rocked me, deeper with every patient thrust, coaxing out sounds from my lips I didn't know I was capable of making. The heat in my belly coiled hard, then tightened and braided itself into every other nerve in my body, until it hurt to hold it in, until I was certain I'd split right down the center from the wanting. He covered my mouth with his, swallowing my broken moans, as if every sound I made was precious and he could never risk letting any of them escape.

His body was so much bigger than mine, strong and broad, thick through the chest and arms, all muscle and wiry scar, but he moved over me like something weight-less, like a summer cloud. He braced his hands around my head, careful not to crush me, but when I clawed at his shoulders, he let me. There was nothing in the world but this, his skin against mine, the wild pulse of his heart, the smell of clean sweat and tobacco and sky, the taste of him, a little like salt and a lot like I'd never get enough.

The second wave crested before I was ready. It took me off guard, so sharp and bright my legs kicked out wild, my hands flailed, desperate to hold on to something, anything, and I sobbed into the thick muscle of his shoul-der. My whole body shuddered, convulsing, and the plea-sure was so sharp I almost thought it was pain, except how it washed away all the fear and left only a wide, clean ache afterward. I felt myself tighten around him, squeezing him in, and that was when his own climax hit.

He groaned, a raw, helpless sound, and I felt him jerk inside me, his hips grinding deeper, and then he was shaking, shuddering, holding me so tight I could hardly breathe.

He didn't move for a long time, just pressed his face into my neck and held me like I was the last safe thing in the world. I stroked his hair, tangling my fingers in the sweat-damp curls at the base of his skull, and neither of us talked at all; we just breathed, listening to the frantic percussion of our hearts, the soft creak of bedsprings, the hum of a city in blackout on the other side of the window.

He shifted after a while, slow and gentle, sliding us up together so we were both propped awkwardly against the headboard, still wrapped around each other. I thought I'd feel shame, or maybe loss, but instead it was like a fever breaking, a heavy, honeyed exhaustion that made me want to sleep for a year. He kissed my hair, my forehead, the tip of my nose, each one softer than the last, and when I finally dared to look up, he was watching me with a kind of reverence I'd never seen on any face before.

He brushed a thumb over my cheek, scooping up tears I hadn't realized were still falling. "You're all right?" he asked in a voice that sounded rough as gravel.

I nodded, not trusting myself to answer. My body was a tingle of aftershocks, my mind a liquid mess. I wanted to say something funny, to make the moment less terrifying, but nothing came to mind except his name.

"Gideon," I whispered.

He smiled, and it was a crooked, broken thing, but it made my heart flip in a whole new way. "That's me," he said.

We lay together in the oversized hotel bed, tangled up in sheets that smelled of fresh laundry and starch, and I allowed myself to believe that maybe there was a future, even if it was just tomorrow. I closed my eyes and listened to his breathing until mine matched it, until the air between us was full of nothing but hope and the promise of morning.

We lay there a long time, warm against the cold, filled up with something new and bright. I never wanted to move again. He stroked my hair until he thought I was asleep, then whispered, "I love you, Inga. God help me, I love you."

I didn't answer. I pretended to sleep, but my heart was wide awake, certain that if I answered aloud, the world would break the spell. I pressed myself closer and let the warmth of him fill all the places the war had left empty.

Berlin — July 26, 1948, Monday

THREE DAYS. Three days had passed, and I still felt like I was moving through someone else's life. A better life. One I hadn't believed I'd ever deserve.

Every night, I lay beside Inga, listening to her steady breathing, her soft sighs, the way she curled into me as though she'd been made to fit under my arm. And every night, she welcomed me with a trust so fierce it humbled me down to my bones.

She wanted me. *Me.* Not the uniform. Not the pilot. Not the hero she thought she saw in that alley. Me, man and dragon both.

I still couldn't believe she'd offered herself so tenderly, so willingly. And that she continued to do so, each night sweeter, braver, more open than the last. She accepted the dragon without hesitation, asking questions with wide, curious eyes instead of fear.

"Does it hurt you to change?"

"No."

"Can you fly in storms?"

"Sometimes."

"Are there more like you?"

"Yes. Back home."

Montana. I told her about Montana. About the wide skies and golden plains.

About my family's ranch nestled against the shadow of the mountains. About the old stories passed down through generations, how our ancestors had come from the Celtic Isles centuries ago, bringing the dragon magic with them across the ocean, settling in the frontier where open sky meant freedom.

"Dragons like high places," I'd said, brushing her hair back as she listened. "My people found mountains that felt like home. And we've been there ever since."

She had absorbed every word.

"And they know?" she whispered. "Your town... knows?"

"They do," I said. "Not all the details, but enough. We don't hide from our own."

Her eyes had gone soft and glowing.

"Do you think... I could be happy there?"

"Yes, sweetheart," I'd said, kissing her forehead. "I think you were meant to be there."

And now—God help me—patience was becoming an impossible virtue. We weren't using protection. Every night, her warmth and trust wrapped around me like a promise. If she got pregnant now, before the papers cleared, we'd be in for scrutiny, and I refused to let anyone question our marriage. Our family. Our future.

I needed that marriage sealed. Now.

I arrived at Tempelhof feeling higher than the sky I flew. But the mood shifted the moment I stepped into the hangar.

"Captain Griffin," called a mechanic, jerking his head toward the admin building. "CO wants you. Now."

Not good. I followed the hallway to Colonel Jamison's office. He looked worn; his usually straight tie was loosened, his sleeves rolled up, the weight of the whole damn airlift sagging around him.

"Come in, son," he said. "Close the door."

I did.

He didn't waste time. "We've had complaints."

My jaw tightened. "From who?"

"OPC," he said, rubbing his eyes. "That intelligence man you've tangled with."

My breath sharpened with heat.

"Claims of ration misallocation. Unauthorized move-

ment outside of mission hours. Reckless flying. Undocu-
mented behavior off-base."

All lies. Every one of them. Jamison leaned back.

"Look, son... I don't buy any of it. But I can't ignore it.
Not when it's official. I've got no choice but to open a
formal investigation."

Rage pulsed inside me, not the hot, explosive kind, but
the deep, coiled kind that made the dragon roll forward
under my skin. Jamison held up a hand.

"Whatever you've gotten yourself mixed up in, it's ugly.
OPC sharks have teeth. And if they think you're a
liability..."

He didn't finish. I already knew. They'd keep coming.
After me. After Inga. After the kids.

Unless I cut them off at the knees.

I inhaled slowly. I could threaten the Spook again with
my father's connections, but a better idea was forming in
my head.

"What if I resign?" I asked.

Jamison blinked. Then sagged back into his chair in
relief.

"That," he said, "would make this disappear."

"Honorable discharge?"

"Yes."

A slow, wild grin tugged at my mouth.

He frowned. "You okay, Griffin?"

"I'm more than okay, sir."

Because suddenly everything fell into place: No more Berlin. No more OPC shadows. No more suffocating bureaucracy.

Just freedom.

Montana.

The ranch.

My family.

My people.

Inga.

Klaus.

Axel.

Hilde.

All of us—home.

A wedding under open sky.

The kids running across grass instead of rubble. Inga breathing fresh mountain air instead of ash. And me—finally—free to shift whenever I wanted.

"Yes, sir," I said. "I'll submit my resignation today."

Jamison nodded slowly. "Good man. Let me know if you need anything."

I left the office practically weightless. I'd barely stepped into the hallway before I found the OPC man leaning against the wall like a smug shadow.

"So?" he said, crossing his arms. "You gonna play ball now, Captain?"

I didn't respond.

He smirked. "That's what I thought. You people only understand leverage. Lucky for—"

I punched him in the stomach so hard he folded like a cheap map. He gasped, collapsing to his knees. Before he could recover, I grabbed his collar and slammed him against the wall.

"You listen to me," I said quietly, voice shaking with restrained fire. "You stay away from me. From Inga. From my kids. This is your final warning."

He tried to speak. I hit him again, not enough to break anything, but enough to make the point.

"You think I won't go darker?" I growled, letting heat bleed out between my teeth, letting steam curl from my nostrils in two slow, deliberate streams.

He paled, turning chalk-white when I allowed him a glimpse of my dragon self.

"You're finished here," I said. "I'm done with you. So stay the hell away."

I released him and let him slide to the floor, wheezing. I didn't look back. The future was waiting. And nothing— nothing—was going to take Inga or the kids from me now.

By the time I finished paperwork with Jamison and handed over the first draft of my resignation, my whole damn body buzzed like someone had plugged me into a generator.

I practically *ran* back to the hotel.

The second I opened the suite door, three tiny bodies slammed into me.

"Kapitän Gideon!" Klaus shouted, arms locking around my waist.

"You're back!" Axel squeaked.

Hilde just threw herself at my leg like a little koala.

And then I saw Inga.

Standing near the window in a soft dress the seamstress had fitted that morning, hair loose around her shoulders, eyes bright in a way I'd never seen.

God, she stole my breath every time. She smiled when she saw me—really smiled—and I felt like the world clicked into place.

"You're home," she said softly.

"Yeah," I answered, tugging her into my arms with one hand while holding the kids with the other. "And I've got news."

Her brows lifted. "Bad?"

"No," I said. "Good. The best."

We sat on the velvet sofa, me in the middle, kids crawling all over me, Inga curling into my side. I took a breath. "I resigned."

Inga blinked. "You… what?"

"Honorable discharge," I said. "I'm done. No more Berlin. No more airlift. No more OPC breathing down my neck."

Inga just stared at me like she wasn't sure she'd heard correctly.

"So… what does that mean for us?" she whispered.

I smiled slowly.

"It means," I said, "we're going home."

"Home?" Klaus asked, bright-eyed.

"Montana," I said. "We're going to the ranch. Fresh air. Space to run. Clean water. Real food. And a family waiting to meet you. And the best part?" I winked at the kids, "Have you ever ridden a horse?"

Inga's lips parted. "Gideon…"

"And," I added, turning to her fully, "we're going to surprise my parents. We'll have the wedding under the Montana sky. The way it should be."

She covered her mouth; her eyes flooded immediately.

"Oh," she whispered. "Oh, Gideon..."

The kids started cheering, shrieking, and bouncing on cushions.

"RANCH!"

"COWS!"

"HORSES!"

"FLYING WITH GIDEON!" Klaus cried.

I laughed so hard my ribs hurt. God, it felt good.

"Before we leave," I said, wiping my eyes, "we need supplies. Warm coats. Mountain boots. Travel trunks. You'll need gear for cold nights, for hiking. The kids'll need heavier clothes—Montana winters aren't kind. And you—" I tilted Inga's chin and kissed her forehead. "You're gonna need a wedding dress."

Her breath broke.

"I... I've never..." She shook her head, overwhelmed. "You're sure?"

"I've never been more sure of anything," I said.

She threw her arms around me, and I held her tight, feeling her whole world trembling with relief and hope.

We were halfway through planning what to buy when a knock sounded on the door.

Sharp. Cold. Wrong.

I felt the dragon stir before I even turned. I opened the door just enough to see him: A Soviet messenger in civilian clothing, his posture as stiff as could be expected, his eyes cold and flat, like there was not a single thought in there that was his own. He extended a sealed envelope.

"Captain Griffin," he said. "I am here at the request of Herrn Weber. He demands the immediate return of his son, Klaus Weber, into Soviet custody."

Inga froze behind me. Klaus whimpered and hid behind her skirt. Axel moved in front of Hilde instinctively.

I took the envelope and opened it. I only read the first line,

Return the boy.

Then I laughed.

Actually laughed.

The messenger blinked. "This is not—"

I held the paper up between two fingers.

"When you go back to whatever hole you crawled out of," I said calmly, "you can tell Gerhard Weber…"

I flicked my fingers. Heat surged. The dragon's breath curled up my arm like a secret flame. The paper erupted into ash.

"…that Klaus is *mine now*," I finished. "My son."

The messenger recoiled. "You—you cannot—"

The kids let out a loud Oh!

I shoved the pile of ashes into his chest hard enough to make him stumble backward. "Tell him he gets one chance to leave us alone." I stepped forward, eyes going molten gold. "One. Chance."

The messenger backed down the hall; he was shaking from head to toe, and his entire visible skin turned white as chalk.

"And if he tries again?" I added, letting steam curl from my nostrils. "I burn," I said, "*everything he stands on.*"

The man fled. Inga sagged against the wall, trembling. I turned back to her immediately, gathering her into my arms.

"It's over," I murmured into her hair. "We're leaving. He'll never touch you again. Or Klaus. Or any of them."

She nodded into my chest, gripping me like I was the only solid thing in her world. Klaus came and pressed his cheek against my side. Axel hugged my leg. Hilde reached up with both hands.

I wrapped them all in my arms. I had a family now. And no one on this earth—Russian, American, dragon, or human—was going to take them from me.

Inga

Berlin — July 28, 1948, Wednesday

THE MORNING WE LEFT BERLIN, the whole city seemed to hold its breath. We boarded the military truck at the side entrance of the hotel; Gideon had arranged everything, down to the last paper. The children and I were wearing our new clothes and shoes. Klaus practically vibrated with excitement. Axel clutched Hilde's hand the whole time, both solemn and excited in that strange way children are when they sense the edges of something huge.

I held onto Gideon's arm the entire drive, afraid that if I let go, everything would dissolve like a dream. When we reached the airfield, a C-54 loomed like a metal giant under the silver skin. The wings were gleaming where the sun's rays hit them in the morning haze. Gideon squeezed my hand once, then led us toward the ramp.

"Ready?" he asked softly.

I nodded, though my stomach flipped. "Ready."

"Home," he murmured.

The word poured through me like sunlight.

We followed the airman up the metal ramp; the children clung to my skirt and Gideon's hand. Inside, the plane's belly was all rivets and steel ribs, the floor lined with canvas seats stretched tightly over metal frames. Cargo nets hung along the walls, bulging with supplies headed back to the States. A faint scent of oil, recycled air, and something metallic filled my lungs, sharp and new and terrifyingly exciting.

Gideon helped Klaus up the last step, then guided me inside. The ceiling was low enough that tall men had to duck. The windows were round portholes, each showing a slice of the sky. Soldiers and families settled in quietly, coats and bags tucked by their feet, murmuring to nervous children. It felt less like boarding a plane and more like stepping into a great migrating bird preparing to leap across the world.

We found our row—wide bench seats with rough straps —and Gideon buckled the kids in, making sure each clasp clicked firmly. When he turned to me, his eyes softened, as if saying *trust me… you'll be safe.*

I took a deep breath and smiled at him. I sat and took his hand as the hatch sealed shut behind us.

The engines stared low, rumbling like thunder trapped in steel. My heart pounded loud enough to drown it out. Klaus grabbed my sleeve. Axel pressed his face to the little window, breath fogging the glass. Hilde curled into my side, clutching her doll.

We lifted.

Slowly.

Gracefully.

Against every law of nature I'd ever known.

And Berlin—my Berlin—began to fall away beneath us.

My breath hitched.

There it was.

The city where I'd been born, learned to walk, and learned to survive. The city where bombs fell, mothers cried, and children starved. The city that stole so much from me, and yet… it was all I had known.

As we climbed higher, the patchwork ruins came into view. Streets like broken ribs, buildings like jagged teeth, whole neighborhoods flattened into patterns I recognized far too well.

"That—there," I whispered, pointing through the window. "That used to be the Zoologischer Garten… the zoo. My mother used to take me to see the elephants. I always thought they looked like old grandfathers."

Klaus squinted. "Where? I only see… broken."

"Yes," I murmured. "But before… it was beautiful."

As we banked left, I caught sight of Tiergarten, once a forested heart of the city, now a bare skeleton of stumps. I saw the scar where the Kaiser Wilhelm Church stood, broken spire jutting up defiantly.

My chest tightened when I noticed movement. A cluster of children running across a courtyard, tiny figures weaving between mounds of rubble. Bare legs. Torn clothes. I knew them, even if I didn't know their names.

Trümmerkinder.

Like Axel had been, and Hilde. Like Klaus might have become. Children who knew hunger better than warmth.

Farther along, I saw the silhouettes of Trümmerfrauen, women with scarves tied over their hair, standing in lines by the piles of debris, passing bricks hand to hand. Their movements slow, weary, eternal.

My throat burned. I pressed my palm to the window. "They're still there," I whispered. "Working. Always working."

Gideon reached over and covered my hand with his.

"We'll help them," he murmured. "Someday, when we can. But right now… it's your turn to have a life."

I turned to him and smiled through tears. Because he meant it. Because he had already given me a life I hadn't dared imagine.

When Berlin became a gray blur beneath us, the children's awe blossomed.

"It's so small!" Klaus gasped.

"It looks like toy houses," Axel said.

"It looks like… nothing," Hilde whispered, unsure if that was sad or wonderful.

The clouds swallowed us, thick and white and endless. I had never imagined anything so soft and enormous. I pressed my forehead to the window and whispered a prayer I hadn't spoken since my mother died.

"Thank you."

Hours later, the ocean appeared.

A great, impossible sheet of blue, stretching farther than my mind could grasp. Waves like shifting silk. Sunlight glittered off the surface like thousands of diamonds.

I gripped the armrest. "Gideon… there's… so much water."

He grinned. "More than you can imagine."

"Will we fall in?"

"No," he chuckled. "Not today."

The children pressed their noses to the glass in unison.

"Water!" Klaus shrieked.

"So much!" Hilde cried.

"Are there sharks?" Axel asked, fascinated.

Gideon leaned over. "Only friendly ones."

I laughed—really laughed—and for a moment, I felt weightless.

Meals were served in metal trays: warm rolls, butter, ham, and something they called *casserole*. The children ate until they were pink-cheeked and sleepy. Blankets were handed out. Cushions too. Hilde curled up in my lap. Klaus fell asleep on Gideon's shoulder. Axel stretched across two seats, snoring softly.

Hours passed in a gentle hum.

For the first time in years, nothing hurt.

Gideon surprised us halfway through the journey.

"You want to see the cockpit?" he asked.

The children nearly exploded with joy. He winked at me and led them through the narrow aisle into the sacred space where the pilots sat. I followed on tiptoes, wondering if I was allowed here too. Gauges glowed softly. Lights blinked. The sky stretched endlessly in front of us, a sea of cotton clouds tinted pink by the sinking sun.

Axel whispered, "It's magic."

Klaus reached out hesitantly. "Can I… touch?"

Gideon nodded. "Only this switch."

Klaus flipped it. A tiny light blinked.

Hilde giggled.

Then the plane shuddered, and I froze.

The captain called, "Turbulence ahead, Captain Griffin."

Gideon squeezed my hand. "It's alright. Just air pockets. We're safe."

The plane rattled again. My breath shortened.

Gideon pulled me gently into his chest. "I won't let anything happen to you. I promise."

And just like that, the fear loosened. We left the cockpit, and the children talked for an hour straight about buttons and clouds and how Gideon was obviously a sky king.

I agreed.

Hours later, the mountains rose from the horizon like a painting coming alive. Deep blue peaks. Silver rivers. Forests rolling in endless waves. And the sky—God, the sky—so open and clean it made my chest ache.

"This…" I whispered, pressing my fingers to the window. "This is our new home?"

"Yes," Gideon said softly. "Welcome to Montana, sweetheart."

Klaus gasped. "It looks like heaven."

Axel grinned. "I want to run everywhere."

Hilde pointed. "Trees!"

I rested my head against Gideon's shoulder and let joy bloom inside me, warm and enormous. Berlin had been gray rubble beneath our feet for so long. Now the world was wide and green and full of promise.

Gideon murmured. "We're almost there."

I closed my eyes and whispered, "Thank you."

For saving us. For loving us. For giving us a sky to fly in.

When the wheels touched down, the whole plane shuddered, rattling through my bones. Klaus stirred against my side, Axel blinked sleepily, and Hilde yawned so wide her jaw popped. Gideon gave my hand a squeeze.

"We're here," he whispered. "Welcome to Montana."

Montana.

The word still felt unreal on my tongue, like a place out of fairy tales instead of somewhere I would actually step onto. Customs was quick—quicker than I'd expected. A few signatures, a glance at our papers, and a smile from a tired official who seemed charmed by the kids clinging to Gideon like ducklings. When we stepped outside, the air hit me like a revelation.

Fresh.

No coal dust. No smoke. No rubble. Just sky. Endless sky. A blue so deep it hurt my eyes.

Gideon inhaled like a man tasting home for the first time after a long exile.

He turned to us, grinning. "Alright. We've got two choices. Stay in the city tonight and rest..." His eyes moved to me, soft and warm. "Or we can make the drive to the ranch now. We'll get there before dark."

My heart stuttered. I leaned into him, my cheek brushing his shoulder. "If it's alright," I whispered, "I would love to meet your family."

His smile softened into something tender and a little mischievous. "Fair warning, they'll likely make us sleep in separate rooms until we're properly married."

I fought a grin. "I'm willing to take that risk."

He raised a brow. "Are you now?"

"Yes," I said, eyes locking with his. "Very willing."

He laughed—warm, rich, relieved—and kissed my fore-head like he couldn't help himself.

He borrowed a truck from a man who greeted him with a hearty clap on the back. "Griffin! Back from saving the world, are ya? Take her for as long as you need." A wink toward me. "And who's this pretty thing?"

Gideon cleared his throat, cheeks turning faintly pink. "My fiancée."

The man whistled. "Well, I'll be damned. Congratulations, you two!"

I blushed, clutching Klaus's hand tighter. They loaded our luggage into the truck bed, then the children, who squealed with delight at sitting among the bags like it was the greatest adventure of their lives.

Gideon opened the passenger door for me with that old-fashioned gallantry he did so naturally, and when I climbed up, he shut it gently, almost reverently. He rounded the truck and got in beside me, thigh warm against mine, the smell of leather and dust and pine in the cab.

"Ready?" he asked.

I nodded. I was more than ready to start the next part of my new adventure. He took my hand as he started the engine. And the world opened.

Montana was… I didn't know a word big enough. It was wide. Endless. Wild. Alive.

Mountains rose on the horizon like giants sleeping under blankets of stone and forest. Pines stretched in every direction, sharp and dark and ancient. Yellow grass danced in the wind, blinking gold under the sun. The sky —Gott im Himmel, the sky—was enormous. Bigger than Berlin, bigger than anything I'd ever imagined. I felt small under it, but not in the way rubble made me feel small.

This smallness was awe.

"This place…" I whispered, unable to look away. "It feels like it goes on forever."

"It does," Gideon said, voice warm with pride. "This is freedom, sweetheart. Real freedom."

I squeezed his hand. "And this… all of this… is truly your home."

He glanced at me with that look he reserved only for me,

soft, hungry, hopeful. "Ours," he said quietly. "If you want it."

I leaned my head on his shoulder, heart full and overflowing. "I do."

He inhaled shakily, like my words hit him deeper than he expected. Outside the window, the children pointed at everything: horses grazing in distant pastures, tall fences, herds of cattle, barns with red peeling paint, and creeks glinting like silver threads. Their laughter bounced through the truck bed and into my veins like light.

"Gideon!" Klaus shouted through the open window. "Are those cows?"

"Longhorns," Gideon called back.

"Are those... American cows?" Axel asked, awed and confused.

Gideon chuckled. "The most American cows you'll ever meet."

Hilde squealed as a hawk soared overhead, wings spread wide. I watched its shadow ripple over the grass. I couldn't help it; my eyes prickled with tears. Everything was so big. So clean. So full of promise.

I stared at everything, at Gideon's hand holding mine. At mountains rising to meet us. At the children laughing in the wind. At a life finally beginning.

"Do you think your family will like me?" I asked softly.

Gideon brought my hand to his lips. "They're going to adore you, Inga. How could they not?"

While the truck turned to rumble down the dirt road leading to the *Griffin Ranch*, its white fences gleaming in the sunlight, I believed him.

I truly believed him.

We drove a little farther in silence, the wind whipping softly through the windows, the children's laughter trailing behind us like ribbons in the air. My hand stayed wrapped in Gideon's, his thumb brushing back and forth in slow, sure strokes that made my chest feel warm.

Then a thought slid into my mind, hesitant, almost embarrassed. "Gideon?" I asked quietly.

"Mm?"

I gestured out the window at the endless sweep of grass-land, hills rolling like a green ocean all the way to the foothills of the mountains. It had been a while since we passed a large gate and a sign reading *Griffin Ranch*. "This land..." I began carefully. "Is all this—" I swallowed. "Part of your family's ranch?"

He glanced at me, a smile tugged at the corner of his mouth, a little shy, a little proud. "Yeah," he said. "Just about everything you see from here to those two ridge-lines, and beyond the creek, across that valley... all ours."

My jaw dropped.

"All of it?" I squeaked.

"All forty-five thousand acres," he said, as casually as if he were talking about a garden plot.

Forty-five thousand acres.

My mind couldn't even comprehend that number. Forty-five thousand acres in Berlin held whole districts. Thousands of families. Blocks of buildings.

Here… it was sky and earth and wind. Open. Wild. Free. And it all belonged to him. To his family.

My breath caught. "Gideon… you're… rich."

He squeezed my hand gently. "We're comfortable. The ranch has been in my family for generations."

"This is more than comfortable," I whispered.

He laughed, warm and a little bashful. "Well… it'll all be yours soon. Yours and the kids, too."

My heart somersaulted. I pressed my hand to my chest as if that could calm it. I had held a feeling Gideon might be better off than I had thought when I met him. I mean, the hotel, the clothes… but this?

I didn't have time to consider what that meant, because just then the house came into view. And whatever thoughts I had vanished completely.

"Oh…" I breathed. "Oh, Gideon."

Because it wasn't a farmhouse.

It was a dream.

A massive two-story home stood at the center of the ranch like a proud white jewel. Crisp white paneling, freshly painted, gleamed in the sunlight. Dark green shutters framed every window, matching the wide wraparound porch that hugged the house like welcoming arms. The roof was steep and elegant, with dormer windows and a tall stone chimney sending up a thin curl of smoke.

Behind it stretched a labyrinth of barns, huge red structures with wide doors and loft windows, some newer, some older and sun-bleached. Smaller outbuildings peppered the grounds in neat rows: workshops, storage sheds, a smokehouse, and a chicken coop as big as a Berlin apartment.

To the left spread a cluster of fenced pastures where horses grazed, tails flicking lazily. Beyond them roamed cattle, hundreds of them, like dark dots moving across the light green fields.

And then—

Cowboys.

Real cowboys.

Riding horses, dusty hats tipped low, lean bodies rocking with their mounts. One lassoed a steer in a practiced arc; another led a string of horses toward the barn; a third shouted something across the field, waving as the truck approached. The kids simply exploded.

"Kühe!" Klaus screamed.

"Horses!" Axel squealed.

"Look! Look! Cowboys!" Hilde shrieked, standing up so fast she nearly toppled over.

The truck hit a bump, and the children bounced like popcorn, laughing, pointing, shouting in three different directions at once. I pressed a hand to my heart. This wasn't just different from Berlin. It was the opposite of it.

I blinked hard as we turned down the long dirt lane toward the house. This was where Gideon had grown up. This was the world that shaped him. The sky. The land. The freedom. The dragon in him. The goodness in him.

"This is…" I whispered, unable to find the words. "Gideon… it's beautiful."

He looked at me then, really looked at me, eyes soft and full.

"Not as beautiful as the woman I brought home," he murmured.

My heart turned to melted butter.

As the truck rolled to a stop in front of the great white house, I knew this was the beginning of my real life. The one I had never dared to dream of. The one I would protect with everything in me.

We had barely rolled to a stop in front of the great house when the screen door snapped open. A woman stepped out onto the wide porch, blinking into the sunlight. She wore her graying dark hair braided and pinned back, an

apron tied around her waist, hands still damp from whatever she'd been doing in the kitchen. Her round face was
warm and soft, the kind of face children would instinctively trust. Flour dusted her cheek. She squinted toward
us, shading her eyes with her hand.

Suddenly, she jolted backward. "Gid—?" Her voice
cracked. "Giddy?"

I felt Gideon stiffen beside me, then smile. Before he
could even open the truck door, the woman's voice rang
out through the warm Montana air, "HANK! HANK!
Get out here, right now!"

She flew down the steps so fast her apron strings trailed
behind her like ribbons. Her feet hit the dirt, and she
sprinted toward us with the speed of someone twenty
years younger. Gideon barely had time to step around the
truck before she crashed into him with enough force to
stagger them both.

"Mom," he laughed, arms going tight around her. "Hi."

"Giddy," she breathed, clutching the back of his shirt as
though she feared he'd disappear again. "Oh my sweet
boy, you're home. My baby's home."

He held her close, face pressed into her hair, and for a
moment I saw him not as the strong, unstoppable dragon
who could level a building… but as someone's son.
Someone deeply loved. Cherished.

Gideon's mother's eyes moved. Past Gideon. Past the
truck. Straight to me—

and the three children clinging to the hem of my coat. Her hand covered her heart. Her eyes filled instantly, as if her heart recognized us before her mind did. "Gideon..." she whispered. "Is that... is that your girl?"

Gideon glanced at me, then back at her, smiling softly. "Mama... this is Inga."

I swallowed hard, nerves fluttering everywhere at once. "Mrs. Griffin," I whispered. "It's an honor."

She did not hesitate. Not even a heartbeat. "Oh, sweetheart," she said, and swept me into the warmest, fullest embrace I had felt in a long time. Not since my mother... she smelled like fresh bread and pine cleaner and sunshine. "Call me Maggie."

"Oh dear Lord," she murmured into my hair. "My Giddy's gone and got himself married. I can't believe it. I thought he'd fly forever and never land long enough to give me a daughter."

I flushed. "We're... not married yet."

Gideon cleared his throat sheepishly behind us. "Well... technically, Mama, we were hoping you'd help plan the wedding."

"Gideon!" I squeaked, pulling back to look at him. "You can't just—your mother has—"

"Oh, honey," Maggie said, gripping my arms, eyes sparkling with delighted tears, "I would *love* to. I have been waiting my whole adult life to throw a proper Montana ranch wedding."

Gideon winced playfully. "Brace yourself."

"Oh, hush," she swatted him. Then she looked down, smiling gently at the three little forms half-hiding behind my legs. "And who are these beautiful babies?"

Klaus peeked out. Axel tried to bow. Hilde clung to my skirt, staring with huge eyes.

"These are… my brother Klaus," I said softly, pushing him gently forward, "and Axel and Hilde. They're… orphans. Trümmerkinder."

Maggie's face broke wide open. "Oh dear," she whispered, already bending down, arms widening. "Come here, all of you. Come here to me."

Klaus hesitated only a moment before he allowed her to fold him to her chest. Axel followed, then Hilde, who whimpered at first but melted the second Maggie stroked her hair.

"You poor little ones," she soothed. "You must be starving, tired to your bones. Well, you're safe now. All of you." She pressed kisses to three dusty heads.

"My goodness, children! Finally, children! I've been waiting decades for grandchildren. Your sister—Lord love her—she won't settle down, stubborn girl."

Gideon snorted. "Molly'll love this."

Maggie looked up at me, eyes shining. "You came bringing me four blessings," she whispered. "Four. I don't know how to thank you."

I opened my mouth to correct her—that the blessings had come from Gideon, not me—but emotion clogged my throat. She smiled softly, wiping at her eyes. "Welcome home, Inga. Welcome home, all of you."

Two riders appeared on the ridge before the house, horses kicking up dust as they galloped closer. The sun hit them just right, and for a moment they looked like silhouettes from a moving picture, tall, sure, powerful. One rider wore a wide-brimmed hat and swung it in a wide arc as they turned into the yard.

The kids gasped.

Hilde's eyes nearly popped out of her head. "Eine Kuh… kuh… Kuhfrau?" she whispered, stumbling over the word.

I couldn't blame her. A cow*girl* was something none of us had imagined outside of picture books. As they got closer, the dust cleared enough to reveal faces.

"Molly?" Gideon breathed beside me.

The woman on the left pulled her horse to a stop, grinning so wildly she looked half-feral. She had a long black braid, sun-browned skin, and the kind of confidence that radiated off her like heat.

"Gideon?" she hollered. "Is that you, big bro?"

She didn't wait for an answer. Molly swung herself out of the saddle mid-gallop, hit the ground running, and *launched* herself at Gideon like she'd been waiting ten years just to tackle him.

He caught her, staggering back with a laugh. "Easy, Molls. You'll break my ribs."

"Serves you right for disappearing across the ocean!" She slapped the back of his head affectionately. "We heard rumors you were coming home, but you didn't send word. You could've at least—"

Her words cut off when she noticed me, then the children peeking from behind my skirt. "Oh!" she said, blinking. "Who's…?"

Before I could speak, another voice joined us. "Well, I'll be damned."

The second rider dismounted smoothly, tall, broad-shouldered, weathered like the mountains themselves. Gray threaded his dark hair, and his eyes were the same warm amber as Gideon's. The resemblance was unmistakable; this had to be his father.

"Hank," Maggie said with a smile, "this is Inga."

He looked me up and down, not in judgment, but in appraisal, the careful assessment of a man who'd lived long enough to recognize truth when he saw it. He stepped forward and pulled me into a strong, warm hug. "Welcome to the family, darlin'," his deep voice rumbled in his chest. "You've brought my boy home. Can't ever thank you enough for that."

I choked up instantly. When he stepped back, he turned to the children. "And who're these young'uns?"

"This is my brother Klaus," I said, guiding him forward, "and Axel and Hilde. They're—"

"Family," Gideon finished firmly. "All of them."

Hank nodded as if that settled everything in the world. He knelt down to their level. "Well, now. Look at you fine little folks."

He shook Axel's hand solemnly, then Klaus's, and hugged Hilde when she reached for him with surprising boldness. Hilde clung to him like she'd known him forever. Hank's eyes softened. "A granddaughter," he murmured, voice thick. "Imagine that."

He looked up at Molly, "Looks like you got competition now, Molly. Maybe I'll have better luck teachin' this one not to break horses before breakfast."

"Fat chance, old man," Molly said, elbowing him.

"Hi sis," she turned to me with a wide, mischievous smile. "I'm sorry you're going to have to put up with him for the rest of your life, but I'm sure glad to have a sister now."

I laughed loudly; I couldn't help it. The love I felt from these people surrounded me like a cloak, and I instantly knew Molly and I would get along; she had too much Gideon in her for us not to.

Molly turned, eyes sparkling at Klaus. "You ever been on a horse before?"

He froze, and a small gasp escaped him, a joyful, magical sound. My eyes stung from threatening tears.

Gideon's hand found mine instantly, steadying me before the tears could fall. Molly didn't wait for permission. She scooped Klaus up as if he weighed nothing, swung him in front of her onto the saddle, and mounted in one fluid motion.

"We'll take turns!" she announced to Axel and Hilde. "Hang on, kiddo!"

And then she galloped off. Fast. Fearlessly. Laughing.

Klaus's whoop—half terror, half pure delight—rang across the entire ranch.

He came back flushed, breathless, shouting in German so quickly I barely kept up. "Es war unglaublich! Der Himmel war überall und—und—das Pferd! Ich will ein Cowboy sein! Ein richtiger Cowboy!"

I translated breathlessly as he poured out his excitement.

"He says it was incredible. That he wants to be a cowboy. A real cowboy."

Hank let out a booming laugh. "Well now," he said, planting his hands on his hips, "first thing we'll have to do is teach him proper English. Horses around here don't understand German." He winked. "And neither does your old grandpa."

Klaus froze. His mouth dropped open. "Grandpa?" he echoed in German-accented English.

Hank grinned and opened his arms. "If you'll have me."

Klaus launched into him like he'd been waiting his whole life for the word. And Hank held him tight, eyes glistening. I covered my mouth to hide a sob.

This—this right here—was the moment everything inside me finally healed.

Montana — July 29, 1948, Thursday, early morning

THE HOUSE DIDN'T SETTLE until well past midnight. Mom had gone on a loving, unstoppable rampage, making up beds, fussing, planning, muttering about quilts and curtains and *those poor babies who need proper pillows, not those hotel things*, while Dad carried trunks upstairs like a man half his age.

Molly kept dragging each kid back outside *just one more time* to show them the barn cats, or the chicken coop, or her new mare.

They adored her. Naturally.

And through all of it, Inga moved with wide-eyed wonder, as if trying to absorb everything at once. Mom had voted—loudly—that Inga and I would sleep in separate rooms.

"It's proper," she insisted. "Not until the wedding, Gideon Boyd Griffin!"

Molly had smirked behind her. Inga had blushed, and though I hated being apart from her after nights of being tucked into her warmth, I didn't argue. It was tradition, and as my mother pointed out, proper. Mom was already neck-deep in wedding plans.

After the last door closed and the house finally exhaled, I found myself wandering. Something in me knew where she'd be. And sure enough—

there she was. Sitting on the porch swing, wrapped in one of 'Mom's quilts, staring out at the dark land under the spill of stars. Her hair was loose, falling over her shoulders like a shadow lit by moonlight. I stepped out quietly, letting the screen door click behind me.

"You cold?" I murmured.

She startled softly, then relaxed the moment she saw me. "No," she whispered. "Just… thinking."

I sat beside her, put my arm around her shoulders, and she melted right into me instantly, leaning her head against my chest with a soft sigh.

"Happy?" I asked, voice rougher than I intended.

She nodded. "So much… it scares me."

My chest tightened. Her voice trembled, "Your family… they're wonderful. I don't know how I'll ever thank you for bringing us here."

I turned her face to mine gently, brushing away the tears with my thumb.

"Inga," I exhaled her name, pressing a kiss to her temple, "you don't ever have to thank me."

"But—"

"No."

I kissed the corner of her eye. Then the other. Soft. Slow. Her tears tasted like relief.

"If anything," I whispered, "*I* should be thanking you."

She blinked. "You?"

"Yes." I cupped her face in both hands, forcing myself to speak the truth I'd kept buried for years. "Before I met you, I was a broken man, sweetheart. I hated everything. Everyone. Myself most of all. I couldn't face coming home. Couldn't even call home. I felt empty and angry and… wrong."

Her hands slid up my chest, gentle, afraid to break the moment. "But you…"

I breathed out shakily. "You taught me how to love again. How to be a man again. How to come home."

Her eyes glistened, reflecting the porch light like tiny stars. Then she reached up and kissed me.

In the distance, wolves howled, low and haunting and beautiful. She jumped in surprise.

"What was that?" she whispered.

I laughed, brushing a lock of hair behind her ear.

"Wolves. They roam the mountain ridge. Don't worry, they're shy. They won't come down here."

Her breath softened. "It's... beautiful."

We sat together in the quiet, watching the moonlight wash over the fields. The barns. The fences. The place that would be our future. She saw everything with new eyes, and because of that, I saw it fresh again, too. Eventually, I pointed toward a distant rise, silhouetted against the sky.

"Dad said we could build a house there," I murmured. "For us. Big enough for all of us. A place that's just ours."

She tilted her head, thoughtful.

"Is that what you want?" she asked softly.

I brushed my thumb across her cheek. "I want you to be happy, sweetheart."

She looked back at the warm lights of the big house behind us—'Mom's curtains glowing softly, 'Dad's boots by the door with Molly's boots right next to them.

"Can... can we all live together?" she asked. "In this house? Or is that too much for your parents?"

I smiled. "I was hoping you'd say that. We always lived together. Even when my grandparents were alive. It's the Griffin way."

She nodded. "Together," she whispered. "I like that."

The word settled over us like a blessing.

Together.

I looked at her, my future wife, wrapped in my mother's quilt, with moonlight in her hair and home in her eyes, and something mischievous sparked deep in my chest. I leaned closer. "You know…" I murmured, brushing my lips against her ear, "they're all asleep."

She swallowed.

"So?" she whispered.

A grin tugged at my mouth.

"You want me to show you the hay barn?"

Her breath caught, but the smile she gave me could have lit the whole Montana sky.

We crossed the pasture beneath a river of stars, the grass black and sparkling with dew. I took her hand and led her into the barn. Inside, the hayloft was cavernous and warm, taking in the moonlight through knotholes and cracks, painting everything in a patchwork of silver and soft gold. We climbed the ladder in silence, my hand never letting go of hers, even as we reached the top and she stumbled on the last rung. I caught her, spun her lightly, and she stifled a giggle against the sleeve of my flannel shirt.

I took her face in both hands and kissed her, slow and searching, the dust motes swirling around us like the inside of a snow globe. My lips traced the edge of her jaw, tasting the salt of her skin, feeling the little pulse at her throat as it fluttered under my tongue. She reached for my shirt, untucking it with steady hands, and I helped, shucking my flannel and undershirt in a tangle.

She was losing her shyness a little bit more every time we made love. Cautiously and deliberately, her hands roamed over my chest, like she meant to memorize every part of me. I did the same, following the rise and fall of her ribs, my fingers brushed across her shoulders and forearms, the fine blond down at the base of her neck. She gasped when I kissed the hollow below her collarbone, and again when my hands learned the secret softness of her waist.

I stopped for a moment to drape the quilt she had brought over the hay and then kissed her again. She opened up to me with such vigor, it made me dizzy. I still had a hard time believing that this amazing woman had chosen me. But I wouldn't question it; instead, I would use every day of my life to live up to what she seemed to see in me. Inga's hands bunched my shirt at the shoulders, knuckles whitening.

"Lie back," I told her, and she did. The moonlight reflected in her eyes, and she watched me as I unbuttoned her blouse, slow, catching the shiver of her pulse at the hollow of her throat. The fabric parted, frame by frame, her collarbones, sharp as table edges; the rise of her breasts under the chemise; the first, soft glint of a nipple through thin cotton. I kissed every inch as I uncovered it, hungry to taste her everywhere.

She tried to hide a gasp when my mouth closed over the tip, tongue flicking gently, then firmer. Her back arched straight off the quilt when I kissed lower, memorizing every gasp, every sound, every part of her: the slope of her ribs, the small, hollowed places the war had left, the line of the scar she wore half-hidden by her side. I lingered there, pressing my lips to it, and whispered, "Beautiful." She made a sound that could have been a laugh, or a sob, or both.

I tugged her skirt down her hips, then her underwear. I kissed down her belly, following the fine dusting of dark hair that arrowed between her legs. I would've gone slow, but I couldn't help it: some primitive thing inside me needed to taste her, right now. I pressed my mouth to her core and licked, soft at first, then deeper and firmer, savoring the way she jolted and her knees flew up around my ears. She tasted like salt and sweetness, like nothing I'd ever had before her, and all at once, I was ravenous for everything she'd give me. Her hands tangled in my hair, her knees were trembling around my ears, every breath a broken prayer.

"Oh God," she said, and it wasn't cursing. "Gideon— don't stop, please—"

I didn't. I held her hips and tongued her clit, first in circles, then with quick, steady pressure, like learning an instrument by ear. She stiffened, her whole body drew taut, and then she came, loud, sudden, and unrestrained. I felt the wet pulse of it against my tongue, the shudder wracking her frame. I wanted to make her come again, and again, until the memory of every bad night was wiped out by this.

But she pulled at me, insistent, desperate, dragging my face up to hers with greedy hands. "Come here," she demanded, and I liked that side of her. Liked the way she pawed at my shirt, half-shoving, half-caressing, until I peeled it off. I kicked off my pants, careful not to crowd her, but she pulled me in, legs wrapping my waist. She reached for me, bold in a way that turned my brain to static. "I want you," she whispered. "I want all of you."

"You have me." I lined myself up, pressing just the tip inside, and waited for her to tense. She didn't. She just tipped her chin up and looked at me like she'd drown if I left her now.

I pushed in, slow as I could, until her heat closed around me and the world dropped away. The tightness was almost painful, but she took it, her nails digging into my skin, her mouth open in wonder. I could barely hold off, every instinct screaming to bury myself in her, but I made myself go slow, to work her open, to memorize every angle of her face as pleasure took her over.

"Inga," I said, "you're perfect. You're so—" But there were no words for this.

She kissed me, hard, and rocked her hips up to meet me. That was it for my patience. I thrust in and out, first gentle, then harder, letting her set the tempo with every moan and gasp. After, I'd try to recall the specifics, how her hair fanned across the pillow, the velvet heat of her, the way she said my name like a secret, but in the moment, I was nothing but sensation, nothing but the glorious, insane fact of her around me, under me, with me.

She came again, legs locked around my back, and I lost it, hips stuttering, choking on her name as I spilled inside her. The whole room went white behind my eyes. I collapsed beside her, pulling her close, my face buried in the wet tangle of her hair.

She rolled and pressed her forehead to my chest, laughing, damp and delirious. "I can't feel my body," she said.

I grinned and kissed the crown of her head. "That's the general idea."

We drifted, blissed out and quiet. After a while, she asked, "Will it always be like this?" in a tone that might have been hope or awe.

I stroked her arm, feeling the future spool out, bright and impossible: morning coffee, reckless Saturdays, her in my arms for the rest of my goddamn life.

"It will be," I promised.

We slept a little. Woke a little. Listened to the ranch wake up around us, dogs barking, a horse whinnying, one of the ranch hands cursing loud enough to scare the chickens. Reality crept in. We had fallen asleep, and now we had to walk back inside. Covered in hay. Looking like sin and sunrise and bad decisions.

We tried to sneak into the kitchen—quiet as you please—when Mom looked up from the stove. She stopped stirring. I'm not even sure she kept breathing; her eyebrows shot straight into her hairline.

"Well," She said, setting her spoon down very slowly, "I suppose my suspicions were correct."

Inga froze. I froze. Mom's gaze slid from what was probably hay in my hair…

to the hay on Inga's shirt… to the hay sticking out of places hay absolutely should not be.

Then she pressed a hand over her mouth. "Oh Lord," she muttered. "We'll need to get that wedding planned and done with as soon as humanly possible."

Inga turned scarlet. Absolutely scarlet. Like she might combust on the spot. I bit my lip to keep from laughing and wrapped an arm around her shoulders, kissing the side of her head.

Mom pointed at me without looking. "Don't you smirk at me, Gideon Boyd Griffin. Don't you dare."

"Wouldn't dream of it," I lied.

She clucked her tongue. "Honestly. The barn, of all places…" Then she shook her head. "Well, the hay is fresh at least."

I choked. Inga made a tiny dying noise.

"Coffee?" I croaked, desperate to change the subject.

Inga stiffened. "Real… coffee?"

Mom blinked. "Is there any other kind?"

Inga's eyes got glassy. "M-Maggie... I—"

"Oh heavens, child, sit down. You look like you're about to faint from joy."

She herded Inga to a kitchen chair like a little mother hen. "You can bathe later. Coffee first."

"But—" Inga tried.

"Sit," Maggie repeated, pushing gently on her shoulders. "Not a word. I'm making you breakfast too. You're too thin by half."

Inga obeyed, still red as a beet. Mom filled a cup with steaming coffee so fragrant it filled the whole room. She set sugar and creamer in front of her like ceremonial offerings.

"Now," she said, beaming, "drink."

Inga lifted the cup with trembling hands, inhaled, and her eyes fluttered closed like she'd just been handed salvation. "Oh," she whispered. "Oh, this is... heavenly."

Mom turned to me with a shooing gesture. "Well? Go on. Shoo. Your fiancée and I need to talk."

I blinked. "Talk? About what?"

Maggie narrowed her eyes. "About *everything*, Gideon."

Inga choked on her coffee. "Maggie—"

"Oh, hush. Go."

She waved me toward the door. "Go feed the cows or mend a fence or... whatever it is you boys do. This is girl time."

I looked at Inga. She looked at me. Her eyes cried: *Help!*

Mine said: *I love you, but you're on your own.*

And the moment I stepped onto the porch, I swear the entire ranch could hear my mother start, "So. When exactly were you planning to tell me I was getting FOUR grandchildren at once?"

Montana —July 29, 1948, Thursday morning

I STARED at Maggie with wide-open eyes. "I'm not..." I stammered... at least I didn't think I was pregnant. I hadn't given the ramifications of what Gideon and I were doing any thought yet. Stupid, I know. Irresponsible.

I wished Gideon were here right now, and at the same time, I was grateful he wasn't. I felt my face heat even more. "I don't think I am..."

Maggie shook her head. "No matter now. You two will be married in no time." Then her face took on a thoughtful expression, and she sat down across from me. She took both of my hands in hers. "Sweetheart, when did your mama die?"

I swallowed. "Four years ago. I was fourteen."

"Hmm, hmm," she nodded as if she was telling herself she was right about something. "Fourteen? I am so, so sorry, sweet child."

"Thank you." I felt tears well in my eyes. No matter how many years had passed, the loss of my mother still hurt.

"Now, did she ever have a *talk* with you?"

Talk?

We had talked about a lot of things, Mama and I. How to stay alive, how to find food for Klaus. What to do about his cough. But somehow, I didn't think this was where Maggie's question was going. And then it hit me, and I think my face turned even redder, something that, before that second, I would have sworn wasn't even possible.

"Uhm…"

"Look now here. Men want certain things…" Maggie began, and sweat broke out all over my body. *Oh dear God.* "Some women like it, some women don't." He searched my eyes. "Do you know what I mean?"

I nodded, my voice was barely a whisper, "I think so. Yes, ma'am."

"My son hasn't done anything you don't like, has he?" There was a glint in her eyes that told me if Gideon had, he would be in a world of hurt.

I bit my lower lip, praying the ground would open and swallow me whole. Even bombs would have been preferable right now. "No, no. Gideon is… the best man I've ever met."

"Good, I'm glad to hear so," Maggie nodded, but there was still some steel in her eyes that almost made me fear for Gideon.

"Now I'm assuming that whatever you two did in the barn wasn't the first time." She didn't pause, and I was thankful I didn't have to answer. "I'm also assuming you two haven't used any kind of protection." I felt like I was folding into myself. This time, Maggie's eyes were probing me, waiting for an answer.

"Protection…" I squeaked.

She nodded vigorously, "I know it's not openly discussed the way it should be for young folks like you. But you need to know that pregnancies don't have to be a surprise," she winked. She actually winked. *Oh please, someone kill me now?* At the same time, I felt a wave of love for Maggie, too. She didn't know me. At all. And she had taken me into her home with open arms. Her only condition had been separate rooms for Gideon and me, and we had… I had…

"I'm so sorry," I whispered, tears flowing down my face.

"Oh dear, no," Maggie's chair scraped back. "Don't cry, sweetheart. Don't cry. I didn't mean to make you cry. I just…" She folded me into her arms, and I held on to her in utter shame and embarrassment. "Hush now, sweet baby. Hush."

It took a minute or two, but I got myself back under control. She handed me a handkerchief, and I blew my nose loudly and very unladylike.

She took my hands again, shaking her head. "That wasn't at all what I was implying. I'm sorry." Maggie lowered her voice without making a fuss of it, the way women did when they were passing along things that mattered. "I just want to make sure you understand how it all works," she said softly. "Bodies, babies, all of it. No surprises you're not ready for."

Heat rushed to my cheeks. I nodded, staring into my coffee like it might rescue me. "We've only... it's only been a few days," I admitted. "I didn't plan—any of it."

Maggie snorted, not unkindly. "No one ever does." She reached over and squeezed my hand. "Listen to me, sweetheart. My son doesn't do anything halfway. If there's a baby, there'll be a ring. If there's a ring, there'll be a wedding. And if there's a wedding—" her eyes twinkled, "—there'll be half the county showing up whether you want them to or not."

I let out a shaky laugh and held up my hand with the ring. Maggie took it and scrutinized it. "Hmm, he did good." She nodded in approval, finally releasing some of the tension inside me, even teasing a slow smile from me.

"He did." I looked at the ring lovingly.

"Do you know what a shotgun wedding is?" she asked, letting go of my hand.

I blinked. "I... assume it involves a gun?"

She barked a laugh, delighted. "It does, metaphorically. Means the groom's so eager to do right by the bride that folks joke someone's holding a shotgun to make sure he shows up." She waved a hand. "Not necessary in your case. Gideon'd walk himself down the aisle if he had to." Something in my chest loosened at that. The fear didn't vanish, but it softened, edged with hope instead of panic. "Well," Maggie said briskly, standing. "Then we'll plan properly. No worrying. That's my job now."

She bustled about, pulling tins from a cupboard. "You need breakfast. You're skin and bones."

She plopped down a plate of biscuits smothered in some white, creamy sauce. I blinked. "What is… that?"

Maggie froze, then looked from the plate to my face, horror dawning. "Oh Lord," she muttered. "You don't have gravy, do you?"

I shook my head slowly. "Not like this."

She laughed, already reaching for a fork. "Well then. Sit. Eat. We'll start with biscuits and gravy—and after that, we'll conquer the rest of your new life one step at a time."

Maggie caught my expression and blinked. "Not your thing?"

I shook my head apologetically. "In Germany, we… um… don't eat that. Not even before the war."

She laughed, a big, warm laugh that filled the whole kitchen. "Fair enough. What do you eat?"

I eyed the biscuit; it seemed edible enough. "Just a biscuit and some jam, please."

"Sounds good, actually. Let me get that for you."

She whisked the plate away, set it aside for someone else, I assumed, and brought out a new one with fresh, warm biscuits and a jar of thick red jam.

"Better?" she asked with a smile.

The first bite had me closing my eyes. "Oh," I whispered. "This tastes… like a holiday."

Maggie beamed. "Homemade. Strawberry. My mother's recipe."

Warmth spread through me, not just from the food, but from the feeling of being *seen*, understood. We sat a moment in comfortable silence before she leaned forward, elbows on the table, chin in hand.

"So," she said. "Tell me everything. How did you meet my son?"

"He… rescued me."

"Of course he did," she muttered fondly. "Soft heart. Takes after me."

I smiled shyly and told her about the alley. The Russians. Gideon appearing, like a myth made real. Maggie's eyes grew soft, then fierce, then soft again.

"Well," she said, "sounds like he found his purpose the moment he found you."

My throat tightened. She took another sip of coffee, then

asked quietly, "And the children? *Trümmerkinder*? Tell me what that means."

I hesitated. "It means… rubble children. Kids who live on the streets. No parents. No homes. Sometimes they sleep in ruins. Sometimes in cellars. Many are orphans."

Maggie's entire face crumpled.

"Oh, dear Lord," she whispered. "How many?"

"So many," I sighed, seeing their faces once again and feeling the yummy biscuit expand in my mouth at the thought of them going hungry. "And no one knows what to do with them. Everyone is trying to survive. They get forgotten."

Her eyes filled, then sharpened. "Axel and Hilde…?"

"They're both orphans. But not siblings."

She reached across the table and gripped my hands. "Oh, sweetheart."

"I know, I wish… I wish I could somehow… help them."

For a moment, she just held me, as though she could somehow absorb every heartbreak I'd ever endured. Then she straightened, eyes blazing with a fire I recognized from Gideon.

"How serious are you," she asked, "about wanting to help those children?"

My breath caught. "Very. Very serious."

"Do you still know people in Berlin? People you trust?"

"Yes," I whispered immediately.

"Good." She stood, marched to the counter, grabbed a notebook and pencil, and slapped them on the table.

"Then let's get started."

I blinked. "Started… what?"

"Fundraising, sweetheart."

"Fund… what?"

"Fundraising!" She motioned emphatically. "Raising money. Organizing donations. Getting supplies. Building houses. Making your dream real."

I stared at her, stunned. "But how—"

"You don't worry about the how," she said, tapping her pencil against my knuckles. "Worry about the *why*. The *how* is my job."

I felt my eyes sting. "Maggie… I…"

She waved away my tears. "Hush. You came all the way from a war-torn country with two orphans and your baby brother. There's a reason the Lord put you in our path."

I swallowed. "You think… we can help them? Truly?"

"Oh, honey," she said, sitting beside me and wrapping an arm around my shoulders, "we're Griffins. We can do anything. And Montana's got space. There's room for more children here. Plenty of women in town would take some in. Patti Baker, especially. 'She'll pretend she doesn't want to, but she will. Her husband'll grumble, but he'll make bunk beds faster than you can blink."

A small, stunned laugh escaped me. We talked.

And then we planned. Oh God, did we plan. She explained to me about fundraising. Big dinner parties that sounded daunting, but the money it would bring in… I thought about the Trümmerkinder, even Bastian, who had never seen something like Montana. Elke could help organize it. We could bring them here. Maybe not all of them, but many.

I started to dream. And the more I did, the more it seemed possible. By the time the sun crept higher, my notebook was filled with ideas: letters to write, contacts to reach out to, possible places to house children, names Maggie rattled off like an army of helpers waiting to be called.

The kitchen smelled of jam and biscuits and hope.

Until the children stumbled in, interrupting us in the best way. Still sleepy, tousled, and adorable. They each got a biscuit shoved into their hands before they could even sit.

Then Hank and Molly came in, dusty from morning chores.

"You're up early," Molly said with a teasing grin.

"Planning," Maggie announced proudly. "We're saving children."

Hank tugged off his hat. "Well, now. Sounds like a fine morning to be a Griffin."

And then— "Uh… may I come in?"

Gideon's head poked around the door frame, cautious as a man approaching a lion's den.

Maggie smirked. "Yes, you may, but your fiancée and I aren't finished."

He raised his hands. "Wasn't planning on interrupting."

The kitchen filled with laughter, noise, biscuits, and easy warmth. I felt myself melting into this new life, absorbed into it like I'd always belonged.

After breakfast, Maggie clapped her hands decisively. "Alright, men. Listen up. I'm taking Inga and the children into town today. Molly's coming too."

I blinked. "Town?"

"For stuff for the bedrooms," Maggie explained. "And wedding supplies. And a dress."

Molly groaned dramatically. "Oh, come on, Mama—"

"No complaints," Maggie said. "You're coming."

Molly rolled her eyes. "Fine. But only if I get to pick the shoes."

Maggie hiked her eyebrow and turned to Hank. "I'll need the checkbook."

He grinned so wide I thought his face would split. "This," he declared, thumping his chest, "is the happiest day of my life. About time the money in this house got spent."

Not much later, we were just about to climb into the truck—Maggie urging us along, the children bouncing with excitement—when the ground began to tremble beneath my feet. Soft at first. Then stronger. A rhythmic thrum that sounded like distant thunder made me look up. Molly paused mid-step, and Hank glanced toward the rise.

And then I saw him.

Gideon.

Riding straight toward me on a golden sorrel stallion, dust curling behind them like a banner. His hat was tipped low, one hand loose on the reins, his shoulders broad beneath his worn denim jacket and sun-faded shirt. Cowboy boots. Coiled rope at his hip. The morning sun was striking him in such a way that, for a heartbeat, I swore I could see the dragon beneath his skin shimmering like heat on a summer road.

Power and grace emanated from him, making my heart beat faster at the sight. I swallowed, unable to believe that this striking man was mine. That soon I would call him husband, and he would call me wife.

He slowed the horse only at the last second, swinging it around in one smooth, impossibly effortless motion. The stallion's hooves kicked up a halo of dust, and I stood there, speechless, breathless, completely undone.

"Good morning, sweetheart," Gideon drawled, removing his hat with a slow sweep that made my knees wobble.

He leaned down from the saddle, the brim of his hat brushing my forehead before he tucked it against his thigh. His eyes—gold-flecked, warm, mine—crinkled at the corners as he smiled at me.

I forgot everything else: Hank, Maggie, Molly, the children. It was only Gideon and me. He reached for my chin with two fingers, tilting my face up.

"Before you go," he murmured, "I needed to tell you something."

I swallowed. "Yes?"

He bent lower. So close I could feel the warmth of his breath. "You're the best thing that ever happened to me, Inga Weber. You saved me. You gave me a family. You gave me a reason to come home." His voice tightened. "I love you. With everything I am."

My eyes burned hot. Tears I didn't even know I'd been holding welled up and spilled over. I reached up, brushing my fingers along his jaw. "I love you too," I whispered. "More than life. More than I ever thought I could love anyone."

His smile broke into something bright and devastatingly beautiful. Then he leaned down and kissed me. A deep, claiming kiss that tasted like morning sunlight, wild air, and forever. The horse shifted beneath him, tossing its mane, as if the earth itself wanted to lift us higher.

When he finally pulled back, his forehead rested against mine.

"Go," he said softly. "Pick out your dress. Build your dreams. I'll be right here when you get back."

I pressed a hand to his chest, felt the strong beat of his heart underneath. "My home," I breathed.

"Always," he whispered.

He straightened, placed his hat back on his head, and gave me that crooked cowboy grin that melted every last piece of me. As Maggie herded me toward the truck and Klaus shouted that he wanted to ride horses again and Hilde clapped her hands in delight, I looked back one last time.

Gideon sat tall in the saddle, turning his horse toward the pastures, sun crowning them both in gold. And I knew—without doubt, without fear, without hesitation: my story had begun the moment he walked into that bar in Berlin.

But this… this was the happily-ever-after I had always dreamed about and never dared to hope for. This was the life I'd fought for.

This was love. And at last…

This—him, his family—was home.

EPILOGUE

Montana — August 16, 1948, Monday, late morning

THE HOUSE BUZZED LIKE A BEEHIVE. Women rushed up and down the hall with flowers, ribbons, and baskets. Somewhere outside, someone was hammering the last wooden arch plank into place. From the porch came bursts of laughter and the thumping hooves of restless horses.

I stood in the center of one of the upstairs master bedroom suites—a suite that after today would be mine and Gideon's—in my wedding dress, hardly recognizing myself.

The gown I had picked was simple but breathtaking: soft ivory, cinched at the waist, the skirt falling in layers that brushed the tops of my new boots. My hair was pinned half-up, the rest cascading in curls down my back. When

I moved, the dress whispered like something out of a dream.

Behind me, Molly groaned dramatically.

"I swear, if one more person tells me how *pretty* I look, I'm gonna throw myself into the horse trough," she grumbled, tugging at the soft blue dress Maggie forced her into.

I laughed. "You look beautiful, Molly."

She pointed at me suspiciously. "You only say that because you're glowing like a saint. It's unfair. Some of us are not made for lace."

She grumbled even harder when Hilde, who was twirling in her tiny flower-girl dress, said, "Molly, du bist sooo hübsch!"

I grinned, "She thinks you're pretty."

"See?" Molly muttered. "Now I can't even argue with a six-year-old."

I reached out and squeezed her hand. "Thank you for being my maid of honor."

She softened instantly. "Of course." Then she added, leaning close, "But if you later want to demote me to bridesmaid, I won't be hurt."

I blinked. "What do you mean?"

She just winked. "We'll see. Griffin men can be full of surprises."

Before I could question that, a sudden commotion erupted downstairs, shouts of surprise, hurried footsteps, and Maggie's unmistakable squeal.

Molly's grin spread slowly, wickedly, as she straightened the bodice of her dress.

"Oh," she said, eyes sparkling, "that'll be your surprise."

"What surprise?" I asked, heart skipping nervously.

But she only nodded toward the stairs. "Go look."

I gathered my skirts and hurried down the hall, then the steps, until I reached the foyer, where I froze. Because standing there, clutching a small traveling bag, cheeks flushed, eyes wide, was Elke.

My Elke.

My oldest friend from Berlin.

She squealed, dropped her bag, and flung her arms around me so hard my veil nearly came off.

"Inga!" she cried, voice thick with emotion. "Gott sei Dank! Look at you! A wedding! A ranch! *Amerika!*"

Tears sprang instantly to my eyes as I held her tight. "Elke… how—how are you here?"

She leaned back, wiping at her face. "Your Gideon arranged it. He sent a *telegram* and a *plane ticket*. He arranged for me to stay in town so we could surprise you."

I felt laughter and tears collide in my chest. "He did that?"

Elke nodded happily and winked. After all the times we'd talked on the phone during the past two weeks, she had never said a word—I called her regularly at Die Ecke so we could make plans for the Trümmerkinder, plans she had fully embraced.

And goodness, the past two weeks had been *full*. Every hour not spent on wedding planning had been spent building the very first fundraiser. Maggie had introduced me to several women from town—Patti Baker, Mrs. Longwell, and the two Burnham sisters—who welcomed me with warm hugs and fierce determination. They were already organizing bake sales, quilt auctions, and a community dance to raise money.

Hank and a crew of ranch hands had begun putting up the first small cabins on the far side of the property, simple but sturdy, meant to house the first wave of children we hoped to bring safely from Berlin. Families in town had already started asking about adoption. Even skeptical, grumbling husbands seemed to soften the moment they saw the photographs Elke mailed over, those wide eyes and thin faces tugging something tender loose in their hearts.

It was happening. Our dream. Their hope.

And now Elke was standing here in Montana, right in the middle of it.

She looked around at the ranch house, Hank grinning from the doorway, Maggie beaming like she'd claimed Elke as a daughter within seconds, the children peeking from behind banisters.

"This is..." Elke breathed, "...more beautiful than anything I ever imagined for you."

I squeezed her hands, unable to keep the tears from spilling. "You're here. I can't believe you're really here."

She grinned, wiping her nose with a laugh. "Wouldn't miss it for the world. Now come. You have a husband waiting, and I need to fix your veil before you walk out there looking like a windblown goose."

Behind us, Molly barked a laugh. "Good luck trying to tame that hair. It's got opinions."

We all laughed—Maggie, Hilde, Axel, Klaus, Elke, Molly —and warmth washed through me so deeply I could barely speak. Today, surrounded by the family I chose and the family that had chosen me right back, I was about to marry the man who'd saved my life in every possible way.

Gideon.

My pilot.

My dragon.

My home.

Molly placed my veil over my hair, kissed my cheek hard

enough to leave a memory, and whispered, "Go. He's been waiting since dawn."

My heart trembled as I stepped through the back door and out onto the porch. And the world… stopped. The backyard had been transformed into something out of a fairy tale, our fairy tale. Rows of wooden chairs filled with neighbors, ranch families, and the women helping with the Trümmerkinder. Children swung their legs, mothers held bouquets, and old men wiped at their eyes as though remembering loves long past.

And lining the aisle on both sides were cowboys on horseback. Standing tall and proud, hats removed, horses still as statues. Behind them rose the mountains, sharp, blue, eternal.

At the far end of the aisle, beneath an arch woven with wildflowers—sunflowers, sage blossoms, white daisies, lavender—my Gideon stood waiting. Axel at his side, tiny but fierce in his little suit, chest puffed out with pride.

But I saw only Gideon.

And he saw only me.

His breath hitched visibly, his hand rising unconsciously to his heart. His eyes—those warm, gold-flecked eyes—shone with a devotion so deep it nearly brought me to my knees.

Klaus took my hand. "You ready?" he asked in German, his voice trembling with importance.

I squeezed his fingers. "Ja, mein Schatz. Let's go."—Yes, sweetheart.

We walked down the aisle together, past cowboys tipping their hats, past women dabbing tears, past Elke, who was openly sobbing, and Maggie, who grinned to hide her watery eyes.

The horses whinnied softly, as if blessing us. And then we reached him. Gideon's hand slid into mine like it had always belonged there.

"Hi," he whispered, voice cracking.

"Hi," I whispered back.

The ceremony began. The priest spoke words I barely heard. Because Gideon looked at me like I was the only person alive. And I looked at him like he held the whole world in his hands. When it came time for vows, he spoke first.

"Inga Weber," he said, voice thick with emotion, "I loved you the moment my dragon saw your soul. And I will love you until the mountains crumble and the sky falls. You are my heart. My peace. My future. My home."

Tears streamed down my face. But I smiled through all of them.

"My Gideon," I whispered, "you saved me. Not just from danger, but from fear. From loneliness. From believing happiness was not meant for people like me. I love you with everything I am, with everything I will ever be. And

I will walk by your side—on the ground or in the sky—
for the rest of my life."

"Do you take this man—" the priest began.

"I do," I breathed.

"Do you take this woman—"

Gideon didn't wait. "I do," he said, pulling me in before
the sentence even finished.

Our lips met—soft, full of promise, full of fire—and the
entire ranch erupted in cheers. And then—

Gideon broke the kiss…stepped back… and with a shiver
of light and heat, his clothes ripped, and he shifted.

Gasps echoed across the yard. Maggie let out a sob of
happiness.

Where my husband had stood now towered a great
golden dragon, scales bright as sunlight, wings folding
with a whisper like silk and storm. But his eyes—those
warm, gold-flecked eyes—were still Gideon's.

My breath caught in awe. He lowered his massive head.
An open invitation. My heart knew before my mind
caught up. I gathered my dress and climbed onto his
back, settling between the warm, powerful ridges of his
spine. My veil fluttered behind me like a banner.

"Ready?" I whispered to him.

He rumbled, deep and affectionately, before he leaped.

His wings snapped open. And then air was rushing past us. The ground fell away.

We soared over the ranch, over the house, over the barns, over the men cheering and the women waving handkerchiefs, over the cowboys who whooped like it was the rodeo.

Klaus jumped up and down, shouting something I couldn't hear. Elke fainted and then recovered, screaming my name. Molly hollered and pumped her fist in the air.

And I—

I laughed. Laughed with pure, unfiltered joy as Gideon swooped and circled, letting me see all of Montana spread out beneath us like a promise we'd been given by the universe itself.

"I love you!" I cried into the wind.

The dragon roared back, fierce and tender and *mine*. We circled once more, then descended gently, landing beside the celebration where people reached out with awe and reverence. The dragon walked off for a moment, followed by Hank, who was holding a bundle of clothes in his arms. They entered a barn, and minutes later, my Gideon reappeared. The tux he had worn was replaced by jeans and a flannel shirt. He was even more handsome than sin. He strutted toward me, caught me in his arms, and kissed me again, breathless, laughing, glowing.

"I love you," he murmured against my lips.

"I love you too," I whispered.

Forever.

Our forever.

In Gideon's arms, with the sky still singing around us, I finally understood. Home wasn't a place. It was him. It was us. It always would be.

THE END

I hope you enjoyed *The Dragon at Midnight*. This book is part of a series called *Monsters in Uniform*. Each one features a unique monster by a different author. Check it out

HERE

ALSO BY BELLA BLAIR

The Intergalactic Alliance Series

1. The High Commander's Mate
2. The Commander's Challenge
3. The Pirates Tribulation
4. The Consul's Taming
5. The Overlord's Sacrifice
6. The King's Choice
7. The Alien Tyrant's Conquest
8. The Barbarian's Fate
9. The Pryxz's Revenge
10. The Scout's Temptress
11. The Spymaster's Story
12. The Alien Pilot's Match
13. The Sphynxian's Destiny
14. The Maraguy's Emergence

The Vissigroths of Leandar

1. Fated to the Vissigroth
2. Promised to the Vissigroth
3. Claimed by the Vissigroth
4. Bound to the Vissigroth
5. Craved by the Vissigroth
6. Returned to the Vissigroth

The Princes of Tartarus

1. Claimed by her Alien Prince
2. Desired by her Alien Prince

Warlords of Thyre

1. Tribute to the Alien Warlord
2. Mated to the Alien Warlord
3. Craved by the Alien Warlord

The Pandraxian Series

1. Conquering the Alien Lord Protector
2. Conquering the Alien Commander
3. Conquering the Alien Emperor

Alien Barbarians of Vandruk

1. Tzar-Than
2. Dzur-Khan
3. Dzar-Ghan
4. Ghan-Zahr

Space Guardian's Mate

1. Space Guardian's Heart
2. Space Guardian's Soul
3. Space Guardian's Destiny
4. Space Guardian's Legacy

Arkhevari Rising:

1. **Zapharos: Legends of the Lost Gods**
2. **Dravok The Celestial War**

3. **Thyros: Blood and Starlight**

Holiday Romances:

1. My Christmas Alien Mate

Collaborations:

MY ALIEN CAVEMAN Series Page

1.Rescued by the Alien Vhar'Khyng

DAD BOD:

1. Dad Bod: Wolf Shifter

FILTHY FAIRYTALES Series page

1. Eliza's Cursed Dragon

2. Rose's Untamed Bear

FATED TO MY CAPTOR Series page

1.Stolen by the Demon

ABDUCTED BY THE RUTHLESS ROYAL

1. Taken by the Zypherian King

MY MONSTER MY PROTECTOR Series Page

1. Protected by the Alien Space Guardian

A TIME FOR MONSTERS

1.Rise of the Gods: Vardor's Desitiny

MONSTER BRIDES ROMANCE

1. Monsters, Vows, and Growls

MONSTERS IN UNIFORM

1. The Dragon at Midnight

ABOUT THE AUTHOR

Bella Blair has been addicted to stories since the cradle. "Again, Mom, again!" she'd demand until her mother finally decided to teach her to read—securing Bella's life-long obsession. Later, with her grandmother's old Royal typewriter (ignoring the crooked letter "E"), Bella started crafting her own stories, complete with daring heroes and fierce heroines.

Inspired by powerful women like Emma Peel, Warrant Officer Ripley, and Buffy, Bella adds a touch of The Witcher and a dash of Khal Drogo to her worlds, creating supercharged characters who practically set the page on fire with romance, action, twists, and a hint of conspiracy.

Originally from Berlin, Germany, Bella moved to the States after falling head over heels for her real-life action hero. Now based in sunny Phoenix, Arizona, she spends her days setting her keyboard ablaze with her latest tales, walking her German Shepherd, Dexter, alongside her very non-alien husband, or catering to an undisclosed amount of spoiled felines ruling the house.

www.ingramcontent.com/pod-product-compliance
Lightning Source LLC
Chambersburg PA
CBHW051940240626
47153CB00005B/1571